GROUND
TRUTH

A Pittsburgh Murder Mystery

GROUND
TRUTH

A Pittsburgh Murder Mystery

REBECCA A. MILES

Light Messages
Torchflame Books

Durham, NC

Copyright © 2022 Rebecca A. Miles
Ground Truth: A Pittsburgh Murder Mystery
(The Pittsburgh Murder Mysteries #1)
Rebecca A. Miles
rebeccaamystery@msn.com

Published 2022, by Torchflame Books
an Imprint of Light Messages
www.lightmessages.com
Durham, NC 27713 USA
SAN: 920-9298

Paperback ISBN: 978-1-61153-464-1
E-book ISBN: 978-1-61153-465-8
Library of Congress Control Number: 2022903158

My husband, David

and

In memory of my colleague and friend
Jerry Rabinowitz, MD
Victim of the massacre at the
L'Simcha Tree of Life synagogue
Pittsburgh, October 27, 2018

ACKNOWLEDGMENTS

A HEARTFELT THANK YOU goes to the entire crew at Torchflame Books for their expertise in bringing *Ground Truth: A Pittsburgh Murder Mystery* to print. Their decency and author support is notable and unusual in the publishing world.

I would also like to thank my two official readers, Kathleen D'Appolonia, Ph.D., and Jayne Kirber, for their plot insights and corrections of my unfortunate grammar gaffes.

John Paine, Independent Editor, took a novel with a mystery at the center and helped me turn it into a proper murder mystery. John is simply a wizard at what he does.

Finally, I'd like to thank my husband, David, for listening to me endlessly talk about Chief Detective Stefan Jablonsky and Kate Chambers, different ways to poison people, and issues of truth, justice, loss, healing, and the depth of the human heart.

CHAPTER 1

CHIEF DETECTIVE STEFAN JABLONSKY, a tall, broad-shoul-
dered man in his early sixties, stood in a deep excavation
site in the university section of town. Pittsburgh's medical
examiner, Dr. Aashi Patel, who was covered in the ubiquitous
crime scene hazmat suit, was quietly giving him an initial
report on the two skeletons that had been unearthed at the
dig. The area had been tented and brightly lit for the forensic
team, who were moving around in their spectral white suits;
Jablonsky thought they looked like ghostly visitors from
another planet. It was January, so the tent helped shelter
everyone from the frigid night air, making the gathering of
evidence a bit easier.

Patel and Jablonsky were bent over, looking at the
partially uncovered skeletons of two human beings. "I know
it is early days, but what can you tell me?" he asked.

"Now Stefan, you know that I do not guess. I deal in
scientific facts. I must look at all the evidence once it is back
at the laboratory. What I can say is that one of these sets of
bones belonged to a female, and one to a male, and that the
skeletons appear to be fairly complete. There are two good
sets of teeth, so if these people were local, theoretically it
should help speed identification."

Patel's Indian American accent always charmed Jablonsky,
and when they were not covered by goggles, so did her large

truffle-colored eyes. He prodded her a little more, "Come on Aashi, can you at least give an estimation as to how long these two have been buried?"

"No, I cannot. Scientific study tells us that an adult body can take somewhere between eight to twelve years for all the flesh to decompose completely, if, that is, the body is not embalmed and is buried in normal soil conditions. Also, we have to consider things like the depth of the burial hole and how moist the soil is—it is hard to say exactly."

"So, these two bodies could have been dumped here, um, around 2006." Jablonsky's speculations were interrupted by the appearance of a tall, sinewy man with longish gray-blond hair, startling azure-blue eyes, and a visage heavily lined from many years of sun exposure. Dr. Patel took off her goggles and gloves and offered her hand to the stranger.

"Thanks so much for coming out, Dr. Fitzroy. We can use your experience in moving these bones to our lab. There is a hazmat suit over there that I think will fit you. Feel free to instruct my young forensic pathologists, most of whom have lots of experience with flesh, but not so much with only bones. By the way, Dr. Fitzroy, this is Chief Detective Stefan Jablonsky." Jablonsky took the measure of the man in front of him, liking his unobtrusive demeanor, his direct eye contact, and the firmness of his handshake.

"We are lucky to have an archeologist here in Pittsburgh who is so familiar with digging up and dating bones. Dr. Eddie Fitzroy is a Britisher, who comes from a rather famous family of archeologists and anthropologists. He studied with Kate Chambers's grandfather in Boston, and of course, knows Kate as well."

So this is Kate's world-traveling man, mused Jablonsky. Stefan liked and respected amateur sleuth Kate Chambers, who made no secret about her long standing, but long distance, love affair with Fitzroy. Their relationship had been going on for almost fifteen years, most of which he had been working overseas at various digs.

"Good to meet you, detective Jablonsky. Kate always talks about you and your detectives in glowing terms." Fitzroy turned toward Patel and addressed the work at hand, "Dr. Patel, I'm going to suit up and have a closer look at these bones."

Fitzroy's knowledge of this type of work was evident to Jablonsky by the way he approached the scene—he moved slowly and carefully around the site, like a shaman divining secrets to the past. Stefan chuckled to himself, thinking, *all he needs is a headdress and some rattling bones.* Patel put her headgear back on and joined Eddie as he began to instruct the team; they cautiously started the tedious job of uncovering all of the skeletal remains and then delicately packing them.

Jablonsky was surprised when a grinning Kate Chambers tapped him on his shoulder. "I made a vat of fresh hot chocolate for you and the crew—Eddie texted me that he needed certain special tools from his gear, so I'm dropping them off, along with this thermos. I hope it's okay that I'm here." Kate had her thick black hair tucked behind her ears; her pale skin was ruddy from the cold air. Jablonsky noted her inquisitive expression as she looked around at the beehive-like activity.

"This is a crime scene Kate, and you are a civilian. I don't want you to linger. It is unclear what has happened, so there might be someone dangerous lurking about. If you hand the tool bag to detective DeVille, he'll take it to Dr. Fitzroy." Kate knew Antoine DeVille so they greeted each other warmly, Kate joking with him about how white he looked in his suit. "This is the whitest I've ever looked, that's for sure," he responded.

Antoine DeVille, Jablonsky's number one, was an attractive black man, born and raised in New Orleans by Creole parents and grandparents. Stefan respected his brains and work ethic, so had begun to promote Antoine, whom everyone called Coupe.

DeVille walked the tools back to the site and Jablonsky, still concerned over having a private citizen at his scene, decided to make use of her presence by assessing her familiarity with, and knowledge of, this part of the university area.

"You know," said Jablonsky, "Early in my career I patrolled almost every neighborhood—this part of the city underwent quite a change, starting in the late 1970's until... well, now. Do you know much about the South Oakland neighborhood?"

"I did my graduate work here at the university. What I most remember was the battle between the residents wanting to maintain their neighborhoods and the desires of outside investors to develop the area—just like they are doing now— tearing down the old hotel and putting up a newer, bigger one. I guess you might like to know who the citizen groups were that resisted the development, correct?"

"Exactly. If it is foul play, which I think we will find it is, I want to know who the leaders were on either side of the development question."

"You know me. I'm your girl for research, plus the purveyor of insider details on university people and politics. Johnny probably can help as well. His mother worked for one of the main bakeries on Forbes Avenue that was in business around the time of the first wave of land development. Between the three of us, we can enlighten you on the history of this community."

Kate's eager voice and excited expression made Jablonsky laugh; he knew from experience that she and her university pals could deliver the goods. He was cordial with Kate and her friends, and happy to use their knowledge when it related to a case, but Jablonsky kept a professional distance. He was a trained police detective; she was an academic with sleuthing interests—Jablonsky correctly saw their worlds as sometimes intersecting, but fundamentally different.

He remarked, "Of course, there are more options than developer malfeasance. Years ago, organized crime owned bars, beer distributorships, and a few private clubs around the university center and the general area of the East End—Shadyside, East Liberty, and such. Dumping bodies at construction sites was certainly one of their modus operandi." Jablonsky rubbed his gloved hands together and pulled his knitted Steeler cap closer over his ears; it was bitterly cold.

"Is Dr. Fitzroy here in Pittsburgh for good?" Jablonsky was a bit shame-faced over his blatant quest for personal information, but he really didn't care. He was the Chief of Detectives after all, so he darn well could ask whatever he wanted; and besides, he was the father of a daughter. Even though his Carly was through law school and practicing in Pittsburgh, he couldn't always stop himself from checking on whom she was dating; it was a protective reflex. He unwrapped a piece of the cinnamon gum he always kept with him, fired it into his mouth, then offered Kate a piece.

She laughed at his transparent dig for gossip—but since they had worked together for a few years, she felt he had a right to know. "Eddie is working in Ligonier at the fort, so he is back and forth. When he's in town, he stays with me." Kate smiled and left the implications of that hang in the air; she handed him the thermos of hot chocolate, took the piece of gum, and then made her excuses to leave.

Patel and Fitzroy crouched in the dirt around the two skeletons. Eddie supervised the pathologists, showing them how to gently brush away soil from the bones, and then, with what looked like pointed garden trowels, carefully dig around each bone to liberate it from its resting place. Right now, they were freeing the tiny bones of the fingers.

"It's remarkable that almost all of the bones are here," commented Fitzroy. "Of course, we have to run the tests, but I'd say these bones have been here for almost twenty years. All the fabric, and the threads holding their clothes together, is fully disintegrated, but over here, it looks like there are some remains of a leather jacket. Leather takes years to completely break down. Right now, just between you and me, I'd say we are looking at two people who were buried here around the early two thousands."

Dr. Patel watched and listened but did not comment. She was not someone who easily speculated, choosing instead to wait for the results of scientific tests. Aashi had completed her residency at the university medical center, so she was familiar with the ethnic enclaves that used to exist in this area. Plenty of crime occurred in those neighborhoods—she knew that it was probable these two people had been murdered.

The bones were packed and ready to be moved to the medical examiner's laboratory. The forensic technicians had used their ultraviolet lights to look for fibers and biological material not readily visible to the human eye, and those findings had been placed in evidence bags, also ready for transport. Dr. Patel stood and stretched, sore from hunching over in the cold air, when she caught sight of Bill Reeves, head of Pittsburgh's estimable forensic center. He and Jablonsky, colleagues and friends, stood with their heads almost touching as they exchanged information about the skeletons. Aashi walked over to them and presented a brief update.

"Dr. Fitzroy has agreed to act as a consultant until we know the particulars. He's heading back to the lab now to see that everything is unpacked correctly, so I want to be there."

"When do you think you will have date, manner, and cause of death?" asked Jablonsky, stamping his feet to keep the blood flowing to his cold toes. Bill Reeves snorted at Jablonsky's push, "I always say to you, Stefan, when she knows, you'll know. You can't rush the scientific process." Patel returned to the tent as Reeves and Jablonsky walked uphill out of the pit.

"You know Bill, there is something familiar about this situation—two missing young people." Stefan wrapped his neck scarf tighter against the cold wind, saying, "It will come to me." As Jablonsky made his way out of the excavation hole, he also made a mental list: *I need to know cause of death; the identity of the two bodies; and especially what was going on in South Oakland when these bodies were dumped.*

CHAPTER 2

JOHNNY MCCARTHY, one of Kate's best friends, let himself in the kitchen door of her condominium. After her grandfather died and Kate had inherited his estate, she was able to buy one of the four condominiums that had been built in an historic mansion on Fifth Avenue. She knew that as a professor of art history, Johnny appreciated both its' beauty and its' place in city history. He also approved of Kate's decorating sensibilities—a curated mixture of her mother's and grandfather's antiques, combined with a selection of modern art and art glass.

It wasn't uncommon for her blond, blue-eyed Pittsburgh friend to stop by her home every day. She loved him like a brother, particularly appreciating his discerning intellect and sharp Irish wit. Johnny always supported her love of solving puzzles, particularly when they involved murder.

"No evening class today?" Kate had just walked home from her office at the university, and was busy feeding her chocolate Labrador retriever, Bourbon Ball. BB, as he was often called, usually met Johnny with wiggly bum and a few head-butts, but right now, his big block head was buried in the dinner bowl.

"No. No class tonight. Where's Himself?" Johnny looked around for evidence of Eddie Fitzroy's stuff but didn't see any.

"He stayed at the morgue most of the night with Dr. Patel, unpacking the bones of the two skeletons they found at the site of the new hotel. He came home, showered, and then went back to the morgue. He is there now and will head out to Ligonier from downtown. He'll be back here at the end of the week."

Ever the romantic, Johnny made his voice theatrically breathy, and asked, "Before he left, did you have some private time for the horizontal mumbo?" John had known Fitzroy for years; whenever he came to Pittsburgh to see Kate, the three of them enjoyed the city together. Johnny knew Eddie to be a decent man, with honorable intentions toward Kate—if only he would stay in one place. It was Kate who refused to follow him around from dig to dig; she had created a full life for herself in the city, one that included meaningful work and good friends.

"Yes. We had some private time together, Mr. Nosy. It's not always about sex, you know."

"Yes, it is." Kate knew that Johnny liked to say that, but he had chosen a partner who was every bit his intellectual equal, and who unfortunately had recently moved to Paris. "I know you miss Julius," she responded.

Along with her friends, Kate was still getting used to having Fitzroy in town. He had been a part of her life since she was a teenager, but as an archeologist, he never stayed in one place for long. Eddie, who was almost fifteen years older than she, had decided to try and settle in Pittsburgh. Luckily, one of his colleagues, who was ill, had asked him to take over a project at Fort Ligonier in the Laurel Highlands. It was only an hour drive from the city, so the job gave them time to see if their relationship would work in a full-time situation.

"What's the story about the two skeletons?" asked Johnny, interrupting her musings.

"Well, Eddie said they were two youngish people, a male and female, who probably were buried around the time you and I were students. The university was expanding into the local neighborhoods and there were land developers and big construction firms, many from out of state, who were pushing multiple projects. Do you remember a group called the Community Alliance? They organized sit-ins and peaceful marches, and negotiated with the city planning department in favor of keeping neighborhoods intact."

"I remember them really well. I worked part-time at Rosalie's Bakery on Forbes Avenue, the one the Rossetti family owned. You remember that my mother worked full-time at the bakery for years. Michael Rossetti, the son of the owner, was the leader of the Alliance. Hey, wait a minute, he and his sister went missing around that time—don't you remember? It was all over the news. Michael and Rosalie Rossetti just disappeared one day—poof, like a smoke ring rising from a cigarette. No trace of them was ever found." Johnny excitedly paced around the room.

"If you think the skeletons might be the Rossettis, we should immediately tell Jablonsky." Kate looked at Johnny with a go-on expression.

"Let's do it. That is, you do it." Kate rolled her eyes at Johnny's sudden shyness, then tapped in the chief's digits on her cellphone. "Detective Jablonsky? Yes, Kate here. Johnny McCarthy was just telling me that around twenty years ago, two siblings went missing in Oakland. They were Michael and Rosalie Rossetti. You remember their names? Of course, you would—it was probably a big case then. It just seemed coincidental that two skeletons were found in South Oakland, where those two lived when they disappeared. Yes. Sure, Johnny and I can come to the precinct. You are at the morgue right now? Well, just let me know when you want us."

To say that Johnny and Kate were excited to be involved in another police case, even one that was cold, was an understatement. They made a fresh pot of coffee and the two sat in the dining room piecing together their memories of twenty years ago.

At the morgue, Patel, Fitzroy, and Jablonsky were standing together looking at the two precisely laid out, complete skeletons. Even before Kate's call, the Chief had already remembered the disappearance of the Rossetti siblings, but hadn't mentioned it to Aashi, preferring to hear the forensic details first. Dr. Patel began.

"So, we have the Mass spectrometry evidence that tells us these two people died around twenty or so years ago, as we had already suspected. This person on the right was a young female in her late teens or early twenties, well-nourished, with normal bone growth, and around 167 centimeters tall. Her teeth are intact, so we should be able to get a match shortly. This person on the left was a young man in his late twenties, also well-nourished, with normal bone growth, and around 185 centimeters tall. We will get a match on his teeth as well. We could only capture a minuscule bit of DNA—what we got was pretty degraded, but we sent it out to be analyzed anyway."

Eddie Fitzroy shifted his weight and looked deferentially at Dr. Patel, whose laboratory it was, and who clearly was the boss. Identifying new bones for forensic reasons was not his usual work. He added his perspective anyway. "I believe these bodies were placed, rather than dumped. Someone took care with them. Additionally, I found this."

Fitzroy opened an evidence bag and took out a tiny object. He used forensic-sized tweezers to handle it. "I found this under the female's skeleton. It appears to be a ring with a semi-precious stone—from my field experience with decorative objects, I'd say this stone is blue topaz. If you look closely, there is an etched figure—could be that of an animal."

Jablonsky looked through a large magnifying glasses to view the object. "I see what you mean—I think it looks like a lion. Does this mean anything to either of you?"

"I'm going to speculate that since it was found under the female's remains, it belonged to her. Semi-precious stones with an engraving of a symbol or an animal typically have a specific cultural meaning. Perhaps the object meant something to her, or it meant something to the person who placed her." Jablonsky listened intently to Fitzroy's speculations.

Patel added, "I think that Dr. Fitzroy is correct. Whomever handled these two bodies showed a certain respect toward them. As of right now, however, we do not have either a cause of death nor a manner of death for either one. There are no bullet holes nor evidence of torture. Neither had ever suffered a broken bone. The common poisons often are difficult to detect once the flesh and organs have decomposed. We will have to wait and see what picture the lab results paint. This is a sad situation—two young people. Do you remember such a case, Stefan?"

"Actually, I do. Bill Reeves and I think that these two might be Michael and Rosalie Rossetti—two siblings from the South Oakland area who went missing about twenty years ago."

"Now that you say it, I do remember the case. I'll use the Rossetti last name to see if we get a hit on the dental records. If it is them, we can confirm identity shortly, but not much else. If the parents are still alive, I would want to personally inform them. It is only fitting."

It was that kind of attitude that endeared Aashi Patel to Jablonsky. He nodded his approval, shook hands with Fitzroy, and headed back to the excavation site. As he drove the snowy Parkway East into the Oakland area, he called DeVille.

"Get me everything you have on a cold case—Michael and Rosalie Rossetti, two siblings gone missing in the early two thousands."

CHAPTER 3

PITTSBURGH'S SUBURBANITES did not know about the Grotto, but university students, congregants at the local churches, and neighborhood residents not only knew about it, but knew how to find it. The Grotto had existed for decades in South Oakland, but someone had to tell you where to look for the narrow path, partially obscured by weeds and grass, which lead to it. At the end of the path was a clearing in which was placed a large statue of the Blessed Mother standing on the globe and crushing a serpent. Several concrete benches were arranged in a demi-lune configuration facing the statue. The spot had been carved into one of the steep slopes that loom above the Parkway East and the Monongahela River, and over the many years of its existence, received a steady flow of visitors. Residents from the small surrounding neighborhoods took care of the Grotto, planting flowers in the spring and hanging evergreen wreathes in the winter.

For many, the Grotto was a pilgrimage site. A litany of requests for help were privately poured out to the statue—old men and women petitioning either for good health or a swift death, young men and woman asking for an intersession with a sweetheart, pleas for good grades or a new job. There were prayers for guidance concerning an abusive spouse or a pedophile priest.

On this particular morning, two elderly women had braved the winding path and were seated together on one of the concrete benches. Each wore a bright wool scarf tied under the chin, a warm winter coat, boots, and gloves. Both came armed with a thermos of coffee, a stadium blanket to sit on, and small brushes to clean the cement benches and the statue. They also had rosary beads tucked into their pockets; after they had had a good gossip, each would silently make a request of the Blessed Mother, and then repeat the rosary's hypnotic prayers. Their usual routine was interrupted today; they were surprised to see an older man approach the Grotto.

"Don't be alarmed ladies, I'm Chief Detective Stefan Jablonsky. I used to come here as a young student and was curious to see if it still existed." Jablonsky had wanted to think over the situation with the Rossetti siblings, so since he was already in Oakland, he decided to visit this quiet place.

"May I sit?" He was very courtly toward the two ladies, having never forgotten his grandmother's etiquette lessons—mostly because they were usually given with the light tap of a wooden spoon on the back of his head.

"So, Mr. Chief Detective, do you think the two skeletons they found are Michael and Rosalie Rossetti?" Jablonsky was taken aback by the question but hid his surprise.

"What makes you ask that, Mrs.? I'm sorry, I didn't catch your name."

"I'm Mrs. Renata Russo, and this is my friend, Mrs. Andrea Brianche. We knew Michael and Rosalie, and we still know their mother, Lisa Marie Rossetti. Gene Rossetti died a few years ago." Seated on the other cement bench, Jablonsky discreetly took out his small paper notebook, balancing it on his knee; his eyes never left the faces of the two Nonas.

"I'm not at liberty to talk about the bodies yet. Police procedure—you understand." He spoke in a conspiratorial tone, hoping it would spark a flow of information about the Rossetti family, which it did.

"The police were never able to discover what happened to Michael Rossetti and his sister, Rosalie. It broke their mother's heart; she was never the same after they disappeared. I think she became, what do you call it when you are afraid to go out of the house? Is it claustrophobic?"

"No. That's not it. It's something like, angoraphobic. No, that would be fear of sweaters." Andrea laughed at her own gaffe, and then continued, "I think it's agoraphobic. Lisa Marie Rossetti can't even go to Mass on Sundays. Once a week, a Eucharistic minister comes to the house and gives her communion. After everything Michael tried to do for this community, and she can't even walk to her own bakery on Forbes Avenue—you know the one, Chief? Rosalie's Bakery?"

In his best empathetic manner, Jablonsky nodded yes, and then asked, "How old were the brother and sister when they disappeared?"

Renata thought for a while. "Well, Michael Rossetti was two years ahead of my Louie in school, so he would have been in his late twenties when he disappeared. Rosalie was in her mid-twenties. What a beauty she was, and smart too! I think she was finished with law school. She was the apple of her father's eye. You know, for years he went every month to the police station to see if they had any new leads."

"Lisa Marie lives in one of the townhouses by the nursery across Bigelow Boulevard. Her youngest son, Marco, lives with her. He's a surgeon at the hospital across the river—he's a big noise," Andrea said, with a smirk that indicated she thought he had forgotten where he came from.

"How did Marco handle the disappearance of his siblings?"

"He had a rough time but, I think he always had it rough in that family. Michael and his friends were so involved in fighting the developers that even before the disappearance, Marco didn't get much attention. As a child, he always seemed on the outside of family life." Renata slowly shook her head side to side, accenting her observations.

"Always on the outside?" Jablonsky repeated.

Renata answered with a long, drawn-out "Well...I thought he was a strange little boy."

"Gifted," interjected Andrea. "He was gifted at his studies. Look, it was like this. Marco was smart but Michael was good-looking and popular, easy to be with. Rosalie was beautiful and smart, sweet and kind, close to her baby brother." Both women's faces were suffused with warmth as they talked about Rosalie.

Andrea continued, "I always thought Marco might have that asparagus disease."

Jablonsky and Renata looked at each other, mystified. "What asparagus disease?" they simultaneously asked. Renata thought for a minute, and then blurted out, "You mean Asperger's syndrome!" In the midst of their chuckles, Andrea continued to talk about Marco and Rosalie.

"Rosalie was a kind, sensitive girl. Beautiful inside and out. Always willing to help someone in need. She was named after her grandmother—actually, their bakery was named for both. She was protective of Marco and he adored her."

Andrea summed up the general view on Marco. "Everyone wanted to help Marco, but it was difficult. He could make you feel embarrassed for even showing interest in him. He's a very well-known surgeon now, but, well, you know... he never married." Both women sighed in unison; clearly being single was a terrible condition, worse than the asparagus disease.

"I might want to talk to Mrs. Rossetti. You could mention it to her, so it wouldn't come as a surprise." Jablonsky gave them his most endearing smile; he was a charmer when he wanted to be.

"Sure, we can do that. Here's a piece of advice, Mr. Detective—you want to visit the mother when Marco isn't home. He'll make you feel like you are intruding. We never visit Lisa Marie when we know he's going to be there. In fact, I'd try seeing him at the hospital."

"Thank you so much for your time, ladies. May I feel free to talk with you again? It would help the investigation if I could have your telephone numbers." It amused the chief that both ladies pulled out sophisticated cellphones. He wrote down their names and numbers and offered each of them his card.

As Jablonsky slowly made his way along the narrow path back to his car, he found himself missing his grandmother, his "Bubba"—a woman whose stern demeanor barely concealed her big heart. "How I miss her nut rolls at the holidays," he thought, even though those baked goods were the last thing his waistline needed. He dialed the precinct.

"DeVille, I'm still in Oakland. I'll expect a detailed report on the Rossetti kids when I get back. Right now, I'm going to stop at the bakery owned by the Rossetti family just to nose around." Even through the cellphone, Jablonsky could feel the smile on Antoine's face at the fact that his inquires would also include sampling the pastries, but since his number one had grown up on beignets, he understood the allure of pastries.

CHAPTER 4

JOHNNY AND KATE were sharing a coffee in his campus office. The office was housed in the university Fine Arts building, a structure that always reminded Kate of an Italian villa, with the semi-circular archways at the entrance and the long wings stretching off either side of the central area. Amid stacks of art books, an oversized computer screen, a modern-looking Tibetan rug, and several well-worn stuffed chairs, was a deluxe Italian coffee machine sitting on a sturdy table. The machine-made Espresso and Cappuccino as well as regular grind. Having studied abroad in Italy, Johnny was a coffee snob.

This office reminded Kate of her grandfather's office, where, when she was young, she would curl up and read while he worked on his anthropology lectures. Sometimes Eddie Fitzroy would stop by the office; he had been a trusted graduate student of her grandfather's. Both of Kate's parents had been killed by a drunk driver when she was just five. Her grandfather, having lost his only daughter, wholeheartedly embraced his little granddaughter, nicknaming her his "Precious Gift." When she was at Johnny's office, she felt that same sense of security and belonging that she had experienced with her granddad.

Kate and Johnny met when they both were working on their doctorates. Her degree was in academic psychology with an emphasis was on cognition and learning. She knew that she had become an academic advisor because she wanted to help students make good decisions, unlike the decision that the drunk driver had made on the night he killed her parents. The career gave her time for her other interests, like sleuthing, working out, and spending time with her friends.

"When we were students, I didn't know that your Mom worked at Rosalie's Bakery. I used to stop in there for Palmiers, you know, the ones sometimes called Elephant Ears. Maybe she waited on me! How well did you and she know Michael Rossetti and his sister?" Kate tucked her long legs under her and settled back to listen to Johnny describe a time in his life about which she knew very little.

"I'm very familiar with Elephant Ears, by the way. I mentioned to you that I worked part-time at the bakery when I was in high school, and then a little as an undergraduate. Lisa Marie Rossetti owned the bakery. Michael was older than me; I remember that he was good-looking with dark hair and hazel eyes. He really was a great guy—friendly to all the staff, who were mostly middle-aged, short, bosomy local ladies. Rosalie sometimes worked behind the counter, and Marco, the younger brother, also came around, particularly when she was there."

"There was a younger brother? How awful that he lost both siblings."

Johnny refilled his coffee cup; Kate watched him repeatedly stirring a smidge of sugar around and around. "Marco was younger than Michael, by probably a decade. He was brilliant—I mean the real deal brilliant. He did odd jobs at the bakery, but never really hung with anyone, me included. I liked him; he knew what I was, but he never took a shot at me the way my dad or some classmates did."

Kate knew that Johnny, as a young gay man in a working-class family, had been badly bullied. She had seen the scars on his legs from a time in adolescence when he used to cut himself. Privately, Kate always wondered why his mother hadn't intervened in her husband's bullying or Johnny's cutting. Her intuition told her there was something not quite right about that family. Kate sent Johnny a loving look and then returned to the subject of the missing siblings.

"When I was a graduate student, I really didn't appreciate the magnitude of building that was taking place—the hospitals and the universities drastically expanded their footprint—more libraries, science towers, and student housing were being built. I naively considered all of that expansion to be progress for the university, but I'm not sure I really understood the other side of it, the resident's side." Kate put down her coffee cup and unfolded her legs. Johnny seemed preoccupied. He was born and raised here and he and his mother personally knew the victims—why wasn't he more forthcoming? She decided to nudge him a little.

"The neighborhood Alliance had marches on Forbes Avenue that would start at the student union and end at one or another construction site. Did you ever participate in the marches or go to their community office?"

Johnny swiveled his desk chair around so he could face her. "You look great today, by the way. It must be either the presence of Himself, or else it is finding the skeletons. You are such a sleuth at heart. But, to answer your question, all those family-owned businesses and tight neighborhoods were slowly being whittled away to nothing, and my mother's job was tied to one of them."

"I hadn't thought about your mom's job. I guess that's what the Alliance was fighting for—everyday jobs like hers."

Once again, Johnny took his time commenting, he seemed wary.

"Michael was so charismatic that he drew all the oxygen out of a room—no one came close to being as committed to the community as he was. He was a born speaker and motivator; everyone admired him. I preferred to be on the sidelines of that power."

"Did you have a crush on Michael Rossetti?"

"No, but I knew someone who did. I don't remember his last name, but his first name was Luca. He was from the neighborhood, started working as a stock boy at the bakery, but then really got involved in the Alliance. He became Michael's gofer. Surprisingly, he was friendly with some of the construction crew who used to stop at the bakery early in the morning for coffee and crullers."

"That's interesting, don't you think? He might have been a mole for the Alliance—buddy up to the workers and then report back to Michael." For the first time in the conversation, Johnny seemed curious.

"I'm going to talk to my mom about who the regulars at the shop were around that time. If I find out anything interesting, we can pass it on to the chief. Let's get out of here. With Julius in Paris, the Slope house is lonely and half empty. I was hoping to stay in your guest room, particularly since Fitzroy isn't here."

Kate just laughed; Johnny almost lived at her condo, whether Eddie was there or not. Julius, Johnny's partner, an attorney who specialized in stolen antiquities, had rented an apartment in Paris to be closer to his work. Kate wasn't sure what that meant in terms of their relationship and decided not to broach the subject today.

Even though it was slushy and cold, they negotiated the several-mile walk along wide Fifth Avenue with alacrity. Not having been raised by a mother and father, she didn't know the ins and outs of marital relationships, so she asked Johnny what his dad thought of the bakery.

"My dad hated my mom working there, but in terms of my being there, he always said that he thought it was a perfect fit—cream puffs making cream puffs."

Kate had ceased to be shocked by the brutish nature of his dad's bullying. "I love cream puffs," she replied. She began to wonder what stories his mother would have to tell about the customers at the bakery; could one of them have murdered Michael and Rosalie? She was definitely tagging along for that visit.

———∽∾∾———

At the same time Johnny and Kate were walking home, Jablonsky was taking an ear beating from the construction manager at the excavation site: "All delays cost money!" But Jablonsky was firm; the site was closed to further activity until the crime scene investigators had gathered every smidgen of evidence.

He walked down to the CSI tent and talked with some of the technicians. Bill Reeves arrived and the two stood together spontaneously sharing their memories of this section of the city. Stefan handed him a piece of cinnamon gum, commenting, "I was a student here from 1976 to 1980. My friends and I occasionally went to the dance clubs on the weekends, and definitely went to the football and basketball games, but once I joined the department, this wasn't my beat."

"When I was a kid, we took the trolley cars from the South Hills to come see the Pirates play at Forbes Field, which was still in Oakland. This section of the university area was a thriving community; ethnically it was mostly Italian and Irish. I went to undergraduate and graduate school here, and then started working for the city at the forensics lab. The missing Rossetti kids was a big case. It was your boss's, right?"

"Yeah. It was his case all right. I looked at his case notes— he never came to terms with the fact he couldn't find out what happened to those two young people. I hope we can do it now."

Jablonsky knew that Reeves would be excited to take on this cold case. Advances in forensic science were nothing short of a string of miracles. His lab technicians could find blood, hair and fiber, soil and DNA clues never thought of twenty years ago. Reeves commented, "Let's get the bastards that killed them. You know as well as I do that this has the smell of murder for hire."

Jablonsky felt like a bullet sitting in its chamber ready to be fired. The possibility that he could bring closure to the Rossetti family, and solve his former boss's case, would make his year. His cellphone rang— it was Dr. Patel.

"We had a hit on the dental records. These are the Rossetti siblings, Michael and Rosalie. No manner or cause of death yet. We are still looking for some evidence of poisoning. I'm ruling both deaths as suspicious. After twenty years of not knowing what happened to her children, Mrs. Rossetti deserves a personal visit. I'll see her later today."

CHAPTER 5

"THE FIRST PERSON WHO WENT MISSING that I was aware of was Jaycee Dugard. It was 1991, and she was eleven years old. She was kept for eighteen years and bore two children as a result of rape. They found her and arrested her captors in 2009. She wrote a book about her experience—I found it tragic and horrifying." Kate poured Dr. James, her senior colleague, another cup of office coffee as they talked about Marco Rossetti.

"Was his siblings' disappearance the underpinning of his problems during his training?"

"Partly. Frankly, many more of his problems stemmed from his brilliance. From the time he was little, he was learning material many grade levels above his own. I think it was overwhelming for him to comprehend so much at such a young age. His teachers and parents were ill-equipped to help him negotiate school and social life as a genius. They were all hooked into the Alliance and what was happening to their neighborhood. Then, when Michael and Rosalie went missing, his mother simply shut down, barely able to accomplish daily tasks. His father spent his time at the police station. I felt that Marco had lost everyone— not just his siblings, but also his parents. They simply weren't emotionally available because of their own grief. He was quite attached to Rosalie; her loss was enormous for him." Kate's colleague shook her head over the human misery visited upon young Marco Rossetti.

Kate responded. "Because of my own story, I'm always interested in loss. I've started casually looking at well-publicized cases of children who were taken—there was Etan Patz, found dead; Elizabeth Smart, found alive; and, recently, the British girl, Madeleine McCann, still missing. How do the siblings of those taken react? I can't find much research on that issue. When my parents didn't come home, I at least knew what had happened to them. My granddad and I had a coherent story to tell ourselves and others as to how and why they had died. Plus, the drunk driver who killed them went to jail." Kate paused, sipped her coffee, and then continued. "I want to ask a clinical question—do you think Marco Rossetti could have murdered his siblings?"

"At the time, I was interviewed by the Chief of Detectives, who asked me about my advising sessions with Marco. Here's the story. Marco had finished almost all of his undergraduate work while he was in high school and so was admitted to medical school at age eighteen. He was still an adolescent—which was why I was seeing him. Anyhow, I'll give you the answer I gave the detective—I'm just not qualified to say, 'yes' or 'no.' Like you, I deal with academic choice and achievement, but unlike you, I do not have clinical training in mental disorders. My honest answer is, I really don't know. I liked him then, and I like him now. After all these years, every so often he still stops in to see me. Marco is a very committed and talented surgeon. He has pioneered several surgical procedures that are used worldwide to save lives in battle zone hospitals."

Kate didn't respond to her colleague's observations but did think to herself that it takes aggression to cut into the human body, even if the cutting is with the intent to heal.

But just because a person can marshal aggression at work, doesn't make him or her more likely to commit a murder. Kate's question to her colleague was specific; could Marco Rossetti have murdered his brother and sister, and further, what would be the motive for that act? Across town, the Chief and his number one were considering the same questions.

———

Jablonsky and DeVille walked toward the interview room where Marco Rossetti sat. Antoine peeled off when they came to the space that housed the closed-circuit televisions so he could observe the interview.

Stefan began by massaging the surgeon's ego. "Dr. Rossetti, thank you so much for coming to the station. I know you are an important man who has many demands on his time." Marco Rossetti stood when Jablonsky entered the room and the two men remained standing, assessing each other.

Marco was about the same height as the detective, clearly fit, with wavy brown hair pulled back into a ponytail, heavy-lidded hazel eyes, and an aquiline nose perfectly shaped for looking down on people. His clean-shaven face was more arresting than handsome. Jablonsky noticed what beautiful hands Marco had; close-cut fingernails tipped the surgeon's long fingers, fingers which appeared ambiguously strong and delicate at the same time.

Dr. Rossetti was dressed in jeans and a white tailored shirt that was open at the neck; his skin was slightly tan. He wore a pair of men's Dansko clogs, with short white ankle socks. *An odd combination for this stylishly dressed man,* thought Jablonsky. Marco had carefully laid his expensive camel-colored wool coat over the back of the chair and now sat quietly, one leg crossed over the other, hands in his lap.

Jablonsky thought the man was both nervous, a state he covered by maintaining a slight sneer, and curious, which he expressed through his direct eye contact and attentiveness.

The chief opened a file and placed the forensic report on the skeletons in front of Marco. "Dr. Rossetti, we do not yet have either a cause of death nor a manner of death, but the two skeletons we found at the excavation site, I am sorry to say, are definitely your brother and sister, Michael and Rosalie." Marco picked up the report and read it carefully, showing no discernible reaction. He placed his right palm on the report and kept it there.

"This has been a long time coming, almost twenty years. We can finally make funeral arrangements. By the way, I should have been with my mother when Dr. Patel told her the news." Surprisingly, Rossetti's tone of voice was not accusatory. This was a man used to dealing with the stark world of irrefutable facts; he wasn't going to waste energy on what had already happened. Jablonsky didn't respond to Marco's statement.

"We will now begin to look at the evidence through the lens of our new technologies and will also be re-interviewing everyone associated with the case. You are an important person in this investigation—I have a few questions for you. For any follow-up inquiries, I will come to the hospital." It was clear to Jablonsky that the good doctor knew he was being stroked.

"For today, then, what are your questions?" The surgeon leaned back in his chair and waited.

"Now, as an adult looking back at that time, was there anyone in your family, any neighbors or friends of Michael and Rosalie, whom you can identify as suspicious in behavior toward your siblings?"

Jablonsky was shocked to see Dr. Rossetti's eyes fill with tears. "Yes. Me. My behavior was suspicious. I resented my brother. I resented his centering our family life on the Alliance. Every night was the same—neighbors and people we didn't even know showing up at our house to talk strategy or just to complain. My mother was constantly on her feet cooking and serving, while my dad poured a thousand glasses of wine. And what did it get the community? The neighborhood was gutted and the shiny new apartments and hotels were built. And are still being built." Sarcasm dripped from his last words, but not rage. *Where was the rage?*, wondered Jablonsky?

"Among the people who came to the house, was there anyone in particular that you think was oily, had some other agenda or was open to being bought off?"

"I've gone over and over this soil, tilling it as if the crop I planted would grow and save my family from its slow, emotional implosion." Marco covered his eyes for a minute, a gesture of sorrow over all that had been lost. "To your point, I didn't see anyone getting rich. Almost all the family-owned shops that existed where the zoning changed went out of business; very few had made plans to relocate. My mother's bakery is still running only because it sits on a main drag." Rossetti seemed sincere in his frustrations, but Jablonsky still had no answer to his question.

"Were there zealots in the Alliance whose enthusiasm struck a false note to you?"

"Michael was a zealot. He believed through his sincerity and through relationships with the city officials, that he could help keep people's homes and businesses in the neighborhood. Once Rosalie started into law, she could present legal arguments, but she wasn't a zealot. Michael never accepted the fact that the other side believed just as strongly in their right to take property, build what they wanted, and get rich, as he believed in his perspective. Nothing stopped the juggernaut that was the Edmonds Land Company."

Jablonsky reiterated, "Yes. The Edmonds Land Company. Dr. Rossetti, I appreciate your honesty but I'm asking a very specific question—was there anyone who you thought was capable of turning on your brother and sister, to the point of murdering them?"

The surgeon's telephone beeped, he looked at it and sent a reply text. "I have to go. I'm needed in surgery. Look, there was a man named Jubas Jones who was the liaison person from city planning. My brother liked him and believed that they were crew members rowing in the same boat; he would know the inner workings of both sides much better than I. There were a couple of friends of Michael's, and one of Rosalie's, who I thought were silver-plated: Rosalie had a friend from law school named Jonathan Price; a guy from the neighborhood, Luca, was Michael's toady. That's all I've got." With that, the surgeon lifted his coat from the chair and walked out of the room.

Jablonsky didn't bother to stop Marco Rossetti because there would be other interviews. His first impressions were that the man was arrogant but also someone who also evidenced sincerity and guilt. It was a surprising mix, and not at all what he had expected. He laughed to himself, thinking that the surgeon didn't fit the profile of someone with the asparagus disease. He called out to DeVille, "Did you get those names?"

Antoine stepped into the room and handed Jablonsky a sheet of paper with the names. "Dr. Patel called to report that she had spent a good deal of time with Lisa Marie Rossetti. When she left, the television crews were already there. She said that between herself and the two older ladies you met at the Grotto, they took care of the reporters—"no problem!" The two grown men both had had grandmothers whom they loved but also feared, so they chuckled at the image of the Nonas sweeping reporters off the porch.

CHAPTER 6

KATE AND JOHNNY HAD FINISHED their workout at Frick Park's obstacle course and were walking back to her condo as a cool-down. Even though the calendar declared it to be winter, the temperature was in the fifties and the sun shone—it was a perfect day to be outside.

"What time is your mother expecting us?" Kate asked as they entered the kitchen door. Bourbon Ball charged toward them for his quota of pets.

"About an hour," Johnny replied, laying on the floor roughhousing with BB.

"She knows why we are visiting, right?" Knowing the circumstances of Johnny's upbringing, Kate never really took to Mrs. McCarthy, but nevertheless, she didn't want her to feel uncomfortable over being asked detailed questions about her life. "I'm going to shower and change."

———

Kate cut a sophisticated figure in her close-fitting black jeans, topped with a black Peruvian wool sweater and matching jacket. Johnny, who liked to look good for his mom, was also sporting jeans, which he had paired with an argyle sweater vest and a tattersall shirt. When he put on his Burberry trench coat, Kate grinned at how amusingly professorial he looked.

Mrs. McCarthy still lived in her home in Greenfield. After Johnny's father died, he wanted his mother to consider an apartment, but she liked her garden and the neighbors. Johnny installed a security system, good outdoor lighting, and called twice a week. Sometimes he went as far as to go to Mass with her, but only on the holidays. The church's stance on gays had alienated him, and then once the extent of the criminal behavior toward children had been uncovered, he completely left the church. His mother understood and never pushed him to attend Mass.

"Hello the house!" Johnny called out as they kicked off their shoes in the entryway and walked down the short hall to the kitchen. "Hi, Mom. Something smells really good in here. What are you making?"

"Wash your hands before you touch anything! Hi, Kate. You look beautiful as usual; you go wash your hands as well." Mrs. McCarthy wasn't a hugger; instead, she turned from the kitchen sink and threw her guests a warm smile. "Go on now. I'm getting some good tea ready, and I have baked some Irish jambon pastries—Johnny's favorite."

They sat around the small kitchen table, savoring the fresh ham and cheese pastries. The only time Kate and Johnny drank tea was with his mother—she steeped her special blend in the old-fashioned way so it had an unusual depth of flavor. Johnny opened the conversation about the Rossetti family.

"You knew practically everyone who came into the bakery, didn't you, Mom?"

"Yes. I guess I did. I'm so relieved that they finally found Michael and Rosalie. I know it is an odd thing to say, but it is good for the family, especially Mrs. Rossetti. I called her to say that I wouldn't be attending the funeral Mass, but that I was thinking of her and wished her well. Maybe she will be able to come out of her house now—you know, Kate, she has the agoraphobia."

"Mom. It's not 'the' agoraphobia, it's just, agoraphobia." His mother swatted away his correction. Kate chuckled to herself, enjoying the banter between them. Her relationship with her grandfather was always loving, but never playful. Kate kicked Johnny under the table for being rude to his mother.

"I'm sorry to hear about her agoraphobia. Before her children went missing, had she been active at the bakery? I mean, as the owner, did she come to work every day?"

"Yes. She came every day. She was the manager—she did all the ordering, dealt with deliveries, oversaw the baking, organized the ladies, and made sure the kitchen and front cases were immaculate. I liked that about her." Johnny rolled his eyes at that comment. His mother was a fastidious housekeeper, and for better or worse, it had rubbed off on him.

"Around the time Michael and Rosalie disappeared, were there any of the construction workmen who regularly came into the store?" To Kate's eye, Mrs. McCarthy's expression changed; she fiddled with pouring more tea and reaching for another jambon.

"Since I worked the first shift, I knew the regulars." She paused, clearly trying to make up her mind about something, and then continued. "Even the owner of the company came in; Andrew Edmonds was his name. I still remember what pastries he liked. His son, Thomas Edmonds, ran the construction sites, so he typically arrived early in the morning with his workers. They all wanted hot coffee, and banana or blueberry muffins or scones." Her voice trailed off, and her eyes had a distant look—she was viewing the movie of those years at the bakery.

Kate remarked, "It is something that the owner himself stopped by—his company was engaged in tearing down parts of the community—the shop must have meant something special to him. I mean, he was out in public where anyone might take a verbal shot at him. You paint a good picture of the energy of the work crews coming in together in the mornings, getting their take-out bags, and flirting with the women. Do you have any pictures?"

"Yes. Yes, I do. Johnny, on the top shelf of my bedroom closet, is an album. Bring it here." Before Mrs. McCarthy agreed to open the photo album, the dishes were cleared away, the table wiped, and another round of handwashing ensued.

"I never saw these pictures before," remarked a surprised Johnny, as he turned page after page of shots of the women who worked with his mom; they all were shyly smiling at the camera, dressed in their white uniforms and hairnets.

"I kept these private. You know your dad never liked me working there.... Oh look, there's Rosalie and Michael with some of their friends." Kate and Johnny leaned in to get a better look at the old polaroid print. "There is Michael, behind him is a boy named Luca; then here is Rosalie, and a girlfriend from law school, and next to her is another friend named Jonathan. The boy in the back is Marco Rossetti, the youngest brother. Now, he is a big-cheese surgeon."

Johnny took personal umbrage at the *surgeon* comment. "What am I, chopped liver? I remember Marco, and I also remember Luca. He was always around Michael—he seemed shady to me. There was something odd about his attachment to the Alliance, and particularly to Michael." With his finger, Johnny traced a slow circle around Luca's face.

"He was shady. And I understand he still is. Just another small-time criminal," Mrs. McCarthy commented in her best all-knowing tone.

"Who are these folks?" Kate pointed to two men, one older and one younger.

"That is Andrew Edmonds, and this is his son, Thomas Edmonds." His mother quickly turned the page and began to talk about more of the young people who had worked at the bakery.

"Mrs. McCarthy, why didn't your husband like you working at the bakery? It was traditional work for a woman, well, at the time. I'm just curious." As Kate closely examined the numerous photos in the album, she was struck by how good-looking the young Mrs. McCarthy had been.

Johnny read her mind, and remarked to his mother, "You were, and of course are, a beautiful woman, Mom. Was Dad the jealous type?"

"Yes. He hated that all the construction men came in and couldn't understand why the owner of the company also stopped at the shop. There was no convincing him that they were all just patrons, nothing else. He went to his death being a jealous man." Johnny and Kate gave out a unified, "Oh." Johnny put his finger to his lips, stopping Kate from pursuing the topic of their marital discord.

While he and his mother talked more about what the neighborhood kids were doing now, Kate was preoccupied with a few questions. Who was Jonathan Price, the man standing next to the stunning Rosalie? And what about that Luca fellow? And finally, was there any basis for Mr. McCarthy's jealousy over the men in the construction crew, and if so, did it have anything to do with the Rossetti murders? Kate decided to mention the existence of the photo album to Jablonsky. It was an interesting chronicle of possible suspects—even the great chief couldn't deny its contribution to the case.

CHAPTER 7

AASHI PATEL AND JABLONSKY were having breakfast at Sophia's Cafe, even though it was a Saturday morning. Since her son, Sai, lived in California, Aashi was free to work whenever she wanted, and she particularly liked working Saturdays—there were fewer interruptions. Both Medical Examiner and Chief of Detectives were careers that had zero work hour parameters, a reality that had contributed to both of their divorces. When a crime happens and a dead body is on the table, Patel and Jablonsky must show up, no matter what hour or day of the week it is. As they sat at breakfast, there was an ease between them, partially because they shared these same work imperatives.

Jeanne, Jablonsky's usual waitress, did not work on Saturdays, but the weekend servers all knew how he took his coffee and how Dr. Patel liked her tea. As the chief triumphed over a three-layer breakfast sandwich of egg, bacon, cheddar cheese slices, tomato, and lettuce, they talked about common poisons.

"Is it possible to detect any evidence of a poison after so many years?" Jablonsky asked, using his napkin to wipe the oozing mayonnaise off the sides of his mouth. The chief was an enthusiastic diner, but also a clean and neat one.

"Your everyday homicidal dose of arsenic or cyanide can often be detected in hair or nails for a few years after death, but not much more. To find anything with the Rossetti siblings will be tough—almost all homicidal doses of poisons would be undetectable in bones after so long a time." As if to put a fine point on her statement, Aashi broke the yolk of her gently poached egg and sopped up its creamy deliciousness with bits of the toasted English muffin.

"As of right now, you, Madame Medical Examiner, have ruled out death by gun shot, knife, or any methods of torture that would leave a trace in the bones. What about strangulation?"

"I considered strangulation, of course. But there was no fracture on either of the victim's hyoid bone. I do have to add that not having a fracture on the hyoid doesn't always mean someone wasn't strangled, but in this case, the young woman probably would have sustained a fracture—she was small boned. I'm fairly confident that they were not strangled."

"I agree. That pretty much leaves poison as our method of death."

"Of course, that is the next logical idea, but we have no blood, organs, flesh, hair or nails in which to find a poison. It is my working hypothesis, however, that poison is the most likely cause of their deaths, but I'm afraid we will not be able to prove it through autopsy or forensics. You will have to elicit a confession from the perpetrator. Mrs. Rossetti and her son, Dr. Marco Rossetti, are pressuring us to release the bones. She wants to proceed with a funeral and burial, and I want that besieged family to have closure."

Jablonsky, now finished with his breakfast, sat back against the orange-red vinyl that covered the seats of their booth. Aashi started to twirl her cup—a habit reminiscent of swiveling her chair when she was at the laboratory. Stefan knew it was a sign that either she was bored or had something else to say.

"Aside from human decency, one of the reasons 1 personally went to inform Mrs. Rossetti that we had found and identified her two children was that 1 wanted to hear her talk about Michael and Rosalie. There are two causes of death that no parent would want to consider—first, for some unknown reason, Michael and Rosalie could have committed a double suicide by taking poison or...." Jablonsky interrupted and completed her thought, "Or, Michael poisoned his sister, and then himself. A homicide and then a suicide."

"Or, Stefan, it could have been the other way around, Rosalie could have poisoned her brother and then herself. But a third party would have to have placed them side by side, and then shoveled the dirt to cover the bodies." Jablonsky found himself thinking about a possible third person; *could it have been the younger brother, Marco?*

Dr. Patel continued. "Aside from the bit of leather found at the scene, there was only that ring that Dr. Fitzroy showed you—we have now confirmed that the gemstone is blue topaz with a lion sketched in it. The size of it rules out that it would be what is called a dinner ring. In Hindu mythology, the blue topaz is used to help one focus in meditation. Sometimes it is worn as a pendant; having it around one's body supposedly helps to give one a long, healthy life. There are other, more romantic ideas about the meaning of the stone. It comes in different shades of blue—Swiss blue is a lighter blue; London blue is a darker blue. The gemstone in the ring Dr. Fitzroy found would be considered the London blue shade."

Their waitress was hovering in the background with a pitcher of ice water, shaking her head at this conversation. *Ugh,* she thought. *Homicides, suicides, poisons, what kind of conversation is this?* She moved up to the table and poured freshwater, then quickly went to get the check; maybe presenting the bill would hurry them out of the cafe.

Dr. Patel was aware of the look of consternation on the waitress's face, so when the check came, she quickly took it and returned the bill with her payment. "It's my turn to treat, Stefan. Let's get out of here, we both have work to do." Jablonsky dropped a few more dollars on the table to add to the tip; he mused that Dr. Patel was consistently stingy in her tipping.

—◊◊◊—

DeVille and Jablonsky wove their way through the Strip District, cut across Shadyside, and finally entered the neighborhood of Squirrel Hill. Except for the ubiquitous lack of parking, it was one of Jablonsky's favorite city neighborhoods. It was a true walking community with college students stopping after class to share a meal at the reasonably priced Asian restaurants, young families shopping at the supermarket, and the elderly headed to the senior center or to the movie theaters. It was an old but thriving city area with a contagious hustle-bustle of energy.

The two detectives were there to interview Jubas Jones, who had been the liaison between the city planning office, the Edmonds Land Development Company, and the Neighborhood Alliance, around the time the two Rossetti siblings went missing. They pulled up in front of a three-story, red brick home which had a large front porch running the length of the house and a precipitous set of concrete steps leading to it. The house had a well-tended look. They sat in the car going over the former Chief Detective's notes on Jubas Jones.

Antoine reported, "Jones was obliging enough on the telephone, saying he understood that since we have found the Rossetti's, the investigation would be reopened." Antoine looked up at the front porch. "Nice house—not as grand as some of the older mansions around here, but it still would have cost a lot of bucks to buy something on this street. I didn't know city planners made that kind of money."

"They make a solid, middle-class salary. Jubas Jones was one of the first black men hired and promoted in that department. I remember seeing him on television—he came across as a clever and articulate guy who personally would have understood the mission of the Alliance. Many city neighborhoods of color were destroyed by real estate greed and gentrification. His wife was a nurse, so between the two of them this house would have been affordable." Jablonsky and DeVille got out of the car, locked the doors, and began the ascent to the front door. Jubas Jones came out onto the porch to watch their arduous climb.

"A mighty effort on both your parts! I try to walk these steps twice a day, just for the cardiac benefits. How do you do, Chief Detective Jablonsky, and Detective DeVille. I'm Jubas Jones. Let's go inside to my study so we can talk in private."

Jones was of medium height with a stocky build and a retirement belly. His skin was a shade of soft brown and his close-cut hair was gray. After asking them to wipe their shoes on the porch mat, he led the two detectives into a good-sized entry hall that opened onto a living room, a formal dining room, and then back into a kitchen. The house was cozy, decorated with family photos, several posters of Pittsburgh, well-worn couches and dining chairs—always observant, Jablonsky noted that there was nothing here that looked more expensive than Jones' preretirement salary could support.

Since there was no obvious space for a study on the first floor, the two detectives kicked off their shoes and followed Jubas to the second floor, where a bedroom had been transformed into an office. The room had been made functional by fully stocked floor-to-ceiling bookshelves. There was a large cherrywood desk that held a computer and a printer. Jones had commandeered the closet for his file cabinets and a small safe. Jablonsky could detect a faint odor of cigar smoke; it was a man's retreat.

"Thanks for seeing us, Mr. Jones. As you surmised, we have reopened the Rossetti case and are interviewing anyone who personally knew Michael and Rosalie, as well as the principals at the Edmonds Land Development Company. I'd like to start first with your impression of the people from Edmonds." Jablonsky settled into his seat and brought out his small paper notebook; DeVille opened his slim laptop to a screen with information on the Edmonds company. Jubas Jones bent forward in his chair, his hands clasped in front of him and began his story.

"I knew Andrew Edmonds, the founder and owner of the company, but I knew his son, Thomas, better. Thomas Edmonds was trying to make his reputation in his father's company through management of the Oakland projects, and so he lived here while those projects evolved. I think he still has a place in Pittsburgh. I was in meetings with Thomas, too numerous to count. And so was Michael Rossetti."

"What did you think of Thomas Edmonds, the son?" Jablonsky asked.

"Well, he was very driven. His father was a powerful and wealthy man who demanded excellence from his workers, and especially from Thomas. The son was an arrogant bastard who looked down on almost everyone except his father, whom I think he actually feared. He and his attorneys always came to the planning meetings dressed in expensive suits. Honestly, I didn't trust him."

"Aside from wanting to please his daddy, and generally being a rich bastard, what was it exactly that you didn't trust about him?"

"I can't legally prove it, but I think Thomas skirted the law in terms of building codes. I also think he was dishonest in how he dealt with the Alliance and with my office. He would promise one thing and do another." Jubas paused, stared at his feet, and then grunted his way out of the chair to retrieve a file, which he handed to Jablonsky.

"When Michael and Rosalie went missing, we all were interviewed by your old boss. Over the several years of negotiations with the Edmonds company, I also kept my own private notes. This file contains both. My unproven suspicions were that Thomas Edmonds never intended on honoring bargains made with the Alliance or the city, and that he had one or more paid plants in the Alliance organization. I mentioned it to Michael."

"What specifically made you think there were plants in the Alliance?"

"Thomas Edmonds, or his flock of legal eagles, would come to the meetings already prepared for Michael's specific objections to their plans. It was as if they had advance knowledge." Stefan nodded in agreement—he would have been suspicious as well.

Focusing on Jubas Jones's private notes, Jablonsky found the same two names that were given to him by Dr. Rossetti—Jonathan Price, a law student with Rosalie, and Luca Lorenzo, a friend of Michael's. He handed the file to Antoine open to the sheet with the names. The two men looked at each other in recognition but made no comment in front of Jones.

"May I take this with me?" asked Jablonsky.

"Yes. I made you that copy. I'll keep the originals for now."

Stefan then asked, "What did you think of Michael and Rosalie?"

Jubas' cleared his throat as his eyes teared. "He was a great kid. He believed that the Alliance could maintain the integrity of the neighborhoods, if all the players involved in the building expansion would agree on certain basic tenets. Michael was an optimist; it was Rosalie who was the realist. She often talked about greed as one of the most powerful human motivations, and that negotiation wasn't a word greedy men had in their vocabulary. She always wanted Michael to hold the line more, to agitate, and to confront—Rosalie felt the Alliance shouldn't give an inch to the company." Jones held out his hand to have Jablonsky give him the file, and then flipped through it.

"Here they are, brother and sister." Jablonsky had seen similar photos in the police file—he passed them over to DeVille, who unconsciously let out a low whistle, "She was beautiful, all right." The two older men smiled at each other over the young man's immediate response to Rosalie's physical attributes.

"Was their relationship as close as everyone indicates?"

"These two siblings were as tight as a Porsche 911 taking a Pittsburgh curve, but as the negotiations for the final architectural plans neared, I occasionally saw them argue. Rosalie would stand up in the meetings, looking like a Botticelli angel, stare right at Edmonds or his attorneys, and point by point go through the legalities; she never believed that the company would honor their agreements.

"And did they?"

Jones let out a snort. "No. The construction sites were far more extensive than depicted in the original plans—Rosalie was right. By that time, however, the two were missing."

"What did you think happened to them? Jablonsky asked, locking eyes with Jones.

"I think they were murdered. I suspect someone from the Edmonds company had hired a hitman, or that someone from the neighborhood had been bought off to kill them. I said the same to your old boss when he first interviewed me."

"Did you like Thomas Edmonds as the person who ordered the murders?" Jablonsky watched Jones struggling to be both honest and clear in his answer, which ended up being "Maybe."

"Do you think it was possible that it was either a double suicide or a homicide-suicide?"

Jones suddenly stood up and paced back and forth in the small study. "By God, I never thought of that! There was never any hint of that idea in the news or around city hall. No, I can't believe that two such passionate and alive young people would do such a thing—what, kill themselves over land development? No." But as he said these words, it was clear that Jubas Jones was not so stunned that he couldn't entertain the possibility, a fact that Jablonsky took note of.

"Thanks, Jubas. This has been helpful. We will talk again."

Jones shook hands with the detectives, assuring them he was available for more questions. Jablonsky and DeVille made their way back down the steep steps to their car and headed to the precinct. After a few minutes of silence, Antoine asked, "What do you think, sir?"

"He certainly is believable, but we will see if there is any consensus of his impressions by others who knew the principals. Interesting that Michael was the dove and Rosalie was the hawk. I also noticed that Jubas seemed to have a soft spot for both of them, especially Rosalie. Let's confirm everything with Marco Rossetti, and also with my two trusty Nonas. I want to wait to speak with Mrs. Rossetti—I've held back interviewing her because I believe she should have some time to absorb the discovery of her children's bodies."

DeVille respected his boss's pacing when it came to when, and how, to interview family members. He knew it was a special "Jablonsky" talent that was both a gift and a skill sharpened by experience. "What about Thomas Edmonds? He keeps a condo here in the 'burgh—I have his personal and corporate addresses. His father, Andrew, is dead."

—◦◦◦—

As the detectives debated the pros and cons of where to interview Thomas Edmonds, Luca Lorenzo, eating lunch at a local diner, was getting a call on a burner phone; the voice said, "You've heard? They found the bodies and have reopened the investigation. But that's not what I'm interested in."

There was such a long silence at the other end of the line that Luca prompted, "Are you still there?"

"Listen closely. Here's what I want." The directions were few, and tersely given.

"And the payment?" asked Luca.

"Same as last time. You can pick it up at the drop spot. Call me afterwards." Luca stepped outside of the diner and walked to his car, where he stamped the cellphone into bits; as he crossed one of the bridges over the Monongahela River, he tossed the remnants into the water.

CHAPTER 8

FIONA MCCARTHY ALWAYS ROSE AT FIVE in the morning. Her neighbors, noticing that her house lights went on, never understood what she did in those excruciatingly early hours, especially in the winter, but they were too polite to ask. They forgot that she used to work the first shift at a bakery. Her morning ritual included brewing herself some fragrant hot tea, then crawling back into bed to read the Pittsburgh newspaper online.

Johnny would be surprised that she also read his academic articles on the laptop he had given her but thought she never used. He didn't realize that his brains and curiosity came from her genes. This morning, she cozily sipped the tea out of her favorite Belleek china cup, completely engrossed in reading an article on the discovery of Michael's and Rosalie Rossetti's remains.

A flat-black Chevrolet Camaro moved slowly toward the house. Since it was still dark, the streetlights cast the kind of chiaroscuro always seen in classic film noir. The driver eased into a full stop, rolled down the car window, and fired two shots into Fiona's front downstairs window. Then he waited. When a figure appeared in the bedroom window of the second floor, the driver took careful aim and fired a third shot. He watched the figure fall backward, then gunned the engine and fled.

The neighborhood erupted into action—with overcoats quickly thrown over pajamas, people came out onto their front porches or into the street, calling to each other and anxiously looking around. Her closest neighbors gathered on Fiona's porch, and when they saw the bullet holes, they started pounding on her front door. "Fiona! Fiona! Are you all right?"

When there wasn't any answer, they lifted one of her flowerpots, retrieved the spare key she kept there and continued to call her name as they entered the house. One neighbor, a medical resident who had been out for an early morning jog before her long shift started, flew up the stairs and found Fiona bleeding and unconscious on her bedroom floor. "Call the ambulance, and get the police," was the cry.

Kate and Johnny were walking around the Highland Park reservoir before heading to work. Their gossipy chatter about the university had run its course, so they kept a good pace in silence, enjoying the crisp air and the beauty of their surroundings. The bright winter sunlight caused the water of the reservoir to shimmer like crystals sewn on a woman's evening gown. The peaceful atmosphere periodically was interrupted by the occasional roar of the big cats at the zoo situated right below the reservoir, or by walking partners sharing a laugh. It was an invigorating way to start the day.

Because they walked so early in the morning, neither typically received calls. Today, however, Johnny's cell pinged, and the name read "Jablonsky." Johnny immediately answered.

"John, are you alone? Kate is with you? Good. Someone took a shot at your mother's house, and I'm sorry to say that she was wounded. She is alive, and on her way to the hospital. Meet me there."

As if in a dream, Johnny turned to Kate, and uttered the improbable, "My mother's been shot. An ambulance is taking her to the hospital. Jablonsky will meet us there. Come on." Kate didn't ask any questions; they both sprinted the short distance to her car and zoomed out of the park, down Highland Avenue to connect with Fifth Avenue, the boulevard which would take them directly to the university hospital. Neither spoke on the quick drive. Johnny leaped out of the car at the emergency department entrance and Kate circled around to find a parking spot.

Before she left the car, she texted Joan. "Johnny's mother has been shot. Can you meet us in the ED?" Joan's immediate response was a simple, "On my way."

Still in her jogging tights, running shoes, and windbreaker, Kate made her way to the emergency department, which was surprisingly busy at this early hour. Kate couldn't find Johnny, but did spot Joan, who was hustling toward her dressed in her surgical greens and comfortable clogs. They grabbed each other in a tight hug.

"I can't find Johnny. All I know is that Jablonsky called and said that someone had taken a shot at his mother's house and that she was hit."

"Actually, one of the emergency physicians just texted me that they had a gunshot wound come in and could I help. There was a bad car pile-up this morning, so the department is slammed. Stay right here. I'll find Johnny." In everyday life, Joan was Kate's closest woman friend, but in the hospital, she was Dr. Weisner, respected and talented surgeon. Kate felt a wave of relief surge over her; if Fiona needed surgery, Joan was one of the best. A few minutes later, a nurse came and guided her back to where Johnny was sitting.

"Joan and her team took Mom into surgery. The bullet is lodged close to her lungs...." Johnny's voice trailed off, too filled with emotion to continue. Kate put her arm around his shoulders and started to ask what had happened when Jablonsky walked into the area.

"I understand your mom is already in surgery. Okay. Here's what we know." Stefan pulled a chair close to theirs and lowered his voice. "Early this morning, around five, someone cruised by in a dark colored muscle car and shot several times at your mom's house. After the first bullets hit the downstairs front window, we believe that she looked out of her second-floor bedroom window—that's when we suspect the shooter got her. I'm really sorry, John."

Johnny made a fist and pounded it into his other hand. With vocal cords pulled tight with his anger, he asked, "Was this just a random drive-by shooting?"

"According to the neighbors, her house seemed to be targeted. No other house was hit, nor were any of the cars parked on the street. If it was just to scare her or the neighbors, more random shots would have been sprayed. They reported that your mom is an early riser, so often lights are on in the house before the sun is up. Apparently, today was no different. Someone had to know that fact, which means he or she has been watching the house."

Kate couldn't stop herself from jumping in. "Did someone see the shooter?"

"A medical resident was out for her early jog before heading to the hospital; she saw the car and could identify it. She also was able to give us half of the license plate number."

"What was the make of the car?" Kate immediately asked.

"That information is part of our investigation; it isn't for the public." If Kate could have stamped her foot, she would have. "But, Chief. This is Johnny's mother we are talking about. I can help, we can help. Come on. I think a little leeway is in order."

"Maybe later on. We are just starting to get a picture of things. Let us do our job—your job is taking care of Mrs. McCarthy." Kate turned her head so he wouldn't see her mouthing, "Screw you." She turned back to face Jablonsky and, in an informational tone, added, "We just had visited his mother, asking about her time at the Rossetti bakery."

"Johnny, did you notice anyone suspicious when you were there?"

Johnny quietly replied, "No. I didn't notice anything. My God, I didn't notice anything. Me, an art historian who notices all kinds of details—I noticed nothing." If Johnny could have punched himself out of guilt for possibly overlooking clues, he would have.

"Is there any reason that someone would want to hurt your mom?" The chief had taken out his notebook and periodically recorded a word or a phrase. Now, his pen was poised, waiting for the answer.

"She's just... my mom. She's a neighborhood lady who worked at a bakery, cleaned and cooked for me and my dad, played bingo on Saturday nights, and went to Mass on Sunday mornings. I can't imagine that there is anything about her life that would engender murderous rage!" Johnny was either on the verge of hitting a wall or breaking down in a crying jag. He got up and walked down the hallway. The chief turned to Kate.

"You were talking with Mrs. McCarthy about Rosalie's Bakery, the one the Rossetti's own? Anything interesting?" Jablonsky had no reservation about scolding Kate one minute for wanting to know information on a case, and the next minute soliciting information from her. *It's all in the service of catching the bad guy,* he thought.

"Yes, there was something interesting. She had a whole photo album with pictures of everyone who worked there, including the young people from the neighborhood. There were pictures of Michael and Rosalie, but more to the point, there were photos of Andrew Edmonds and his son, Thomas Edmonds, and plenty of their construction crew. She had lots of stories about the people who were regular customers around the time Michael and Rosalie disappeared. I believe the album presents a line-up of possible suspects. And she appeared to have had it hidden in the bedroom. Neither Johnny nor his father knew about the album. I find that interesting."

Kate paused, then decided to move beyond the stop sign that the chief had placed between her and the unfolding investigation. Wanting to elicit his theories, she said, "You don't think this shooting has anything to do with the Rossetti case, do you?"

"It might. Look Kate, this is a criminal case. The stories Mrs. McCarthy told about the people in the photo album will be a big help, but someone wanted to kill her—you understand? You and Johnny cannot go snooping around. It is an unsafe situation." The chief's message was definitive, and his tone, curt. He put Kate back in her lane—the amateur sleuth lane. A wave of defiance came over her, but she didn't act on it. "I understand, Sir. You are just looking out for us."

Johnny had returned, so Jablonsky advised him about the procedure. "Bill Reeves and his forensics team are at your mom's house now, processing the scene. Whenever you can manage it, I'd like to talk to you about your mom's stories concerning the bakery. Forensics will take the photo album and perform their magic. Then I'll have it at my office for whenever it's convenient for you to stop by."

"What would my mom being shot have to do with the Rossetti's?" Unlike Kate, who felt that Fiona knew more than she was saying about the people in the photos, Johnny seemed completely blindsided by any possible connection. *Boys and their mothers,* thought Jablonsky. *Sons never think that their mothers have any life outside of taking care of them.* From years of investigative experience, he knew that plenty of moms had secret lives.

Since they were given a beeper that would alert them when Fiona was out of surgery, Kate and Johnny went to the hospital cafeteria. They drank some bad coffee and pushed scrambled eggs around their plates. Kate called her office, explained the situation, and rescheduled her advisees—she wasn't going to leave Johnny's side.

Hospital waiting time is always experientially longer than clock time; although the beeper went off two hours later, it seemed like it had been days. Joan was waiting for them at the surgical suite. "Johnny, your mom is alive. We were, however, unable to retrieve the bullet because it is too close to her lungs. I must warn you that she is quite weak because she lost a lot of blood. You can see her, but she isn't fully awake. The next twenty-four hours will be critical. I'm afraid she is not out of the woods. I'll walk you back to her."

Kate mouthed, "Thank you," to her friend and sat down on one of the long benches outside the surgical unit. Having been an orphan most of her life, she felt empathy for what Johnny might be facing. Even though he still had aunts, uncles, and cousins, losing both parents is, for better or worse, one of life's big transitions.

Her mind drifted back to the shooting. *What would his mother know that would cause someone to want to murder her?* Kate believed the answer was somewhere in that photo album.

CHAPTER 9

THE FUNERAL MASS FOR MICHAEL AND ROSALIE was packed. People's compulsion to attend the Mass had nothing to do with religion, but rather was a recognition of what the Rossetti family, and the South Oakland community, had suffered during the years that Michael and Rosalie were missing.

Two caskets sat side-by-side in front of the altar and were literally blanketed with woven casket covers made of lilies, carnations, snapdragons, orchids, roses, and gladiolas. The altar flowers consisted of tall branches of lush French white and blue lilacs. The symbolism of the spring flowers was not lost on the attendees; even Stefan was emotionally moved by the beauty of the arrangements that honored the youth of the lost siblings.

Dr. Patel and Bill Reeves sat together. Jablonsky joined them before the funeral Mass started, sliding in at the end of their pew. They knew he was working, so were not surprised when he excused himself and walked to the back of the church. He had stationed DeVille at the double doors of the large cathedral to observe people as they arrived.

"Anything?" Jablonsky quietly asked.

"Yeah. I spotted Jonathan Price, and that rough looking fellow slouching over there is Luca Lorenzo." Pretending to read the funeral bulletin, they glanced toward Luca, who himself seemed to be scanning the crowd.

"Put a man on him; don't let him slip through our fingers. And ask detective Lemon to grab Price when he leaves. I want both of them for an interview." As everyone stood for the start of the service, the chief noticed that Kate was sitting a few rows behind Patel; he wasn't surprised to see her, he knew that she wanted to be in the mix—he liked that about her, and he also feared that quality in her.

When the funeral Mass ended, Jablonsky was lurking in the side isle of the cathedral, watching Lemon and DeVille walk out two men; he noticed Kate watching as well. "You look like you know those two guys," he remarked as he caught up with her.

"I don't know them, but I recognize them from Fiona's photo album—that's Luca Lorenzo and Jonathan Price." The forensic crew had already delivered Fiona's work album, but he was still waiting to go through it with both Johnny and Kate. "When Johnny is available, let's meet at my office to talk about the photos. Kate, the sooner the better." The chief left the church, drove back to the precinct, and prepared to interview Price and Lorenzo.

—∿∿—

Jablonsky stood in the bullpen arranging pictures on the murder board: Jonathan Price was there, pictured as a young law student and friend of Rosalie, along with a recent photo of him as a high-priced real estate attorney. An early mug shot of Luca Lorenzo, petty thief and small-time criminal and friend of Michael, was also pinned to the board. A picture of Andrew Edmonds, the deceased owner of the Edmonds Land Company was placed next to that of his son, Thomas, who now kept a very expensive home on Mount Washington.

From the university student newspaper, they found and pinned up old photos of members of the Neighborhood Alliance, and also one of Jubas Jones, the retired city planner. No lines connected any of those people to the pictures of Michael and Rosalie; the investigation was just beginning. In a separate panel was a picture of Fiona McCarthy.

In the interview room, Jonathan Price had broken out in an unprecedented flop sweat and was in the process of wiping his face with a monogrammed handkerchief when Jablonsky entered. Price didn't bother to stand up.

For some cosmic reason, real estate development, in all its job permutations, attracted people who are in some way smarmy, and Jonathan Price was no exception. He was rumored to occasionally transfer funds from his clients' accounts to cover losses he incurred at the poker table; he always put back the money, so in his mind, he hadn't done anything wrong—it was just creative accounting. And, of course, there were other moral infractions, usually having to do with providing "escorts" to out-of-town developers. DeVille had made Jablonsky aware of this attorney's seamy reputation.

"Thank you for coming from the funeral service, Mr. Price. As you know, we are reexamining the Rossetti case. I have your statement from when they first went missing. I only have a few questions to ask about that statement, but feel free to add anything that comes to mind as we talk. This is strictly routine." The little paper notebook lay on the table next to his old boss's case file. Jablonsky flashed Price his most sincere smile, all the while thinking that the man in front of him was guilty of many things, the least of which was wearing a wildly patterned tie to a somber funeral.

Jonathan Price relaxed back into his chair; *Good,* thought Stefan, *I want him to think he's safe.*

"Ask away, Chief. My life is an open book." Price vigorously rubbed his two hands together, clicking his ostentatious pinky rings together. At the heart of the Rossetti case were young people in the midst of both the ideological stage of life and the normal mating urges; Jablonsky would start the questioning there.

"In your original statement, you talked about the last time you saw Rosalie Rossetti alive. The two of you had been studying at the law library in Oakland. She left to meet a friend and you stayed at the library. Do you now remember the name of the friend she was meeting?"

Jonathan Price appeared to grind his teeth, then he straightened his tie and ended with smoothing both sides of his hair with the palms of his hands. "Well, at the time, I didn't want to say who it was because Michael would have killed him."

"Oh? Who was it then?" Jablonsky was surprised at Price's forthcomingness.

"It was Thomas Edmonds. You know, the son of Andrew Edmonds, owner of the development company. It was like Juliet dating a Montague. Thomas was a slime-ball, but a successful one. I admired that." Price started twirling one of his rings.

"This is very interesting, Mr. Price. You say that she kept this relationship secret from her brother? Did anyone in the rest of the family or the Alliance know about it?"

"I don't think so. I don't know about old man Edmonds. Maybe he directed Thomas to get close to Rosalie, you know, to get information. I don't think much got past the old man."

Jablonsky paused, looked at the file, and then in a subdued tone of voice remarked, "You cared for Rosalie. In your earlier statement you said that the two of you were close. It must have bothered you that she chose to have this clandestine relationship with the enemy, and a man you didn't respect. Were you jealous?" Jablonsky lowered his eyes back to the file, then wrote in his notebook, appearing to make his question seem casual.

"Have you seen pictures of Rosalie? Everybody wanted her. Everybody wanted to be next to her, if you take my drift. Yeah, I had a crush on the girl. But I wasn't going to force myself on her." Price straightened some imaginary wrinkles out of his suit jacket with his hands. "I'm a good guy."

"Indeed," replied Jablonsky, his sarcastic tone going over Price's head. Stefan carefully worked through Jonathan's original statement. "Did you know any of Rosalie's women friends from law school?"

"Not really. There were a few girls in our study group, but I had the impression she was always too busy to do chick stuff. She sometimes would grab a beer with me and a couple of the girls in our study group—I think that was about the extent of it. Don't get me wrong; everyone liked her, she just was really focused on her studies."

Jablonsky's daughter, Carly, who was now a practicing attorney, retained several very close girlfriends from law school. Why hadn't Rosalie? He took out four pictures, one old and three relatively new.

"Do you recognize any of these women?"

Jonathan carefully placed his pointer finger on each photo, then picked up one. "This girl was in our law class and study group. Um, she had three names, it was Jane something-something. I haven't seen her for years. I don't know the other three. Who are they?" Jablonsky didn't reveal that they were women unrelated to the case.

"One more question. You knew Marco, the youngest brother. What were your impressions of him?"

"He was a weird kid; apparently brilliant, but really weird. Rosalie watched over him. They were tight."

"Do you think he knew that she was seeing Thomas Edmonds?"

"Now, that's a good question. I'm afraid I don't know the answer. It's possible he followed her one night and saw them together—and then, who knows what he would have done. But I really don't know who would have had a motive to kill Michael and Rosalie."

"You believe they were murdered?"

"Of course. Everybody does. Why else would you be involved?" Jonathan Price stood up. As far as he was concerned, the interview was over, and he had aced it.

"Before you leave, I want you to look at these photos." Jablonsky placed two pictures on the table. One was of a young Fiona McCarthy, and one photo was current.

"This one looks familiar. I think this is one of the women who worked in Rosalie's Bakery. I guess this is how she looks now. I don't remember her name."

Jablonsky thought, *This guy is really something—he's a person of interest and at the end, he gives me Thomas Edmonds or the teenage brother as possible killers. And he lies about knowing Fiona. You've got to admire the degree to which he thinks he can manipulate the narrative.*

"We will be in touch with any follow-up questions." Jablonsky left the room thinking, *Gotcha,* and Price left the room thinking, *Like taking candy from a baby.*

Luca Lorenzo was squirming in his seat. Visually, he was a skinny, weather-beaten white guy, with almost every inch of skin covered in tattoos. On one forearm was a five-card spread with a prominent ace of spades, dice, and stacks of cash, and on the other, skull and crossbones. He wore several bracelets on both arms. His neck had snake bodies running up each side, their open-mouthed heads curling around his ears. Peeping out from his tee shirt was the top of some elaborate, dystopian scene that probably covered his chest and wrapped around to his back.

Jablonsky sat down and, as he did with Price, he opened Luca's old file and then placed his notebook next to it. "Mr. Lorenzo, thank you for coming in with my detectives. Since you were at the Rossetti funeral today, I'm sure you are aware that we are re-interviewing everyone who gave a statement at the time of their disappearance. This is routine; you are here simply to go through your original statement or to add anything that you now know but didn't know at the time."

"Yeah. Okay." Luca grimaced, then slightly twisted his neck from side to side, his vertebra reacting with rebellious cracking noises.

"Tell me about you and Michael." Once again, Jablonsky was after the relationships between the major players in the Alliance.

Luca seemed both surprised and moved by the question. "Mind if I smoke?" he asked, pulling out a pack of cigarettes. "You can't smoke in this building," replied Stefan. "We can get you some coffee."

"Yeah. Coffee. Lots of sugar and cream."

"Go ahead. Tell me about Michael while we wait for the coffee." Jablonsky settled back in his chair and waited.

"Michael was the best friend I ever had. He treated me with respect, you understand? He treated me like we was equals. I was his guy in the Alliance, like, second-in-command. He could count on me, day or night, to do whatever the Alliance needed. He really cared about the neighborhood, you know? He gave a crap." Coffee arrived, and Luca systematically stirred four packs of sugar into his cup.

"You cared about Michael, you loved him... like a brother."

"Loved him? Hey, watch your mouth, I'm no finocchio! But, yeah, I loved him...like a brother." Jablonsky took note of Luca's protestation that he wasn't gay—it seemed a bit too ferocious. Was he? Was Michael? And why would it matter? Was his gayness a motive to murder him?

"Was there anyone around in the Alliance, or the general neighborhood, who would have had a motive to kill Michael?"

"I don't really know. Michael was trying to make the Edmonds' company come to the table, negotiate-like, but their mouthpieces always seemed to be one step ahead. Michael was tight with that city-planner guy, Jones. All that hard work and look what happened. The old neighborhood is gone, ain't it?" To the chief, his words echoed Marco Rossetti's sentiments.

"What about Rosalie? Was she seeing anyone who would want to use her, or get to Michael through her?"

Luca sipped his coffee. "I didn't know much about Rosalie's private life. I was Michael's friend, not hers. But she was smart; she finished law school. She stood up to the Edmonds's attorneys, and sometimes, if necessary, she stood up to Michael. Nothing got past Rosalie, that's for sure."

"Luca, what do you mean by 'nothing got past her'?" Jablonsky opened the palms of his hands in an encouraging gesture.

"Well, Rosalie knew everything that went on at the bakery—it had been her grandmother's shop, and then was her mother's. She knew the construction guys who came in, she knew Andrew and Thomas Edmonds, she knew all the boys who worked part-time, and she knew all the ladies at the counter. Like, people confided in her. She knew where all the bodies were buried—oh, sorry, I didn't mean no disrespect." Luca's sensitivity was completely unexpected.

"Are you thinking of secrets that she knew, and nobody else did?"

"I don't know. I'm just sayin' that people told her things—I don't know what they were." Luca began to crack his knuckles.

In a neutral manner, Jablonsky went through the rest of the original statement. "You know, Luca, you haven't always been a good boy. I'm looking at your sheet—lots of criminal activity over the years. You must know people who conduct business, shall we say, off the books. Did Michael ever ask you to do things for the Alliance that involved criminal activity?"

"No. Michael lived in the straight world."

"Did Andrew or Thomas Edmonds, or any of their crew, ask you to do something bent?"

"Yeah. When Thomas Edmonds was hiring local workers, he asked me to find out who would look the other way, you know, for some coin." *Now we are getting somewhere,* thought Jablonsky.

"Thomas knew that you were close to Michael and the Alliance. Did he want you to be a mole for him?"

"Yeah. He asked me to snitch. I said no. Nothing was going to get between me and Michael. I said I would help out with the workers, but not with the Alliance. I had my standards."

"I can see that. So, just to summarize: The Edmonds Land Company was engaged in paying you for information about workers; They paid certain workers to look the other way on building codes; They paid people to lie about complying with the city planning regulations. And it is possible that Rosalie knew about some of the company's malfeasance. Close enough?" Jablonsky kept his expression and tone even, non-judgmental.

"That's the skinny." Having finished his coffee, Luca started tearing apart the paper cup, bit by bit.

"Just one more thing." Jablonsky took out the two pictures of Fiona McCarthy. He turned them around to face Luca and slid them across the desk. "Do you recognize this woman?"

Luca took his time scrutinizing the photos. "Well, she looks like one of the women who worked at Rosalie's bakery a long time ago. I don't remember her name."

"Do you own a flat-black Chevy Camaro?"

"That's my ride; everybody knows the car. My baby is in the shop, though. There were a few chips on the paint. It is over at Diamond Detailing."

"Your car was identified on the morning that Mrs. McCarthy, this woman, was shot."

Luca was clearly shocked. "That ain't true! My baby has been in the shop for a couple of weeks. Ask the owner of Diamond Detailers."

"Is this your vehicle registration and license plate number?"

Luca looked at the registration document. "Yeah. That's mine. But whoever told you my car was on the street the day of the shooting is lying. Absolutely." He stretched his arms over his head and let out a deep breath. "We done here, Chief? I got appointments."

"We're finished. Luca, I'm sure Michael would be proud of how helpful you've been. Shows that you really were a brother to him. Don't, however, leave town. I may want to speak to you again."

Jablonsky left the Lorenzo interview feeling like the man with the criminal past was more honest with him than Price, the ostensibly well-known attorney and officer of the court. *If everyone was confiding in Rosalie, I wonder if she knew something that got her and Michael killed?* Jablonsky unwrapped a piece of cinnamon gum and wedged it into one cheek.

After the two interviews, Jablonsky and DeVille began to formulate motives and note connections on the murder board. Luca Lorenzo, Jonathan Price, Thomas Edmonds, and even Marco Rossetti, were all in the frame. In his illegible cursive, the chief wrote: Who ordered the hit on Fiona? Who was driving the Camaro? What were people confiding in Rosalie? Was Michael closeted?

CHAPTER 10

KATE WAS FINISHED with her appointments for the day. She looked at her cell to read the latest texts from Johnny—he said that he was leaving his office to go to the hospital to see his mom. They decided to meet and trek what was affectionately named "Cardiac Hill."

They arrived at the hospital winded but refreshed from the exercise and made their way to his mother's private room. Both were relieved to see the guard sitting next to her door. They asked him how everything was and then slowly entered the room. The sounds and sights inside the room immediately transported Kate back to the days before her grandfather's death—the beeping of the machines, hydrating liquid being slowly dripped into the IV, the craggy lines on the monitors tracking blood pressure and heart rate, the small cup of water with its bent drinking straw, and the overheated atmosphere. It was all too familiar for her and all brand new for Johnny.

Kate busied herself with putting the flowers she had brought into a vase. Johnny pulled his chair close to the bed, reaching out to brush his mother's hair away from her face.

"Hi, Mom. How are you feeling?" Fiona opened her eyes and attempted a smile. She pointed to the area of her chest where the bullet had entered, whispering, "Pain." Kate knew that one word was like a sharp knife cutting into Johnny's heart. "I'll be right back, Mom." He hurried out to the central nurses' station to talk to her team about his mother's pain medications.

Kate sat down and tried to distract Fiona by chatting about how much she had enjoyed the ham and cheese jambons. Mrs. McCarthy gave a hint of a smile at the compliments. She gestured to Kate to move closer, and then took a surprisingly strong hold of Kate's hand. "You take good care of my boy. He will need you, you more than that Julius. You stand with him against what is coming."

"Of course, Fiona. I will always be there for Johnny. But what do you mean by what is coming?" Kate leaned closer to hear the sick woman's weak voice. "In my basement, you will find a Manilla envelope taped to the back of the freezer, and inside, a sealed freezer bag. It says "pork chops" on it. Get both. The evidence is there."

Fiona ran out of breath just as Johnny and the nurse came back into the room. Mrs. McCarthy wasn't thriving as everyone had hoped she would; her skin was the color of porcelain, and she had no appetite. Today, as if they were a talisman, she had laced her rosary beads through her fingers. When she drifted back to sleep, Kate and Johnny talked about the shooting and Jablonsky's call asking them to come to the precinct. Kate did not tell Johnny, yet, what his mother had said. It was such a curious phrase, "against what was coming."

—⁓—

"Detective Jablonsky. Didn't mean to distract you." Stefan quickly covered the murder board, and steered Jubas Jones into his office. Even before Jablonsky could begin his follow-up questions to the meeting at his house, he observed that Jubas looked like he had something to say. "Has something new come to mind?" he prompted.

"Well, I remembered something that I forgot to tell your old boss. At the time, I didn't think it was relevant, but maybe it is. In the middle of the negotiations between city planning, the Alliance, and the Edmonds Land Company, a colleague and I were having dinner at an out-of-the-way place we often went to. I saw Thomas Edmonds sitting at the restaurant's bar having a drink with Rosalie Rossetti." Jubas paused, and Jablonsky moved his chair forward, interest writ large on his face.

"Really? I thought they were on opposite sides." The chief didn't reveal that Jonathan Price had already mentioned this unlikely liaison.

Jubas nodded in agreement, saying, "At first, I thought she was continuing to negotiate with him, but then at some point, he reached over and put his hand on her shoulder, then moved in close—it was intimate."

"How did she respond?"

"She didn't move away from him. I watched them until our entrees came, and then around that time Edmonds helped with her coat and they left together. Plus, I recognized another person sitting with a group at a back table; the guy rubbernecked when Rosalie and Thomas left together."

"Did you know this person from the Alliance?" Jablonsky already knew the answer to his question.

"It was a friend of Rosalie's from law school. His name was Jonathan Price."

"Did you recognize anyone else at his table?" This was a new group of possible suspects.

"No. Price was there with a guy in a suit and a girl. The suit had a briefcase with him, and he and Price were engrossed in examining what I thought looked like legal documents or legal contracts. You know, certain pages had those little blue sticky arrows that point to where you sign. Like that."

"Did you recognize the girl at the table? Jubas shook his head in the negative. "Did Thomas Edmonds see them?" Jablonsky didn't know the answer to this question.

"I'm not sure."

"Jubas, wouldn't an affair between those two have been completely out of character for her, a fervent member of the Alliance and loyal to her brother? An affair would have betrayed everyone she was close to and put into question everything she said she believed in. Am I right?"

"Absolutely! Even more so because Rosalie wasn't just liked—she was beloved. She was a beautiful, warm, witty person, whom both men and women wanted to be around. For her to hook up with a slime like Edmonds would have been unthinkable to those who cared about her."

Jablonsky quietly asked, "Is that why you didn't mention it in the original inquiry?"

Jones looked down at the floor. "Yeah, now that you put it that way, I guess it was the reason. You know, everyone was half in love with her, me included. I never saw her flirt with any man, young or old—but there was something about her presence that made you feel taller, smarter, better looking— you're a man, you know what I mean." Despite his years, Jones blushed at his own susceptibility to the alluring pheromones of a young woman's presence.

"I think I can remember back that far. Jonathan Price was known to have a crush on her. Was that your take as well?"

"I really didn't know him. He was just the law school friend who hung around with Rosalie. Others would know better than I; if they were romantically linked, it would have been common knowledge. The Alliance was a gossipy group—like all groups, I guess."

"Jubas. Do you know this woman?" Jablonsky laid out the two pictures of Fiona that he previously showed Price and Lorenzo.

"That's a woman who used to work at Rosalie's Bakery. I still stop in there for pastries, but she has been retired for quite a while. Um, she had an Irish name... wait a minute... is this the woman who was shot in Greenfield?"

"Yes. You knew some of the main characters in the company, but did you know anything about members of the construction crew that stopped there in the mornings?" Jablonsky cast his line and went fishing.

Jubas Jones's eyebrows were raised so high that they could have taken flight over the top of his head. "I don't know. I really didn't know the woman; she was just someone who waited on me at the bakery. She was a good-looking woman; many of the patrons flirted with her, including those constructions workers. Maybe that's a link—but what would the motive be—I mean, to want to kill her?" Jablonsky sat back and let Jubas Jones speculate.

"I guess this means you will be talking to Thomas Edmonds. He's got to be your prime suspect." After having spent his career in city planning, where he was always in the loop about what was going on politically as well as with the police, it was hard for Jubas not to ask about the investigation.

Jablonsky gave him a crumb from the table, "I will be talking to Edmonds."

Jubas left the office, stopping to say hello to Antoine. Jablonsky noticed that Jones, an older, professional black man, always stopped and talked with Coupe, his rising black detective. *That's good,* thought Stefan, *even though I'm not sure I completely trust Jones.*

Before Jablonsky talked with Edmonds, he wanted to stop at the hospital to check on Mrs. McCarthy and then see Kate and Johnny. "Coupe. Get in here. Listen, I want you to find out about Lorenzo's Camaro. You heard him say that it was supposedly at Diamond Detailers when Fiona was shot. Then I want you and Lemon to canvas the neighborhood again to see if anyone remembers anything else."

Antoine nodded as he typed his notes into his slim laptop. The chief continued. "Jones confirmed some facts for us. Jonathan Price definitely knew that Rosalie was seeing Thomas Edmonds. Jubas saw Price at the same restaurant the night he saw Rosalie and Thomas together. If Jonathan Price was signing some contracts or legal documents, I want to know what they were. I'm heading over to the hospital to talk with Fiona."

CHAPTER 11

AS HE WAS DRIVING TO THE HOSPITAL, Kate called him. "Chief. I want to report an odd conversation I had with Fiona McCarthy a few hours ago. When Johnny was out of the room, she asked me to stand by Johnny for, quote, 'What is to come.'"

"Do you know what she meant by, 'What is to come?'"

"No. I don't know. But then, she went on to say that the evidence, yes, that's the word she used, "evidence," was in her basement freezer; there is also a manila envelope taped to the side of it. A bag, actually inside the freezer, is marked, pork chops." Kate couldn't resist saying that last sentence again, "A bag marked pork chops."

"Okay. You grab Johnny and the two of you meet me at Fiona's house. I'm going to call DeVille and the forensics people. He will bring Fiona's work album. Don't go into the house before we all get there—I don't want anything touched or moved on the outside, either. You understand, Kate? We don't know who else might be there looking for the contents of the pork chop bag. Stay in your car and wait for the police. Hear me?" Jablonsky was authoritative in his commands, trying to communicate to Kate that her safety might be on the line.

Kate held her hand over her cellphone so the chief wouldn't hear her derisive, "Yes, Daddy." Then she continued.

"Of course. I'll call Johnny right now, and we will meet you there. Detective Jablonsky, I haven't had a chance to tell him about all of this yet. It will be new information to him. I'm glad you will be there, you know, to help him, if the content of the freezer bag is damning in some way." Kate ended the call feeling like she had massaged the chief enough that he would let her stay in the game. *Hey,* she thought, *I'm the one bringing the pork chop bag to the party.*

Jablonsky knew that his normal boundaries around civilian participation in criminal cases was doubly necessary when it came to Ms. Chambers. Kate had been raised by her grandfather, had been a favorite of her swim coaches (male), and had been close to the director of her dissertation, also a man. While her grandfather gave her appropriate guidelines about personal security, he never talked to her about dating and how dangerous men can be.

A mother knows that her daughter must always be vigilant concerning predatory men, particularly a girl with striking looks and intense energy. Unfortunately, without much female guidance, Kate never developed the antenna for danger that other women had. It was a deficit that Johnny, and Eddie Fitzroy, understood about her, and about which they worried. Jablonsky was unaware of her fundamental lack of education when it came to wolfish men and personal safety—he just didn't want any civilians hurt.

When Kate and Johnny arrived at his mother's house, it was lit up like a Christmas tree. Forensic technicians carried their bags into the house and began to process the basement and the outside of the freezer. Everyone was waiting until the chief arrived before looking into the freezer.

Kate took the opportunity to tell Johnny what his mother had said. By his mystified expression, he clearly thought she was speaking in Klingon. "You mean we are here to look in my mom's freezer for some kind of evidence to some unknown crime?" Johnny's voice cracked. He looked terrible, with dark smudges under his blue eyes and hair that stood up as if it had been electrified. He slouched in the car seat and covered his face with his gloved hands.

Jablonsky and DeVille finally arrived, and they motioned for Kate and Johnny to come into the house. Everyone trooped down the steep wooden steps to the immaculate basement and moved right over to the wall where the freezer stood. As directed, the team had located a manila envelope taped to the side of the freezer. Jablonsky opened it and began to rifle through the sheets. "These look like Xerox copies of invoices for electrical work, roofing, plumbing, and so forth. They are for the townhouses on Delilah Street. There is a list of checks, signed by Thomas Edmonds, for payment on the invoices." The chief handed the material to the technicians to bag.

He then lifted the lid to the freezer—even the forensic techs commented on how clean and organized its contents were. Jablonsky began to move the bags around. "There it is!" Johnny shouted like he had just seen a unicorn jump out of the opening.

Jablonsky already had gloves on, so he lifted out the pork chop freezer bag and carefully opened it. "Chief," said DeVille. "There are multiple items in this freezer bag." He pointed to several small boxes, individually wrapped, also secured in even tinier freezer bags. "Okay. Let's open these boxes over here on the laundry table." When the lids came off, everyone stood still, held captive by their glittering contents.

"Do you recognize any of this jewelry as belonging to your mother?" Jablonsky held up a diamond and ruby ring, then a thick solid gold necklace, two large-carat diamond earrings, and finally, a diamond tennis bracelet of the style popular in the nineteen nineties. Johnny opened his hands, palms up, and made an "I can't believe it" gesture.

"There are notes in the boxes. Look." Kate pointed to small sheets of ladies' notepaper, with dates on them: "Christmas, 1998;" "Our anniversary, 1999;" "Just because he loves me, 2000;" "Valentine's Day, 2010."

"That's my mother's handwriting. I can tell you that my father never had the money to buy anything like this. What is going on? I feel like I don't know my mother at all." Kate and Jablonsky watched as the import of these items took hold of Johnny's imagination. "Do you think all of this has to do with her being shot?"

"Maybe. Let forensics bag these and take them to the lab. If you are up to it, I'd like to go over your mother's photo album right now. We could sit at the kitchen table. Jablonsky put his hand on Johnny's shoulder as a gesture of support. Kate knew the Chief didn't need to ask; he could just command their presence. But given that Johnny's mother had just been shot, he clearly didn't want to do so. He was decent like that.

"It's okay, chief," replied Johnny.

Jablonsky brought out his little notebook and Johnny placed Fiona's photo album of work colleagues on the table. Kate made all of them some strong hot coffee. After being fortified with caffeine, Johnny moved the album closer to him and began to slowly turn the pages once again, this time with an eye to who might have wanted to hurt his mom.

"John, did your mom have anything to say about these photos that you didn't know, or that surprised you?" Jablonsky thanked Kate for handing him another steaming cup of coffee.

"First of all, I never knew this album existed, so that was a surprise in itself. I remembered that my father didn't like her working at the bakery, but never realized why until we started flipping through the pictures. She indicated that my dad was jealous of the men who came into the shop. Mom was a good-looking woman in her day." Johnny looked to Kate for confirmation of his statement.

"She was very pretty. Your dad clearly thought it was odd that Andrew Edmonds, in particular would stop in the bakery. I thought your mom focused on him more than on the construction workers. Look how many pictures of Andrew Edmonds are in the album—there must be five or six. I myself find it curious that he was at the bakery so frequently, and that he allowed his picture to be taken with the staff." Kate eased the pictures out of their holders and laid them side by side on the table.

"He is smiling in each one of these, and in half of them, he is looking at your mother." Jablonsky pointed to three of the photos where, to his eye, the two were either flirting or sharing a private communication together. "You are right, chief. I didn't see that the other day," remarked Johnny. Jablonsky glanced knowingly at Kate.

"John, we are going to have to talk to your mom. I want you to be there, but if she asks you to step out of the room, you have to agree. I need her to feel comfortable opening up to me about the meaning of the things we found. Agreed?"

"Of course. I understand. You should do it soon, maybe tomorrow. She has not been awake that much." Everyone suddenly became aware that a few of the neighbors were lurking on the street in front of the house.

"DeVille is outside asking for any new information that someone might have remembered about the morning your mom was shot."

"Do you want me to talk with them as well?" Johnny looked so exhausted that it was hard to imagine him moving at all.

"No. We'll take it from here. Go home with Kate. We will talk tomorrow." Jablonsky almost pushed the two academics out the door so he could confer with DeVille in private.

"Bingo. Not only do we have the jogging medical resident's identification of the car and part of the license plate number, but a guy on the other side of the street was putting his garbage out early that morning and confirmed the rest of the plate number." Antoine flipped the cover of his laptop shut in obvious satisfaction.

During the drive home, Jablonsky considered the possibility that Fiona McCarthy's request that Kate stand by Johnny for "What is to come" might mean that there was more to be discovered than just the invoices.

CHAPTER 12

"TELL ME WHAT YOU FOUND OUT." Even after the long night at Mrs. McCarthy's house, Jablonsky and DeVille were at the precinct early talking about their research into the Edmonds Land Company. They reconnoitered in Stefan's office, but before they began, both stood at the window watching a rainstorm that was pelting the building. The dirty piles of slush and the old frozen snow on the sides of the streets were suddenly made even dingier by the steady rain.

"Hurricane Katrina was over a long time ago, but even so, whenever there is a hard steady rain, it makes my skin crawl." Every so often, Jablonsky could detect a slight drawl in DeVille's speech, like now, when he was thinking about his hometown.

"Okay, Coupe. Give me the details on this family-owned business."

"Andrew Edmonds incorporated the company in New Jersey in the nineteen sixties. He built projects all over that state and New York, then moved into Philadelphia, and finally Pittsburgh. Edmonds senior and his attorneys worked with each city-county planning department in order to get the necessary permits needed to build housing, convention centers, hotels, and so forth. He was at the height of his career in the nineties. In our university area, he built a few hotels, but he mostly built townhomes. These townhomes took the place of the row houses, row houses that had stood in the local neighborhoods since the eighteen hundreds." Antione paused to drink some coffee. Coming from New Orleans, he abhorred what passed for that hot drink in the precinct's machines, so like Johnny, he brought in his own deluxe coffee maker, completing his brew with some chicory for a kick of flavor.

"Was the company ever sued? If there was nothing to hide, why would anyone keep twenty-year-old invoices?" Jablonsky mused, "Their work in this city must have been compromised."

"It gets really interesting. Around the time Thomas, the son, took over running the construction crews, there were complaints about the quality of the work. Inspectors filed reports that certain safety codes were not being followed. There were reports on the Delilah Street townhomes specifically, indicating that electrical boxes were not to code. Another report said the concrete wasn't the correct mixture, and, finally, some roofing beams were considered structurally inadequate."

"It's odd that city planning, and the city inspectors weren't able to make a legal case around these specific violations. What about the family?" Jablonsky prompted, wanting to hear about the father/son relationship.

"There is Thomas, who went into the business, and a sister, who lives in New York, and who didn't have a role in the company. The wife, Eugenia, is also in New York, and is still living at home, but has nursing care. Andrew died in 2015. Eugenia came from "old money" in upstate New York, somewhere around Saratoga Springs. It was her family's money that started the business. As the company flourished, Andrew traveled all the time, so I'm not sure about their relationship."

"That is a good starting point for our interview with Thomas. Now, what about the Delilah Street townhomes?" Jablonsky knew he remembered something but couldn't quite bring it forward.

"About five years ago, there was a fire in one of them. The fire department records indicate that it began in an electrical box. Even though they knew the origin of the fire, since so much time had elapsed from the original construction, they couldn't prove negligence on the part of the Edmonds company." Antoine paused, waiting for his boss to respond.

"It would be hard to pin that on the Edmonds company—over the years, the boxes could have been replaced by several other electricians. What about his personal life?"

Antoine smiled. "Well, he has been married and divorced four times. With three of the ex-wives, he settled one lump sum on each lady, a sum large enough that the wife did not ask for alimony. And, he has the one daughter who is currently in medical school."

"Does Thomas see this daughter?"

"I did speak with Jane Louise, the first ex-wife, and I asked her that question. She commented that Edmonds is not as attentive to the daughter as he should be. I had the impression she was holding something back. There are no other known children. When I spoke with the other ex-wives, none admitted to having any contact with him after their divorces and monetary settlements."

Annie Lemon poked her head in the door, saying, "Chief, Mr. Edmonds is here. I put him in the interview room. He's an unhappy man." She rolled her eyes to indicate her amusement.

As usual, Antoine stationed himself in the closed-circuit television room. Jablonsky grabbed two fresh cups of coffee and entered the interview space.

"Mr. Edmonds. Thank you for coming in." He placed one coffee in front of Thomas, then laid packets of sugar and creamer on the table. Stefan busied himself with opening the old file on Thomas, placing his notebook beside it. He began right away, not giving Edmonds a chance to complain.

"You are aware that we are reopening the case on Michael and Rosalie Rossetti. Here is the statement that you gave almost twenty years ago. Is there anything you now know that you didn't then—any suspicions about who the perpetrator might have been?

Jablonsky's immediate question succeeded in interrupting Thomas Edmonds's annoyance at being summoned to the precinct. While Edmonds read through his old statement, Stefan took the measure of him. Thomas was now well into middle age. He was of medium height, with thinning, blondish-colored hair and high color from too much Scotch. His cold blue eyes were surrounded by pouchy skin pockets. Thomas was nicely dressed—monogrammed cuffs peeped out from a matching cashmere sweater. He wore tweed pants and expensive shoes. He looked prosperous and acted entitled.

"I don't think I have anything to add to my original statement. I had, and have, no idea why the Rossetti siblings died." There was no arrogance in his tone of voice, just disinterest. This was a man who was in a business where he was often questioned by various professionals, so he knew how to evade. Jablonsky noticed, however, that his eyes narrowed when a question came at him.

"Okay. I would like to ask you about the history of the Edmonds Land Development Company. Your Father, Andrew Edmonds, started the business with some money from your mother, Eugenia. Is that correct?" Jablonsky's tone was conversational, a tone designed to make the interviewee believe he was asking about everyday information.

"Yes. My mother's family were wealthy industrialists in upstate New York, so she was able to initially fund my father's ambitions." In his paper notebook, Jablonsky wrote, "Rich boy, private schools, definitely a bully."

"Would you describe your father as ambitious? Hard-driving?"

"I'd say he was both hard-driving and ambitious. He had a vision, or a belief, really, that he could provide good quality housing at a reasonable price, especially to older cities that could benefit from gentrification." Jablonsky was surprised that there was no tone of pride in Thomas's description of his father's mission.

"By the time he was here in Pittsburgh, your father had achieved his vision, and you were working with him. He must have been away from home a great deal." Jablonsky continued his chatty tone.

"Yes. I'm afraid that is the price my mother paid for his success. Once I graduated from college, I traveled with him. Chief Jablonsky, I'm not sure where this is leading. What does my company have to do with the Rossetti's disappearance?" Thomas's right eyelid began to intermittently twitch.

"I'm pursuing a line of inquiry, Mr. Edmonds. At the time the Rossettis went missing, you were your father's right-hand man, correct? I've seen photos of you and your crew taken in Rosalie's Bakery. Your crew stopped in there in the mornings before heading to the construction site. You knew both Michael and Rosalie." Thomas reached for his coffee and drank. His eye twitch became worse; he casually placed a finger on the lid.

"I did know both of them. Michael was the president of a neighborhood group and Rosalie worked with him. It was common for neighborhood organizations to want a say in community development—it was something the company was used to dealing with. I mean, we were familiar with those kinds of organizations, and of course, city planners." Edmonds gave Jablonsky a worldly smile as if to say, "Oh, those little people, I've dealt them all before."

"You had a relationship with Rosalie, did you not?"

There was a long pause. Thomas furrowed his brow, pursed his lips, and then, making up his mind, answered. "Yes. I dated Rosalie Rossetti. She was a beautiful and smart girl. Why not? I wanted to get information from her as to her organization's moves. Is the affair important?" In other words, "It wasn't significant to me."

"Did she reveal any strategies to you over pillow talk? Or was it you who revealed things to her?" Jablonsky's question was meant to create a wink and a nod between two men at how beautiful women can lower a man's defensives. Tiny beads of sweat broke out on Edmonds's brow.

"There was nothing for me to reveal. The project in the university area was like many others in various cities. Nothing unusual was going on—if that is what you are implying." Edmonds spoke as if the conversation was over.

Jablonsky laid the found invoices on the table. "Tell me about these bills, please."

Thomas Edmonds picked up each individual invoice, reading each one thoroughly. "These are almost twenty years old; where on earth did you get them?"

"A source. Tell me why someone would want to keep these invoices, in particular?" Jablonsky pointed to the sheets.

"I have no idea." The small beads of sweat on Edmonds's forehead grew larger.

"There was an electrical fire in one of the Delilah Street townhomes that was deemed suspicious. Were you, as site manager, cutting corners on city codes?" Edmonds's expression gave away his anger that he would be held responsible for improper construction protocols.

"Absolutely not! My father would never have sanctioned such a thing. He ran a clean shop." Thomas took out a handkerchief and dabbed at his brow.

"Perhaps he did, but maybe you didn't. If you bring the cost down on any given building site, you win your father's approval and pocket more money. We have information that you hired workers who were willing to look the other way over code infractions."

"Prove it." The two words cut through the air like a charge of engagement parry in fencing. Jablonsky, however, was ready for him.

"I can, and I will, prove it. Mr. Thomas Edmonds—don't leave the city." Edmonds slowly stood, eyeballed the chief in a last gesture of distain, then left the interview room.

Jablonsky was amassing many bits of information, but he wasn't going to paint the picture just yet. This first interview was partially to let Thomas know that he was under the microscope for code violations, probably hiring the shooter at Mrs. McCarthy's, and, finally, being a person of interest in the Rossetti murders. At the next interview with Thomas Edmonds, Jablonsky would lay out his case.

CHAPTER 13

THE RAIN HAD STOPPED but the temperature began to fall. The lighted university buildings appeared as shiny cubes against the gray dusky sky. Kate was still at work and feeling uncharacteristically antsy so she called Joan. "Are you finished with your surgeries? I wondered if you wanted to work out before there is another change in the weather. Eddie is going to be in town for the next couple of days. He has to see a colleague at the anthropology department and then he asked Jablonsky if he could walk the excavation site again, just to make sure nothing was missed. I feel agitated; we've been arguing a lot lately."

"Sorry to hear about the arguments, but, well, you know my thoughts about you and Indiana Jones. Look what happened between Johnny and Julius; Julius's work took him to Europe all the time. Now he has an apartment in Paris, and they barely see each other." Kate always found it interesting that Joan worried that Eddie would break her heart, never considering that it might be the other way around.

"I know. Once the job is finished at the fort, what is he going to do for work? My anxiety is about the future—I just can't see us together in this city. It is the reason for the arguments."

Kate knew that Joan always kept several changes of clothes at the hospital so she could easily head to a Pirates game, dinner, or a workout. "Since you have your car at the hospital, I'll jog over to meet you."

"Where do you want to run?" Joan asked.

"Why, through Oakland to the excavation site, of course." Both women laughed, knowing full well that destination would be part of their running route. Thirty minutes later, Kate and Joan were jogging in unison on the back streets of Oakland, trying to avoid the students arriving for their night classes, who were either driving around looking for parking spaces or executing mad antics on their bicycles. It was an obstacle course. "The park trails would have been easier," complained Joan.

Kate and Joan had met at the university when Joan was in her surgical residency and Kate was finishing her postdoctoral residency. Aside from looking alike, two tall, fit, dark-haired women, they shared a view of life and relationships that was distinctly pragmatic and unsentimental. Joan was possessed of a Jeopardy-like store of knowledge on just about every domain of human learning and had been a Scripps Spelling Bee finalist. Equally important, she was in the loop on all the best gossip at the university hospitals. That knowledge, and those connections, had often been helpful to Kate's sleuthing activities.

They finally arrived at the excavation. The site was lit and they could see Fitzroy, along with several technicians from the forensics team. The weather had morphed into what the meteorologists call a "wintry mix," so their hazmat suits were welcomed.

"Hey Fitzroy! Did you find anything?" Kate yelled.

Eddie walked over to the two women, taking off his hood and googles. "Kate. What are you doing here? If these techs mention it, Jablonsky will have a fit. You know that the chief didn't want any civilians on the site."

Joan pulled Kate's jacket and pointed to an SUV that had just arrived, out of which came Jablonsky and DeVille. "Merde," muttered Kate under her breath.

"Dr. Fitzroy, how is it going?" DeVille gave Kate the kind of look that a friend gives when the principal of the school is coming down the hallway toward you. "Kate Chambers, and the good Dr. Weisner. What are the two of you doing at this crime scene?" Both women felt the sting of Jablonsky's accusation.

Joan spoke first. "Nothing. We were out for a jog, and just ran by to say hello to Dr. Fitzroy. We are leaving." She grabbed Kate's arm, and the two of them returned to their run. Kate continued to whine, "It's not fair that Eddie gets to be there and I don't."

"You sound like you are ten years old. Let's have a good run home, and then order some pizza."

Fitzroy was a well-known and well-published archeologist. It was part of his job to worry over the detritus found at any excavation site, and this site was no different. Since it might be a clue that would help to find the murderers of the Rossetti siblings, he wanted to be extra thorough in his search. Jablonsky and Reeves had suggested that several of the forensic team assist him in his search. After Kate and Joan left, the chief stood off to the side watching their careful labors.

Eddie directed the techs to divide the work area into four quadrants, starting with the spot where the skeletons had lain, then fanning out to the immediate surroundings. They slowly and methodically walked, squatted, or sifted through the soil. It was tedious work, made harder by the fact that the ground was partially frozen. After about an hour, Fitzroy shouted to his colleagues, "Eureka!" Grinning from ear to ear, he held up a small object.

Everyone crowded around. "What is it?" asked Jablonsky.

"It is a woven leather bracelet. It's fairly large." The techs gave Fitzroy some "attaboy" back pats. Jablonsky said, "Why don't you go back to the lab and follow through with the evaluation of the object."

Eddie looked like a boy who had just won the golden ticket to the Willy Wonka candy factory. "Thanks, Chief. I will!"

———

Kate and Joan played with and fed the rambunctious Bourbon Ball and decided on Pizza Margherita for themselves. While Kate served up the pie, Joan waxed poetic about the new pitcher the Pirates had signed. "He is from Chicago. His name is Cheeks Maloukas. He is twenty-two years old, with a fabulous strikeout-to-walk record, and an excellent earned run average. I can't wait until spring training starts!"

Kate listened as she poured Pellegrino for herself and Joan, adding both lemon and lime to the sparkling water. To love Joan was to accept that you would be hearing all about baseball: pre-season, in-season, and post-season. At a point where Joan paused for a bite of her pizza, Kate asked about Fiona McCarthy's condition.

"She isn't doing as well as we hoped. I've tried to be perfectly straight with Johnny over her failure to gain strength—I'm not sure she is going to come out of this. She's getting excellent care, but she is an elderly lady who took a bullet to the chest." Joan's involvement with patients typically ended after the procedure; this time, it was more complicated.

As they worked their way through the twelve-piece pie, Kate talked about the invoices they found at Mrs. McCarthy's house, and especially about the jewelry.

"Clearly, Fiona had a lover, and one with means. These are substantial pieces of jewelry. Johnny hasn't said much to me about them. Speaking of jewelry, which I know you love, they found a ring with an oval blue topaz gemstone at the site. It had what looked like a lion etched into it. I know how interested you are in symbols. Does the lion etching mean anything to you?"

"The lion is a symbol used across different cultures. It is associated with courage, power, control; someone who dominates. In Egyptian mythology, the lion was seen as the king of the yearly flooding of the Nile. Do you know the phrase, king of the beasts? Well, human kings often wear garments that have a lion on them. If a human king is good and just, the lion represents wisdom, the law, protection of the people. I can look into it further. The blue topaz stone might be important in itself." Joan looked like a dog given a juicy bone.

"Great! Speaking of kings, Jablonsky feels that there is a connection between finding the Rossetti siblings and someone attempting to murder Fiona." Kate pushed away her plate, stopping at two pieces of pizza—no sense making the next workout any harder. Kate was a person who knew how much was enough.

"It is difficult to think of parents as having lives separate from being Mom and Dad. My brothers would be shocked, I mean really shocked, to think that my mother was canoodling with another man. Anyhow, who do you think the lover might be?" Taking her cue from Kate, Joan stopped eating at two slices; she decided to take a few pieces home so she could eat them later, in private. Joan liked to indulge.

"This is just speculation on my part, but, judging from the photos in Fiona's work album, I'd say it was Andrew Edmonds, the owner of the land development company. There was just something about how they were looking at each other that appeared sweet and loving. But how that relationship would be linked to Michael's and Rosalie's deaths, I don't know."

Joan switched the conversation to Marco Rossetti. "Since I have brothers, I'm aware of the ties that bind them—exceptional loyalty and irrational competition. I'm sure Marco felt loyal to Michael, but was he in competition with him?"

"Speaking in professional confidence, one type of doctor to another, a senior advisor in my department helped Marco negotiate those long years of surgical training. She felt that he had lost everything when his siblings disappeared because his parents were consumed with their grief. You wonder how someone like him processed his own feelings of loss. It is an unusual type of grief because his brother and sister just disappeared; no one knew if they were dead or alive. Until they were found, it would have been an emotional wound that would never fully heal."

Joan always deferred to Kate in matters related to loss and grief. Kate had lost both parents as a child, and then her grandfather died, making her an orphan by the time she was in her twenties. And each time Eddie Fitzroy left to work at another dig, his absence created yet another empty space in Kate's life; Joan wasn't sure if Kate understood that.

"Why didn't Marco stay at the university instead of going to the hospital across the river?" Kate was always curious when a surgeon like Rossetti, who was offered the moon to stay at the university hospitals, chose to leave.

"Because of what had happened to his family, he was a figure in the Oakland community. I think he needed a fresh start—and he was offered a king's ransom to make the move." Joan, who made a great living doing what she loved, theatrically put one hand on top of the other and pantomimed peeling off dollars.

"Johnny said that Marco had worked a little at the bakery. He felt that Marco knew he was gay, but never tortured him the way his father did. All in all, Johnny thinks Marco is a stand-up guy."

"Because no one really knows him, rumors swirl around Marco. Even though he gives his mother's home as his address, some colleagues say that he has a snazzy condominium downtown. I've never known him to date a woman, or a man—no special someone to take to his condo. There is another rumor that he goes out at night, along with a few general practitioners, and helps treat the homeless."

That rumor ignited Kate's imagination. "He's a world-renowned surgeon, making a zillion dollars a year. Why would he do such a thing? He risks being stabbed by a needle, or getting mugged, or becoming infected with some bad disease. It makes no sense—unless he is terribly guilty about something."

"You mean, if this rumor is true, which I doubt, he is expiating some sin?" Coming from the Jewish tradition, where everyone gets a daily serving of guilt, Joan found guilt-driven behavior to be perfectly understandable.

Kate continued developing her theory. "Well, logic would lead us to think his guilt would mean that he either had something to do with Michael's and Rosalie's deaths or he suffers from survivor's guilt. The senior advisor said she didn't believe he had the nature to hurt his siblings, particularly Rosalie. Could his motive be reduced to the brotherly competition you mentioned? I wonder if Jablonsky knows about Marco's extracurricular activities?"

Joan announced that she would set the drums going at the hospital. "I'm going to find out what group of physicians works with the homeless; they might know if there is any truth to this rumor. Or, if you are game, we could tail him some night."

Kate and Joan laughed together over the image of the two of them, dressed in black, peering under the city bridges for the elusive Dr. Rossetti. They decided to walk Bourbon Ball and were pleasantly surprised that the wintry mix had turned into snowfall. BB loved snow, and immediately busied himself with plowing his nose through the white stuff.

As they watched the snow begin to pile thick on the branches of the trees, Joan returned to the topic of Eddie. "Do you think you will marry him?"

"We love each other, there's no question about that. You know, he's the only person alive who knew me as a young girl, and who knew my grandfather. That means something to me. We do talk about getting married. It is hard for me to envision the whole wedding drama—a white gown, bridesmaids, walking down a church aisle—my parents are dead, my grandfather is dead, and I'm not in my twenties. I'm still getting used to having him around!"

There had never been any tension in the friendship between Kate and Joan except around the topic of Eddie Fitzroy. "Look, I love you like a sister. I want your happiness. But Fitzroy has always followed his career interests, and I'm not sure he will change. I do believe, though, that he loves you."

Kate was silent. Then, in a hesitant manner, she responded. "He loves me. I know that for sure. I'm just not sure I feel the same romantic rush I used to. I know it is hackneyed to say, but I love him. I'm just not sure I'm in love with him." Kate had never voiced her reservations to anyone; she felt slightly out of breath from the admission.

The two friends walked on in silence, any residual tension between them resolved by their mutual appreciation of the aesthetics of the snowfall, now artistically backlit by the headlights of the passing cars.

In the quiet of the evening, Joan said the oddest thing. "There is something strangely attractive about the possibility that Marco Rossetti might be guilty, if not of killing his siblings, then of something else."

"Attractive? You've lost your mind," responded Kate.

Brisk air and falling snow always create an atmosphere ripe for contemplation, so after Joan left, Kate and BB cuddled together on the small couch in her sitting room. Kate's thoughts didn't return to Eddie Fitzroy, who had texted her about his discovery and that he would be at the forensics lab, but rather to the rumors about Marco Rossetti's behavior—what if his nocturnal ministrations turned out to be true? What would be the motivation? Does his unusual behavior have anything to do with the suspicious deaths of his siblings?

Kate wasn't someone who gave much credence to altruism; it would have to be proven to her that Marco Rossetti might simply be that selfless. As she played with BB's silky ears, she opened her laptop and began a search on the famous surgeon.

CHAPTER 14

THE WEATHER CHANNEL meteorologists started widening the sweep of their arms in describing the path of the snowstorm blowing into the city. Jablonsky knew that he had better head to the hospital to interview Fiona before the roads were jammed with fearful, hesitant drivers. *The city of Pittsburgh has many things to recommend it,* Stefan thought, *but effective snow removal is not one of them.*

The guard at Mrs. McCarthy's room stood when he spotted the boss. "Everything is calm here, Chief. No one entered who shouldn't be here." Stefan found Fiona sitting up in bed, flanked on either side by Kate and Johnny. He re-introduced himself and dragged a third chair closer to the bed.

"You are looking better, Mrs. McCarthy. That's a pretty bed jacket you are wearing."

"My son just brought this in." Johnny grinned at Stefan, clearly enjoying being the s-o-n, and the s-u-n. Fiona's voice was filled with more breath than previously; her hair was combed, and she had enough energy to preen a little in her new jacket. Jablonsky took note of the skeptical look on Kate's face; she had intimated that she considered Fiona to have been a less than stellar Mom.

"I'd like to ask you a few questions. Do you feel up to it?" Jablonsky approached Mrs. McCarthy with the same respectful, gracious attitude that he had given the ladies at the Grotto, and she responded to it. "I want to talk to you about some of the pictures we found in your work album. Here are a few in which I am particularly interested."

Kate rolled the mobile hospital table across Fiona's bed and cleared it of magazines and the water cup. She took the pictures from Stefan, laying them side by side so Fiona could easily view them. Jablonsky began his questioning at the heart of the matter. "What can you tell me about this man, Andrew Edmonds?"

"Andrew Edmonds was the owner of Edmonds Land Company. He often came into the bakery, as did his son and the construction crews. They were building the Delilah Street townhouses then." Wistfulness filled her expression, as she held up each picture.

"I'm going to ask you a personal question about Andrew Edmonds. Did you have a special relationship with him?"

"Chief! What are you implying?" Even though Jablonsky had warned Johnny that he was going to ask personal questions, John's reaction was harsh and accusatory. Jablonsky quietly replied, "I'm asking about the nature of their relationship."

Fiona looked at her son. "I'm sorry you have to hear these things, but someone tried to kill me, so I think I must answer the detective's questions honestly." Johnny slumped in his chair like a sullen teenager, and then mumbled, "Go ahead, Mom. I'm sorry."

"Andrew Edmonds and I were involved with each other for more than twenty years."

"What? What are you saying?" Johnny's shock forced him to his feet.

"John," said Jablonsky, stern as a Dutch uncle. "If you can't hear this story, I want you to leave the room." Johnny sat back down, looking over at Kate for support; she put her finger to her lips and mimed locking them.

"Tell me about the relationship." Jablonsky was encouraging and calm, just what Fiona needed to continue.

"I was married, he was married, so at first, we would chat at the bakery counter as I filled his order. I liked how he spoke to me; it was friendly and respectful. After a while, several of the ladies said they thought he had a crush on me. Well, his attention was flattering—I wasn't Miss America, but I used to look pretty good. One day, he passed me a note as I handed him his check. I'll never forget it. "Will you do me the honor of having dinner with me? It will be private and discreet." He had his telephone number on it so I could make the call if it suited me." Fiona stopped and asked for a drink of water; she took a sip and then continued her love story.

"The first dinner was in a small restaurant somewhere in the North Side. No one I knew ever would have gone there. I was very nervous—I tried on three different outfits and thought about not going. But once I was with him, I had a wonderful time, and so did he. He kept an apartment over by the baseball park. It became our place. I helped decorate it, I cleaned it, and he and I spent many happy times there cooking together, laughing at television shows, or just talking. Months turned into years. We loved each other."

Fiona glanced at Johnny, who was looking down at his hands, avoiding eye contact with everyone. Jablonsky intervened in the tense moment. "Did his son, Thomas, know about you?"

"I was never one hundred percent positive. Andrew said he thought Thomas did know—we were together for a long time. How could he not know?"

"Tell me about the invoices. Why do you have them?" Stefan's pen was poised over his paper notebook.

"I kept them because they were Andrew's. I should have turned them over to his attorneys when he died, but frankly, I didn't want any attention put on me. Andrew was an honest man. Before his son came into the business with him, there were never any complaints filed about violating construction codes. Once Thomas took over the crews, there began to be issues. I believe that Andrew wanted evidence of his son's wrongheaded business practices."

"You mean he was collecting information to use against his own son?" Except for Fiona, everyone in the room was startled.

"Yes. That's the kind of man he was." Fiona lifted her chin in pride. She wanted her son, and Kate, and even Jablonsky, to know that her lover had been an honest man.

"What did he intend to do with the invoices?" queried Jablonsky.

"I'm not really sure. I do know that he spoke with his attorneys about them. His wife also knew that he was gathering information and, as you can imagine, they quarreled over it. Thomas was her special boy."

Before the chief could continue, Kate couldn't stop herself from asking the next question. "Did his wife know about you? I mean, you two were together for a really long time."

"Yes. She knew." Fiona hesitated, and then added, "Except for her children's sake, I'm not sure she cared." Stefan returned to the business questions.

"Did Andrew continue to gather information? These invoices are from quite a long time ago—as far as my detectives know, Thomas was never convicted of anything related to the projects the company had in this city." Once again, Jablonsky wondered if Jubas Jones knew who in the city might have been paid to look the other way concerning code violations.

Suddenly, Fiona's face grew very white, almost like she was going to faint. "Mom, lie back on the pillows. Are you in pain?" Johnny fussed over his mother's comfort while Kate went out to find Fiona's nurse, who motored into the room scolding everyone for having taxed her patient. Johnny stayed, but Jablonsky and Kate left.

In a low voice, Kate said, "Let's get a coffee. I have a few things to tell you about Marco Rossetti." By now, Kate knew the route to the cafeteria by heart. They secured a table that separated them from listening ears.

"I'm sorry Johnny had to hear about his mother's affair in such a manner." Jablonsky looked to Kate for her reaction.

"It was a bit more than an affair, wouldn't you agree? All those years! I'd say it was more like leading a double life. It does sort of explain why Fiona seemed so detached from the bullying Johnny took from his father and cousins. Did she even know about it, or was she too involved with Andrew and the bakery?" Somehow, no matter what the explanation, Fiona's lack of attention to her only child clearly made Kate angry.

Jablonsky let her stew. "From your perspective, Kate, do you think she was right that Eugenia Edmonds wouldn't care about the relationship?"

"Eugenia Edmonds may have fallen out of love with her husband, but most people care about being betrayed. I'd have to believe there were confrontations over the years."

Jablonsky nodded his head in agreement, and then prompted her. "There was something you wanted to tell me about the Rossetti case?"

"Oh, yes. Joan said that there is a rumor that Marco Rossetti goes out at night with a group of doctors and gives treatment to the homeless. Now that may sound like a good thing, and it is, but I'm just wondering why someone like him would do it?"

"You think he is guilty of something. I agree. It is my suspicion that Marco is somehow implicated in the disappearance of his siblings. This is a good tip. We also know that he keeps an apartment in the city, although he claims his main residence is at his mother's house."

"Joan said that no one knows if Marco dates. She and I are trying to stoke the hospital gossip fires." Jablonsky smiled at his young sleuth. She could be counted on to give him insider information, information he could use, and had used, in his interviews.

Kate returned to Fiona's room and Jablonsky tried to head back to the precinct. The snowfall continued and the roads had yet to be plowed. Instead of being agitated, Stefan gave in to the barely moving traffic situation, relaxed, and called Antoine. He filled him in on Fiona's interview and Kate's tidbits about Marco.

"I want us to focus on whether Thomas knew that his father was collecting evidence of malfeasance. If he did, that gives him a possible motive to have someone shoot Mrs. McCarthy. And what did Rosalie know about his building practices? If either she or her brother knew something, were they murdered because of it? In other words, did the same motive underpin both the Rossettis' murders and the attempted murder of Fiona?"

CHAPTER 15

JABLONSKY AND HIS DETECTIVES proceeded as if Michael and Rosalie Rossetti were victims of a homicide, although Dr. Patel had not listed it as the official manner of death. But really, two bodies dumped at a construction site? What else could it be? This morning, he and Antoine stood in front of the murder board, talking through new information and speculating on the meaning of the new connections.

Antoine had placed pictures of Michael and Rosalie in the center of one panel and surrounded them by the current persons of interest: Luca Lorenzo, Jonathan Price, Thomas Edmonds. Then off to the side he placed a photo of their brother, Marco Rossetti, with a question mark beside it.

On a second panel was a picture of Mrs. McCarthy. Next to her was a photo of Andrew Edmonds, one of Thomas Edmonds, and one of the construction crew that frequented the bakery. There was an empty circle in which Antoine had placed a question mark for the unknown shooter. He also included that the Diamond Detailer shop confirmed that Luca Lorenzo's Camaro had been in the shop for repainting at the time of the drive-by but couldn't say absolutely that it was there all night or the early morning time of the shooting. The car had been tucked in a corner, outside of the range of the security camera.

Jablonsky took a picture of Jubas Jones, placed it between the two panels, and then wrote, "What did he know about violation of construction codes, and when?" Not looking at his boss, Antoine asked the obvious question. "Is Johnny McCarthy implicated in the shooting?"

Stefan sighed under the weight of having to consider the question about someone he knew. "I can't see how. I watched him closely when his mother revealed the affair—he was stunned. I'd put money on his ignorance of the whole situation. I do not see any reason he would want to murder the mother he's been taking care of all these years. He may not always have liked her, but he loves her."

"What about people at the bakery?" Antoine's impression of Johnny's innocence mirrored Jablonsky's, so he placed Johnny's picture on his desk as Jablonsky continued to talk through facts. "Luca Lorenzo worked there the longest. Marco also worked in the back of the shop, but only for short periods of time. Jonathan Price frequently stopped into the bakery with Rosalie."

"Boss, here are snapshots of Thomas Edmonds's ex-wives." Antoine pinned the small photos off to the side of Thomas's picture. "As you know, I've spoken with all four of them. I mentioned to you that, with the exception of number one, the others hadn't been in contact with him in years. Most are remarried. His first wife, Jane Louise, is a retired attorney living in Key West. She is the mother of their daughter, Eleanor, and is in touch with Edmonds. She was agreeable to speaking with us via Zoom. I can call her right now."

"Set it up. I'll meet you in my office."

A woman around the same age as Thomas came on screen. She had dyed blonde hair, a tan, and lots of heavy pieces of gold jewelry. The former Missus was outfitted in Lilly Pulitzer's bright south Florida colors. During the interview, she didn't hold back in her negative portrayal of her ex-husband.

"I just spoke with him. He's a bastard! Here are some things to understand about him. I have to fight for every penny of our daughter's medical school tuition. She's such a smart, hardworking girl. I try to keep the conflict with her father away from her so that she can love him, even think well of him. Luckily, I'm a retired attorney, so I have ways of threatening him that some others wouldn't know about."

Jablonsky was naturally curious about the situation. "Thomas Edmonds is a rich man. Why do you think he doesn't want to pay for his only daughter's education?"

"His withholding is aimed at me, not her. Thomas just wants to torture me. You should know that he can be cruel. He doesn't care that when he hurts me, it hurts her. I fight for our daughter to have what is her due as a part of this rich family. He should pay for her education!" Jablonsky thought she sounded like many divorced mothers who are in the unenviable position of trying to collect money from derelict fathers. *Except,* he thought, *Jane Louise is empowered by her education and financial stability.*

"Jane Louise, when my detective spoke with the other ex-wives, they all said that they divorced because of infidelity. I'm sorry to ask, but was that also true for you?"

"Yes. He wasn't faithful to me. It's an old-fashioned word, fidelity, but I believed in it, and in him. I'm sure all of the other wives had the same experience—in the end."

"What do you mean by, "In the end.""

"Oh—I guess I mean, eventually, all of us realized that he wasn't going to be a faithful husband, that's all." Clearly there was something she wasn't saying.

"Did you know much about how he conducted his business?"

"Not really. He would complain about difficulties with the city inspectors, but he always seemed to find a way around their regulations. Frankly, I'm not sure that Thomas was very honest in his business dealings, but I'm sorry that I can't give you any substantial details. Are you after him now for building code violations?"

"As detective DeVille explained to you, we are contacting everyone who knew Michael and Rosalie Rossetti. We do have several lines of inquiry that concern your ex-husband— as an attorney, you know that I can't talk to you about them."

Jablonsky asked a few more questions in order to build his psychological picture of Thomas Edmonds and then he ended the Zoom interview. But, the phrase, "in the end," stuck in his mind. She wasn't telling the whole truth about its implications.

Antoine DeVille remarked, "What a control freak this Edmonds guy is. However, I know plenty of men like him, men who want to hurt their ex-wives and don't care if their children get in the way. I feel for her."

"Yes. But isn't the control thing usually because the wife is seeing another man? In this case, she broke it off with him because of his philandering. Maybe she is lying. Or maybe they both had something on the side. Anything is possible. Here's what we learned from her: Jane Louise is still in touch with Thomas concerning their daughter; She remains angry and resentful over his infidelities; She fights for her daughter's rights but tries to protect Eleanor's relationship with her dad. Jane Louise paints a picture of Thomas as a man who is vindictive and narcissistic in that he puts his needs over those of his only child, and that he cheated with other women, and she suspects, in his business. I'm going to want to circle back to her with more questions as the case narrows."

Jablonsky changed the subject. "I want to talk to Mrs. Rossetti to get a sense of Michael's and Rosalie's mental health, and also that of our esteemed surgeon, Marco. I called her, and this morning seems to be a good time if I can get there with all this snow. In the meantime, I want you to speak with Jubas Jones again about the code violations. I'm just not sure he is telling us everything he knows. Thanks, Coupe."

"Okay, boss. You be careful. The roads were terrible when I came in."

Jablonsky smiled, knowing that having come from New Orleans, Antoine remained a novice driver in the snow. Stefan drove a heavy, four-wheel drive vehicle and still was skidding around on the yet unplowed streets. Luckily, there were very few cars about as he headed into South Oakland for his visit with Mrs. Rossetti.

CHAPTER 16

THE CHIEF ARRIVED at Lisa Marie Rossetti's home and rang the bell while he tapped the snow off of his shoes. To his surprise, Renata and Andrea, the two Nonas from the Grotto, answered the door.

"Chief! Come in, come in. Take off those shoes, please." The two ladies bustled about, putting his shoes on a boot tray in the hall and taking his overcoat and gloves. They led him into the living room, where Mrs. Rossetti was sitting in a recliner.

However attractive and energetic Lisa Marie Rossetti had been, the years of not knowing what had happened to two of her children had taken its toll. She was a thin woman, the dark smudges outlining her eyes spoke of ineffable suffering. Lisa Marie was dressed in an ironed and starched blouse, with a sweater vest that matched her pants. The townhome evidenced pride of place—the furniture was dusted, the area rugs vacuumed, and the windowpanes were clean. The walls had a few pictures of Italy, one of the current Pope, and many, many photos of all three of her children and her deceased husband. The pictures represented life before her children disappeared.

"Thanks so much for taking the time to see me, Mrs. Rossetti." Jablonsky tried to start his interview, but Renata and Andrea brought in a tray filled with fresh cups of coffee and some delicate looking Sfogliatella pastries, or, as they are called in English, lobster tails. Instead of reaching for the pastry, Stefan took out his small paper notebook and a pen, signaling that he was there to work.

"The funeral Mass was beautiful, Mrs. Rossetti, and very moving. I want to ask if there was anyone that you saw at the church whom you believe in your heart might have wanted to harm Michael and Rosalie?" All eyes were on Lisa Marie; her friends neither prodded her nor interfered with her answer.

"No. I wish I could have helped more at the time, and even now. Over the years, many people have stopped here at the house to see me, especially since I haven't been going out. It was mostly the same friends and neighbors at the Mass. I didn't see anyone new." Mrs. Rossetti seemed distracted, as if she were struggling to stay in the present.

"Luca Lorenzo and Jonathan Price were there. Do you remember either one?" Jablonsky could see the Nonas clutch each other's hands, actively restraining themselves from answering for her.

"I do. Luca worked at the Alliance with Michael. He was here at our home for all the meetings. Jonathan Price never came to the house. He was a friend of Rosalie's from law school. He would stop in the bakery with her. I didn't really know him."

Lisa Marie slowly rose out of her recliner, and like a family docent, began a tour of all the pictures hanging on the wall. Stefan settled back to give his full attention to the stories of her children while sipping coffee and giving in to the allure of the pastries.

Off to the side of the living room, a statue of Saint Anthony sat on a small occasional table. Stefan knew that Saint Anthony is considered the patron saint of lost causes, lost things, or lost people. In front of the statue lay a card printed with "The Miracle Prayer to Saint Anthony" and a lit votive candle.

There was something in the atmosphere of the Rossetti house that reminded Jablonsky of his grandmother's home, where side by side there existed a combination of Roman Catholic religious mythology, flavored with a pinch of mysticism and a heaping cup of magical thinking. Jablonsky instinctively knew that out of her prayers to St. Anthony, Mrs. Rossetti had woven a net of maternal hope and daily cast that net into the universe, wishing for a catch, years after the search for Michael and Rosalie had ended.

Lisa Marie saw him looking at the statue and asked if he knew the short prayer. At the same time, all four recited the singsong invocation: "Tony, Tony, look around, something's lost and must be found." The shared moment seemed to lift everyone's spirits, and for Jablonsky opened the door for some of the harder questions he had come to ask.

When she sat back down, Lisa Marie seemed more plugged into the reason he was there. "When Dr. Patel came to tell me where they had found my children, I felt vindicated. I always thought that Michael's work, and Rosalie's, were the cause of their murder. Don't you agree, detective?"

"I do. Was there anyone from the city, or from the Edmonds company, that you thought might be guilty?"

"Yes. I told your old chief and my husband that I thought it was Thomas Edmonds." Lisa Marie's voice and visage filled with intensity. As if she were a figure in a Vermeer painting, her skin was lit from inside. "He was in love with Rosalie. I know everyone says that all the men liked her, but he was crazy for her. I could see it in his eyes. Crazy, as in loss of reason. He thought he could hide it, but a mother knows." Renata's and Andrea's heads bobbed in confirmation of what they saw as a universal truth. Jablonsky waited. He hated to ask this grieving mother the next question, but he had to.

"Was Rosalie involved with Thomas Edmonds?" Her nonplussed response shocked him.

"I think she was. I'm just not sure why she was. He wasn't much, you know. The only thing he had going for him was that his father owned the company. Rosalie could have had someone much better. Besides, she didn't really want a man; she wanted a career in law. Just like my mother, who started her own business from nothing, my Rosalie was ambitious. She had dreams and goals. Don't you think?" Lisa Marie turned to her two friends, who couldn't wait to join in.

Renata took the lead. "Oh yes! If she was seeing that Thomas Edmonds, then she had her reasons, and they had nothing to do with love."

"What do you think her reasons might have been?" Jablonsky gestured, opening the response to all three ladies.

Everyone agreed that Rosalie must have been seeking information about the construction business, information that she could use in negotiations with the city planners, details that would give the Alliance more clout. He was a bit surprised at their sophistication concerning dirty business practices and Rosalie's private behavior.

"Were there any papers of hers that weren't turned over to the police? Papers that she might have hidden in her law school notes, or at the Alliance office? Papers with information she might have gotten from Thomas Edmonds about the company?"

"No. Not that I am aware of. You could ask my son, Marco. He might know something about her school papers. If my husband were still alive, he would know. He followed every detail of the investigation, and he kept diaries. My husband was, well, what's the word, compulsive? He wrote everything down—everything about his business and the investigation."

Jablonsky couldn't believe that his old boss had missed the fact of the diaries. "Mrs. Rossetti, do you have these diaries?" All four trooped down steep stairs to another immaculate basement, just like the one at Mrs. McCarthy's. *These ladies and their husbands knew how to keep a house,* he thought. Along a back wall were bookcases where Stefan saw rows of notebooks, methodically arranged by month and year. Not able to contain his admiration, he remarked, "Your husband was an organized man. He would have made a good detective. Remind me again, what did your husband do for a living?"

"He owned a beer distributorship over on the North Side. He sold it when he retired. The bakery is mine, so he knew I would be taken care of financially."

The chief located the diaries for the years the Edmonds company was active in the city and, with permission, bagged them to take to the precinct. Back in the living room, Jablonsky had the unwanted task of palpating around the outside chance that Michael's and Rosalie's deaths might have been a murder-suicide.

"Was there a time when either Michael or Rosalie wanted to give up the fight, or got depressed, or argued?" The room grew silent.

"I know what you are asking. Dr. Patel asked me the same question. My Michael and my Rosalie were Catholics. Neither one would ever take their own life, or the life of someone else. Neither one would commit such a mortal sin. There's an end to that, detective." The two friends added their opinions, "That's right. We used to see them together at the Grotto, even when they were grown. They'd go there to make special requests or say private prayers."

Hmm, thought Jablonsky, *special requests? I wonder what those were?* He continued, "You mentioned your son, Marco. He lives here with you?"

"Yes. But he has another place. He is a grown man; he has his own condominium. I've never been there, you understand, since I don't go out. I've been thinking that now that Michael and Rosalie have been found and properly buried, I might be able to go see his place, or even go to the bakery." Renata and Andrea spontaneously clapped their hands in joy over the idea that their friend's traumatic agoraphobia might be coming to an end.

"One last question, please. Did you all know Mrs. Fiona McCarthy?"

Lisa Marie spoke with authority. "I hired her. She was a good worker, a good baker, and nice to have around. I haven't seen her in years, but she did call me with her condolences when Michael and Rosalie were found." It was as if the proverbial light bulb went off over Lisa Marie's head. "She must be the Greenfield woman that was shot, otherwise you wouldn't be asking about her." All three ladies reflexively made the sign of the cross.

Andrea commented. "She used to wait on me when I stopped in the bakery. She always remembered what I liked. Is she going to be all right?" Jablonsky commented that he wasn't sure, and then added that he couldn't say more because of the investigation. Amusingly, all three ladies put a hand across their mouth, signaling that they understood the hush-hush nature of the investigation.

Mrs. Rossetti said, "Now that we are talking about the Edmonds company, I always thought the father, Andrew Edmonds, was sweet on Fiona. I'd be in the back looking over orders, and he would be at the counter kibitzing with her." The Nonas agreed that everyone at the bakery thought that Fiona and Andrew Edmonds were flirty with each other. Jablonsky made a mental note. *At the bakery, the ladies knew that Fiona was flirting with a married man. I wonder what that behavior provoked?*

"Do you believe that he wanted to find out about the Alliance?"

"No. Fiona McCarthy didn't live around here. She wasn't involved with Michael and this neighborhood. No. I just think they had a thing for each other."

Jablonsky left the Rossetti house with a bakery box filled with pastries. Luckily, one of the neighbors had shoveled the sidewalk, a thankless job, considering the snow continued to fall. He laughed at the kitchen chair that the neighbor had placed alongside the curb marking his parking spot; the chair-marker was an honored winter habit in Pittsburgh. Driving back to the precinct was treacherous and slow going, giving the chief a chance to review what he had learned from Mrs. Rossetti and her friends.

The diaries were a real find—decades earlier, beer distributorships typically had minor connections to organized crime—perhaps Mr. Rossetti had made notes as to any connection between the Edmonds company and men he knew to be bent.

There were fewer secrets in this family than what he originally thought there might be: Lisa Marie knew about Rosalie and Thomas Edmonds; She knew that Thomas was crazy for her daughter; She also knew that Marco had his own place; She was aware of Jonathan Price and his friendship with Rosalie; And finally, she didn't think it was odd that Rosalie might have hidden evidence of bad business practices perpetrated by the Edmonds's company.

Two women, Fiona and Rosalie, one involved with the father, and one with the son. Fiona kept Andrew's secret files on his son; did Rosalie have a similar stash on Thomas? Jablonsky kept one hand on the steering wheel, and with the other, unwrapped a piece of cinnamon gum, enjoying the chew for the rest of the drive.

CHAPTER 17

EDDIE FITZROY HAD BRAVED the interstate from the Laurel Highlands into the city in order to see Kate. He was on a mission to persuade her to go to France with him. As they luxuriated on her couch, he slowly and methodically presented his case. Kate liked listening to him talk and watching his striking face change expression from love, to frustration, back to love, ending in his just amorously grabbing her. If logic didn't work, perhaps sex would. Today, she didn't fight the obvious manipulation.

"Once this situation with Johnny's mother is resolved and my work at the Fort is finished, let's go away. Let's go someplace warm, where we can swim and sail, like we used to do with your grandfather in Nantucket."

"I'd love that, Eddie. But my agreeing to go doesn't mean that when we come back I'll be heading to the south of France with you, or that I'm giving up my interest in helping to solve mysteries."

"Whatever you say, my darling girl. Do you want to get something to eat, or shall we just stay here on the couch?" Eddie attempted to pull her closer, but Kate's mind was elsewhere. She had agreed to meet Johnny at the hospital, so she maneuvered herself out of Eddie's reach and went into her bedroom to change into more presentable clothes. She left a frustrated Fitzroy snuggling on the couch with BB.

The chief was also on his way to reinterview Mrs. McCarthy. When he arrived the police guard was there, and so were Kate and Johnny, who were trying to distract and amuse Fiona. "I had a few more questions I wanted to ask you, Mrs. McCarthy. Are you feeling up to it?"

"I think so. Give me a minute to arrange myself." Fiona pushed herself upright on her pillows, quickly brushed her hair, then straightened her pretty silk bed jacket. Sprucing up always made for clearer thinking.

"Did you know any of Thomas Edmonds's wives? Here are their pictures." Jablonsky placed four photos in front of her.

"Thomas Edmonds's wives? Well, I didn't expect that question. I guess I kind of knew the first one. This could be her," she said, pointing to one of the photographs. She looked over the other three. "I don't recognize these other women."

"How did you know her?" Jablonsky patiently waited as Fiona cast her memory back over the twenty-odd years.

"I think that she was a friend of Rosalie's, from law school. Sometimes she would come into the bakery with her and that young man, Jonathan Price. I didn't really know her— know her, if you know what I mean. She was a customer, and a friend of the boss's daughter."

"I do understand." Jablonsky retrieved an old yellow polaroid photograph from his tiny paper notebook. He placed it next to the first one and took away the other three. Johnny and Kate angled closer over the bed railing to get a better look.

Fiona picked up the photo. "This could be her. She had two first names; one was Jane. I have the impression that there was something special about her...I just can't remember what." She pointed to a young smiling girl, standing together with Rosalie and Jonathan Price, all three mugging for the camera. Jablonsky clarified. "She went by Jane Louise Smith."

"Yes. That's her. You know, Chief, you could also ask Mrs. Rossetti. She would remember more details." Jablonsky nodded in agreement but didn't say that he wanted to spare Mrs. Rossetti having to look at more pictures of her dead children. If need be, he could show the photo to the Nonas.

Fiona turned to her son. "Do you remember this girl, Johnny? She sometimes came into the bakery." Johnny shook his head in the negative. "I can't say for sure. She looks kind of familiar." He looked at the chief, letting his voice trail off.

"Here is another photo, more recent. Do you recognize either of these women?" He produced a picture of Eleanor, Thomas Edmonds's daughter, standing with her arm around her mother, Jane Louise.

"No. Wait, is that Jane Louise Smith today? Well, she looks weathered. So, that's the daughter. She looks like her mom." Always attuned to nuance, there was something in the phrase, 'So that's the daughter,' that caught Stefan's attention.

Before he could pursue it, Fiona bluntly continued. "I want to talk to Kate, alone, please." Kate looked at Johnny for some clue as to what his mother wanted, but he just mouthed, "I don't know," and left the room.

"And Chief, I want you to stay as well. Johnny, make yourself scarce."

Fiona looked very frail. She was still receiving medications through an IV; the thin skin of her hands was purple around the entry site of the needle. Even though she had been interested in the questions, her energy seemed to be waning, and clearly, she wanted to say something before that energy ran out. Kate scooted her chair closer to the bed. "What do you want to tell me, Fiona?"

With a tone infused with disgust, Fiona answered with a question. "Has Julius called Johnny? He hasn't called me, not once." Kate couldn't resist a smile, which she hid by turning her head to look at Jablonsky. "What makes you ask, Fiona?"

"Because I know people. I don't think he really loves my boy. Anyway, I wanted to tell you, and the Chief, about two things, both of which you can help Johnny with after I'm gone."

Kate never treated old people like children, calling them honey or sweetie, nor did she deny their reality when facing death. *She must think she is dying,* thought Kate. "Okay, Fiona. Go ahead."

"Andrew Thomas was a very wealthy man. Through my talking about Johnny, he came to understand how difficult a gay man's life could be—not getting promotions, or being let go, just because of sexual orientation. Until he was dying, I never knew that he had put away money for me. In my bathroom at home, in the right-hand drawer of the vanity, there is a false back. If you take that out, you will find a bank book. Andrew's attorneys paid the tax on the money in that account for all these years. When I die and Johnny inherits that money, there might be more taxes. One of the attorneys will take care of it. Their names are written on the bank book."

Yet another secret being revealed, mused Kate. Then she asked the obvious question. "Why not just tell Johnny about the money now?" Jablonsky was content to let her take the lead—Fiona clearly trusted her and so would be more forthcoming. Civilian or not, Kate was in the mix with his shooting victim, and was doing a good job getting information.

"He is too angry with me, and because of that, I don't think he would accept the money. I fear he will think that

I was a "kept woman." It is a lot of money. It will give him security."

Kate looked at Jablonsky, who gave a slight nod, so given the go ahead she asked, "How much money is it, Fiona?"

"Three million dollars." In her surprise, Kate spontaneously clasped Fiona's skinny arm, and the two of them burst out laughing. Fiona, short of breath after the mirth, added, "That is lots of bingo money, don't you agree?" All these years, and Fiona had never touched the account; she had saved it all for her son. Kate might have to revise her opinion of Mrs. McCarthy.

Jablonsky made no attempt to hide his shock. He immediately thought, *That's three million reasons for someone to shoot her.* He asked, "Who else knew about this bank account? Did Thomas, or his mother Eugenia?"

"I don't know the answer to that. I wondered about it myself. I did know that the account was separate from his official will. No one contacted me or my bank after his will was probated. Both could have known but not said anything. Do you think someone wanted to kill me because of that money?" It seemed impossible, but Fiona's skin color grew even more pale.

"Mrs. McCarthy, at this point in our investigation, it's hard to say. Three million is a lot of money—which means it could be a motive." Fiona held up her hand to stop him from going any further into the case. Kate and Jablonsky watched her struggle to maintain her energy.

"Kate. There is one more thing. Johnny and I want you to have the jewelry Andrew gave me. Don't say no; it is my wish. I don't have a daughter, and, well, I know how much you love my son. Also, I want you to get the bank book and keep it until I pass. Then, you must help Johnny to accept the money. You are a smart girl, persuasive, and kind. You will find the right time to tell him. Knowing you will be with him brings me comfort." Kate knew that Fiona wasn't a demonstrative lady, so her emotion-filled voice moved her.

She hoped she would have Johnny close to her until they were both old, but her own life story had taught her that all human life is ruled by change, anticipated or unexpected. Her philosophy was that everyone came with an unknown expiration date; her young parents' sudden deaths, and now Mrs. McCarthy's being shot, reinforced her point of view.

Jablonsky didn't interject that the bank book was now evidence, and that the police would take charge of it until the crime was solved. And there would be no keeping it secret from her son. Johnny came back into the room, so any questions Kate or Jablonsky had would have to wait. Fiona waved her arm at all of them, saying, "Go home, have something to eat. I'll be all right."

Outside of Fiona's hospital room, Jablonsky took a few minutes to tell Johnny about the bank book and the money. He watched as once again Johnny was hit with a thunderbolt. His only utterance was, "You are joking, right?" He walked in silence, trying to take in the reality of how his mother had kept that much money secret, and how it would impact his life.

Kate's and Jablonsky's minds were alive with questions. *Had Thomas Edmonds discovered the account, and, in anger and greed, decided to eliminate any sign of his father's relationship with Fiona? What about the wife, Eugenia, who knew about her husband's double life? Did she have knowledge of this substantial bank account, and, before she died from old age, decide to do something about it?*

Jablonsky called Antoine DeVille. "Coupe, meet Johnny and me at his mother's house as soon as you can. Mrs. McCarthy has hidden more materials there."

CHAPTER 18

ONCE JABLONSKY AND DEVILLE HAD SECURED the house, the chief allowed Johnny and Kate to enter, along with a few of forensic technicians. Johnny showed them the way to the vanity his mother described. The drawer was carefully emptied of all its contents, then pulled out altogether. Sure enough, there was a false back in it. Once they removed it, they found an old-fashioned savings account book.

DeVille whistled when he saw the size of the account. "My parents do fine, but this, this can buy enough pralines to last a lifetime."

Jablonsky looked carefully at the bankbook. "John, the last deposit made was the same year that Andrew Edmonds died. There must be bank statements of accrued interest on the money. Would you have any idea where those statements might be? I'm assuming they would be paper statements."

"I have no idea where she would have kept them. The forensics people went through her desk the last time. If there were statements, that's where she would keep them."

"We took your mom's laptop. I think Annie Lemon is going through it. I'm going to call her right now."

"I bought mom that nice laptop, but I don't think she ever used it. I doubt detective Lemon will find anything on it."

"Lemon, do you have Mrs. McCarthy's laptop? Good! Is it password protected? You're already in. Okay. Go to the most recently opened files and see what is there." While they waited, Jablonsky remarked to Johnny, "Your mom was using the laptop regularly." Lemon began to announce the titles of the files as she moved down the list.

Jablonsky stopped her, saying, "Is there a file entitled bank statements? Excellent! Now we are cooking with a spoon. Lemon, I'm going to put you on speaker."

"My mother had bank statements on her laptop? Who is she?" Johnny continued to look shocked as revelations about his mother's daily life continued. First, there was a secret lover, now a secret bank account.

"Not only were there bank statements, but also it seemed that she routinely read your published academic articles. Your mom is quite something. You know, John, women of that generation weren't stupid. Their talents were never developed because the church saw them only as wombs, and men saw them only as sexual objects or housekeepers. I have a daughter, and I had a wife. I've been schooled."

Johnny turned away, hiding his tears; he had been in the dark about so much of his mother's life, all the while thinking they had been close. Jablonsky gave him a minute, then asked, "If your mom wanted to keep something hidden on her computer, what name would she give the file?"

"That's a good question. Um... I would look under something to do with baking or cooking. Something like Baking Recipes." Detective Lemon immediately searched but found no files by that name or any name close to it.

Kate spoke directly into Jablonsky's phone. "Detective Lemon, try looking for a file named Bingo Winnings. When Fiona told us about the bank account, she mentioned that it was "a lot of bingo money."" Lemon was quiet, then everyone heard her say, "Here it is, Bingo Winnings. I'm going to open it now. Wow. There are old copies of citations for electrical violations on the Delilah Townhomes."

"Pay dirt!" Good intuition, Kate. Johnny, are you staying here tonight, or at your own place? Here?" The chief turned to DeVille. "I want a guard outside all night, watching the house." Antoine turned away and made the call.

Once back at the station, Jablonsky and DeVille were greeted by a grinning Annie Lemon. She had printed out several sheets of the city's citations for electrical violations.

"Remember when the fire chief said they thought the fires at the townhomes originated in faulty wiring? This might be the proof. We can at least question the suppliers. Someone might know something about that era. Now we have some invoices from most of the suppliers, and we have city citations." Jablonsky couldn't believe their luck. He said a silent "Thank you" to Fiona McCarthy.

When Kate arrived home, she excitedly told Eddie of their latest find at Fiona's house. Eddie had been busy printing and examining photos of the leather bracelet and the ring he had found at the excavation site. Kate looked over his shoulder, commenting, "To me, the setting of the ring is too thick for a piece of fine jewelry. It's more like a lodge ring, or a sports ring—you know, like a Super Bowl or Stanley Cup ring."

"I think so too. I'm not sure about the Super Bowl thing. The forensics people said they would let me know if they come up with any additional information." Kate ordered some Chinese takeout and began to move from the dining room to the kitchen, setting the table. She had changed into a comfy pair of old jeans and a university sweatshirt; her thick black hair was pulled casually into a ponytail. Kate was as excited about Fiona's surprise bank account as she was over the new citation evidence—her fervor made her even more appealing and vibrant than usual.

She could feel Eddie watching her as she moved about the room. "You know, my darling girl, I love to watch you walk and move. One of my most vivid memories of you is when you were competing at swim meets. Your grandfather and I would go together and sit high in the bleachers for the best view. I'd see you kidding around with your schoolmates, relaxed and laughing, and then you would get up on the block, place your goggles, and off you would go, just like a streamlined rocket. It was a thing of beauty. And you always were the victor. You set so many school and state records."

Kate leaned against the kitchen doorframe, enjoying his description of her as a teen. "Yeah, those were halcyon days. Until someone pushed me and broke my shoulder. That ended college recruitments and beyond. I remember you staying with Grandfather in my hospital room. Before they took me to surgery, you two were the last faces that I saw before the sleep of the anesthesia."

As they shared the Moo Shu Chicken and Spicy Shrimp with Broccoli, they reminisced about Boston, her grandfather, and the old neighborhood. Eddie poured them some Martell and Kate threw her legs over his lap as they sprawled on the couch, listening to old jazz recordings by Pittsburgh's Ahmad Jamal. Eddie circled back to the morning's topic.

"I can see that you love the sleuthing work you do, and that you are good at it. But now you are skating on the edge of violence. You were only one degree of separation from Mrs. McCarthy's shooting. You and Johnny could have been in the house when that guy drove by. Your professional work is so rewarding; why do you do this other?" Kate watched the azure blue color of his eyes deepen with frustration.

"My academic advising helps people make good choices. The sleuthing helps bring justice to victims of crime. These two satisfactions come directly from my life experience. The man who killed my parents had a police record of drunk driving—that is, a history of making multiple bad choices, finally ending in lethal circumstances. He had a trial and was sent to prison—and that was justice. These preoccupations are part of who l am, Eddie."

"Look, the dig in the south of France is a fully-funded grant from your grandfather's and my alma mater. I make no bones about the fact that l want to take it. Won't you please come with me?" Unlike her mood in the morning, tonight Kate listened with an open mind.

"Of course, you should accept the grant. It's the work you love, Fitzroy. Oh, l know, l know that you love me." She got off the couch and stood in front of him. "l knew that you weren't going to stay here. And the sad part is, l understand why you can't remain in Pittsburgh. I'm not one of those women who would take you at any cost—l want you to be happy and fulfilled." She ran her hands over her hair, twisting the ponytail into a knot, trying to keep from telling him to go to the devil and get out of her house.

"l want us to be together, to get married. Look Kate, l worry about you all the time. Would it be so bad to spend a couple of years in the spectacularly beautiful south of France? You'd be safe there. You'd find something to do." It was that last sentence that confirmed what Kate had suspected about Eddie—he believed that his work was more important than hers. Bile rose in her throat.

"Oh, I'd find something to do? Thanks a lot. We've been having this same argument since l was in my twenties. l told you then that l wasn't going to be the girl who traipsed around from dig to dig, following her man. I'm not desperate to be married to anyone. l   wanted, and have built, a settled life. And yes, maybe my sleuthing can be dangerous. Get over it, Fitzroy."

She walked through the kitchen and out onto the patio, slamming the door. Not used to a tense home, Bourbon Ball followed her out when the door bounced open and leaned against her and licking her hand. "And how would I get you to the south of France, my best boy?" she whispered to BB.

As Kate stood on her patio, her anger subsided, but her mind didn't return to Eddie, who had stayed inside. Instead, it turned to the discovered files on Fiona McCarthy's computer. *I wonder what else is in those files?"*

CHAPTER 19

THE CHIEF WORE HIS WARMEST OVERCOAT, gloves, and a pair of winter boots as he walked from the precinct to Sophia's Cafe. After one of their murder cases last year, Aashi Patel and he had had their first dinner together as private individuals rather than as colleagues. Their mutual respect, affection, and attraction did not immediately culminate in romance, but instead moved glacially toward it through their weekly routine of meeting for breakfast.

Stefan always wanted to look his best when he was seeing Aashi. He wasn't one of those older men who owned a MMMD—the Men's Magical Mirror of Denial. A mirror that told an older man, "You haven't changed," or, "You look better than ever," and "You've still got it." No hair plugs, toupees, tight jeans, or twenty-five-year-old baby wives for him. Jablonsky lived in reality—he knew exactly what was appropriate for a man his age.

Today, he wore a dark blue sweater vest with a striped shirt and red tie. His light wool pants were gray. Stefan's father had worn Bay Rum aftershave, so he began to wear it at these breakfast dates. Dr. Patel commented that she liked the faint, spicy fragrance, and that put a spring in his step and a second bottle in his medicine chest.

Aashi Patel was thoroughly westernized in her attitudes and personal style. She had the good looks of Indian women

124

but never wore uncut long hair or saris. She liked well-tailored pantsuits, contemporary jewelry, and a bob hairdo. This morning, she wore a plum-colored suit with a soft pink cashmere sweater, and, on the practical side, winter boots. Sitting across from her, Jablonsky thoroughly enjoyed the view.

"Have you finished with the model of the USS Missouri yet?" Aashi was one of the few people who knew that Jablonsky built replicas of famous warships. The sloweddown pace of model building appealed to him, as did the precision needed to make an accurate facsimile. Stefan liked engaging in an activity where, if you did everything just right, the result was guaranteed. The hobby was the antithesis of his work life and a healing antidote to it.

"Not finished yet but getting there. I'll text you a photo. On another topic, you know that Dr. Fitzroy went back to the site and found a woven leather bracelet, the size of which is more appropriate for a man's wrist. It could have belonged to Michael. Young men wear those kinds of things. Any news yet from forensics about the ring?"

"Nothing significant. The setting was ten carat gold, sturdy, but not worth much monetarily. They have dated the setting to the late nineties, or early two thousands. It is American made. They think it is a piece that would be given to a school student or an athlete to mark an achievement." Jablonsky nodded but added nothing.

"I visited with Mrs. Rossetti and came away thinking that a murder-suicide scenario is probably out of the running as the manner of death. Was that your impression, Aashi?" While he waited to hear her response, he squeezed a thick ribbon of Heinz catsup over his mushroom and Swiss cheese omelet.

"I felt the same way. She made it clear that the siblings quibbled, but in the end, I saw the Rossettis as a close family. Were there any new facts that emerged?" Jeanne, their usual waitress, knew Aashi's preference for a gently poached egg, perfectly situated on a toasted English muffin. On her side of the table was also a small bowl of seasonal fruit and a pot of hot water for tea.

"Yes. Mr. Rossetti had started to keep a daily diary when Michael and Rosalie first went missing. The diaries were organized by month and year, and the Missus kept them on a bookshelf in one of the cleanest basements I've ever been in. You could have had a picnic on that floor—but I digress. I've started to look through the diaries. The notes were much more detailed than even those of my old chief's, and that is saying something."

"Anything interesting?" Unlike their ex-spouses, Aashi and Stefan enjoyed arranging tiny bits of information and larger human patterns that would be put together to form a picture of the crime and the perpetrator. For them, it was an enjoyable jigsaw puzzle. In that aspect, Kate Chambers was the same.

"Mr. Rossetti owned a beer distributorship. In the old days, a distributorship meant you were doing business with organized crime types—they were the expeditors of the product. I wonder, and so did he, if there was a link between certain illegal activities by dishonest men in the Edmonds construction crew and his kids' disappearance." As soon as Stefan finished his breakfast, Jeanne brought him a fresh cup of coffee and a to-go cup, with a combination of regular drip and two shots of espresso. The timing couldn't have been better because his cellphone rang. It was Antoine.

"Chief, two roofs collapsed at the Delilah Street townhomes. The firemen are there and they think that the culprit was the weight of all the snowfall we've been having. So far, there are no reports of anyone hurt. I'm on my way now. Should I pick you up, or will you drive yourself?" Dr. Patel urged Jablonsky to hurry to the scene. She would talk to him later.

—◁∿▷—

Schools had cancelled classes because of the weather, so getting into Oakland wasn't difficult. The fire trucks had pulled close to the townhouses and already had their men high up in the aerial work platforms, sometimes called buckets, trying to assess the damage. It was a startling sight. Not only had two roofs caved in, but the beams that held the roof joists had splintered and collapsed, and some of the interior ceilings were crushed and gaping open.

Jablonsky parked where he could and made his way through the neighborhood crowd—everyone was either looking up or pointing up. The fire chief recognized him, walked over, and shook his hand. They too looked up as the fire chief explained that the weight of the snow had caused the roof beams to crack and then collapse, taking the joists with them.

"Is anybody hurt?" Jablonsky asked again.

"Not that we know of. It's lucky the cave-in only affected the third floor. The work to clear the debris will go on for days. Right now, tarps have to be positioned on both roofs to keep out the weather. It is supposed to continue to snow throughout the day but stop this evening." Even while giving the report, the fire chief never took his eyes off of his men.

Jablonsky watched the firemen try to tie down the tarps, and also perused the gathered crowd for anyone he thought was suspicious or out of place. He saw DeVille and motioned to him. Coupe offered his greetings to both senior men. They filled him in on what had happened, and what must happen to safely contain the debris.

"I have the names of the owners. Both are on their way. Each owner said their children were either at a grandmother's or at a friend's, but we are not positive." Antoine shivered as he gave the information; today, New Orleans seemed like a piece of heaven.

"Hey, guys! Children live in both houses. Make sure your search is thorough! Owners are on their way now." The fire chief barked the orders, and then rubbed his hands together, both to warm them and in worry.

Jablonsky said, "Chief. I have a quick question. I know homes suffer damage from heavy snow, but have you ever seen support beams collapse like this?" The fire chief looked directly at Stefan, shook his head in the negative, and expounded.

"No. Roof beams must meet certain load requirements in order to pass inspection. These buildings are only twenty-some years old. Someone's ass is going to be in a sling for this one." He left Jablonsky and hurried over to talk to the men who had been lowered to the ground in the bucket.

Stefan, sporting a large grin, turned to his number one. "The Edmonds Land Company built these. Have Jubas Jones point you in the direction of old inspection records having specifically to do with the roofing. I can't wait to get that arrogant son of a bitch, Thomas, back in my interview room."

"Will do, boss. Also, I have some news on Marco Rossetti. We trailed him for the last week to see if he does go out at night with other physicians, to help the homeless—and, he does. Interesting isn't it."

Jablonsky reiterated Kate's theory that Dr. Rossetti's behavior might be about guilt, then added, "Right now, everyone seems guilty of something related to Michael's and

Rosalie's murders, and of the hit on Mrs. McCarthy. It is as if when they dug up the two skeletons, they dug up a spider's web woven out of lies, infidelities, jealousy, and greed. Everyone has been, and is, hiding something."

CHAPTER 20

JOHNNY'S MOTHER DIED the morning the roofs collapsed. He was at her bedside and so was Kate. Joan had called Kate very early that morning to say she had checked with Mrs. McCarthy's internist and was told that Fiona wasn't expected to last another twenty-four hours. Kate called her supervisor to tell her the situation, then went to the hospital to sit with Johnny.

A few hours before she died, Fiona began a cycle of breathing rapidly, and then stopping; the pattern repeated for some time. Kate remembered all these irregular breathing sounds from when she had sat next to her dying grandfather. Periodically during the vigil, she shared some of her memories with Johnny—she conveyed that Fiona wasn't in pain, but rather this type of breathing was a prelude to death. Understanding that his mom wasn't in any distress seemed to help John's anxiety about what was happening.

When they pronounced Fiona dead, Johnny was still holding her hand—he laid his head down onto the bed and wept. Kate left him alone and went to talk to the nurses. She then spoke with the police guard who had been stationed outside the door since Fiona's admission; that officer called DeVille, who was at the Delilah Street townhomes. She texted Joan and Eddie. Johnny could decide what to do about Julius.

After her grandfather died and she had sat for a while with his body, Kate had had the experience of time bending back on itself—present and past somehow magically touched each other. It was as if she had entered a house in which each room was a stage in her life—a tenth birthday party where her grandfather had hired student-actors to dress as fairies, his beaming face as he stood next to her at one of her four graduations; his wet eyes when he dropped her off at the college dorm; his approval of her love affair with Eddie.

Kate knew who and what her grandfather was, so her grieving had been uncomplicated. Johnny, however, would have to merge a picture of what he referred to as good-Fiona with the newly arrived mystery-Fiona. The other day he had remarked to Kate, "I don't know my own mother anymore."

Kate's advice was, "You have this time with her to ask your questions about her other life. Don't hold back. Fiona wants you to know her before she dies." Kate initially thought he would, like most people, be overjoyed to inherit such a bundle of cash. But maybe Fiona was right, and his first instinct would be to reject it. She chuckled to herself, *If he doesn't want it, I'll take it!*

Kate's phone rang, it was Jablonsky. "I'm sorry about Johnny's mother. You know, since her case is now a murder, her physician cannot sign the death certificate. Dr. Patel must first do an autopsy. She the only one who can sign the official certificate of death citing cause and manner. I hope Johnny understands about the autopsy. How is he?"

"He is still sitting with her. I heard about the problems at Delilah Street. Are you there?" Kate and Jablonsky were likeminded in their belief that Mrs. McCarthy's murder, and Michael's and Rosalie's deaths, were either linked to the people who worked at the Edmonds company or at Rosalie's Bakery—maybe both. She was determined to do more research in order to help with the case. Whatever her original feelings were about Mrs. McCarthy, Kate was driven to help give her, and Johnny, justice.

Jablonsky interrupted her thoughts. "I'm heading over to the morgue. Please give my condolences to Johnny."

"I will. I'll also tell him that you are going to get the bastard who did this to his mom." Kate made no attempt to hide her anger.

———

The wheels of the forensic process were now in motion. Dr. Patel began the autopsy by looking at the hospital's chart on Mrs. McCarthy. Joan's surgical report noted that the bullet had lodged too close to the lungs to be removed—Patel would remove it now. The tiny bit of metal would identify the caliber and maybe the make and model of the gun used to shoot her. The notes from Mrs. McCarthy's internist stated that other than the normal wear and tear of living, Fiona, age 75, wasn't actively being treated for any of the big three causes of death—heart disease, cancer, COPD (chronic obstructive pulmonary disease). *Her life was definitely cut short,* thought Patel.

As she and her medical residents stood over the body, Dr. Patel became the teacher and the philosopher. "Unless there is something upon physical exam, cause of death would be complications from a gunshot wound, and manner of death, murder. Our efforts today are righteous because our findings may help catch Mrs. McCarthy's murderer."

When he entered the morgue, Jablonsky unwrapped a piece of cinnamon gum and popped it in his mouth. Dr. Patel had finished with the autopsy and was seated at the row of microscopes, peering at something. She rotated her chair around and greeted the chief.

"You are here for the bullet? I have it for you. I'm not a ballistics expert, but I'd say this is a .380. What do you think?"

Jablonsky rotated the bullet in his fingers. "The .380 is much smaller than the .38, and this bullet is small. Two gun manufacturers, Lorcin Engineering and Raven Arms, produced cheap revolvers that were used in the eighties and nineties. They are out of business now, but their guns are desirable because they are old and hard to trace. A revolver made by either one of them would fit the bill for this crime; let's see what Bill Reeves's technicians make of this." Jablonsky pocketed the evidence bag, then talked about the roofs at Delilah Street until Aashi started to swivel her chair back and forth—the sign she had work to do.

Back at the precinct, Jablonsky and Antoine stood in front of the murder board, waiting for their neurons to spark new connections. Fiona McCarthy's case was now "officially" a murder investigation.

Jablonsky began. "Who else knew about the three million dollars Andrew Edmonds left Fiona?" He moved the photo of Thomas Edmonds next to Mrs. McCarthy's. "Thomas is our prime suspect."

Below Thomas's photo, Stefan drew a straight line and wrote the name Eugenia Edmonds. "Fiona said that Eugenia Edmonds knew about her relationship with Andrew. After he died, and Mrs. Edmonds was settling the estate, I believe she would have asked about any monies that went to Fiona. It's only human nature that she would want to know if he had given the woman with whom he had almost lived for twenty years anything of consequence."

"Agreed," Antoine said with his hint of a drawl. "I had mentioned to you that Eugenia still lives in her home but has health care workers who look after her. I couldn't find any report of dementia—she is just really old. At this point in her life, what would be her motive for hiring someone to kill Fiona?"

"My current working hypothesis is that Thomas Edmonds hired a trusted local hood to shoot Fiona, in part out of loyalty to his mother and in part because he suspected Fiona might have information about building code infractions. When the Rossetti siblings were finally found, and it was at one of his building sites, he decided to close the loop. Before their bodies appeared, he felt safe." Jablonsky opened another piece of gum—the taste of cinnamon always spurred new insights.

"You mentioned that in the past, beer distributorships dealt with lower-level mafia types who controlled access to the products via the trucks and the drivers. The same used to be true in New Orleans. Do you see a connection between Mr. Rossetti's business and either of these murders?" Antoine accepted the piece of gum offered him, stuffing it into his cheek; he liked the slight cinnamon burn.

Jablonsky turned, cocked his head to one side, and then said, "Everything seems to center on Mrs. Rossetti's bakery and the people who either worked there or were customers. But Mr. Rossetti might have been following a line of inquiry known only to him—that's why we are going through the diaries. For instance, did any of Edmonds's construction crew get their beer at Rossetti's, and happen to connect with a guy who knew a guy who could "fix" things, like alter or make the paperwork disappear on code violations? Mr. Rossetti's beer business, Mrs. Rossetti's bakery, Michael's and Rosalie's disappearance, and now, Fiona's murder—the past is still very much present."

Antoine commented, "So, you think that Thomas Edmonds could have gotten the names of people who were willing to look the other way when it came to codes and other acts of malfeasance, and that he still might have those contacts. Someone he could call in the present day—murder for hire."

"That's one possibility. Then there is Luca Lorenzo, Jonathan Price, and our dear surgeon, Marco." Their theorizing was interrupted by the clerk announcing that Jubas Jones had arrived.

Jablonsky had decided to talk with Jubas in his office rather than in one of the interview rooms. Jones was not on the short list of suspects, but he was in the mix. Stefan knew that he would get more information from him if Jones felt he was part of the team.

"I was sorry to hear about that Mrs. McCarthy. After seeing her picture, I remembered her from Rosalie's bakery; a pretty and charming lady, who always had a smile and a witty comment." Jubas, dressed in business casual attire, settled himself in the visitor's chair, clearly a man who was used to dealing with many types of people and meetings. He was relaxed.

"DeVille asked you to brainstorm about the Edmonds Land Company and their record of code violations. We have copies of violations with electrical and lumber suppliers, and I'm hoping you can provide us with more. Do you remember being in city planning meetings where any other violations were discussed?"

"I went back into my personal files, and then made a few calls to the inspectors who would have been around then. Everyone's memory aligns—the father was clean; the son was dirty. It went like this—the city sent numerous inspectors to the hotel site. They would find violations and Thomas would correct some things, but then other problems would arise. The same was true with the Delilah Street townhomes. The hotel and the townhomes were built around the same time—excavation for the new hotel is on the old hotel site."

"Correct. Where the bodies were found. While the original hotel was being built, were there any employees in the inspectors department who could be bought?"

"Yes. There was a guy named Al Sweets who was rumored to be on the take from several construction firms, Edmonds among them. The department attempted to go after him for accepting bribes but couldn't get any evidence that would legally hold up. Unfortunately, he is dead. I did bring you a list of the electrical, plumbing, concrete suppliers, and the lumber yards that gave product for both the hotel and the townhome projects." Jubas slid a piece of paper over to Jablonsky.

Jablonsky wrote the name Al Sweets in his small notebook and thanked Jones for the list. "I'm going to switch topics for a minute. Did you frequent Rossetti's beer distributorship when it was open? I know my father did. Every Saturday morning, he   drove over and bought a case of Rolling Rock beer." Stefan hoped that sharing a bit of personal history would spark some heretofore forgotten information from Jubas.

"I used to go there all the time. Rossetti would have types of beer you couldn't get anywhere else, and he was a fair man. He treated white and black customers equally—outside of black neighborhoods, that used to be rare in Pittsburgh. After Michael and Rosalie disappeared, many black bar owners took their business to him, a 'burgh show of kindness. What makes you ask?"

"Just following a line of inquiry. Did you know if he kept a clean shop? I mean, was he known to be involved with organized crime?"

Jones looked surprised. "No. I mean, organized crime ran the trucks that hauled the beer, but the city never had any complaints about that business; Rossetti was a straight shooter. You can't be thinking that he had something to do with his own children's deaths!"

"No. Absolutely not! I'm trying to find out how the Edmonds company connected with bent construction workers." The chief gave Jubas Jones a look which meant, "That's all I'm going to say." Jones left the precinct, and DeVille immediately poked his head into the chief's office and was handed Jones's list.

"This is a list of suppliers to the old hotel and Delilah Street townhomes. I want you to snoop around and see what infractions there might have been in goods and services, especially from the lumber yards. Roof beams just don't collapse under a bit of snow—something was wrong."

CHAPTER 21

UNLIKE MICHAEL'S AND ROSALIE'S FUNERAL, which was held at the diocese's grand cathedral, Fiona McCarthy's Mass took place at her local church and was attended only by family, neighbors, and her bingo buddies. The priest's remarks were bittersweet; sweet because his reflections on Fiona's life were personal and humorous, but bitter because he was at a loss to explain why an innocent like her would be gunned down in her own home.

Jablonsky attended the service. He parked himself in the last pew of the church in order to observe the congregation. The neighborhood church he grew up in was much like this one—small, gossipy, always struggling for money. It felt familiar, but not in a good way; the sheer numbers of the sexual abuse cases had destroyed any good memories he had of church.

The chief headed to the basement hall where he saw Kate and Joan sitting together at one of the back tables; they were watching Johnny, with Eddie Fitzroy at his side, moving around the room fulfilling his filial duty. Jablonsky noticed that Fitzroy seemed to know how to strike just the right tone with Fiona's elderly friends—sympathetic and sometimes irreverent. His years of dealing with elders from other cultures served him well.

Stefan overheard Joan ask Kate, "How is Johnny doing?" Kate folded and refolded her napkin, so preoccupied that she did not answer Joan's question. "Ladies, I'm going to give my condolences to John, and then I'm going to have to leave."

Jablonsky looked longingly at Kate and Joan's food; Fiona's friends had prepared a luncheon filled with ethnic favorites, which were also the chief's favorites. Rosalie's Bakery had sent a fabulous spread of pastries, enough so that the funeral guests could take some home. His hungry look brought Kate out of her machinations—she offered to make him a plate of food to take back to the precinct.

The chief encircled Johnny in a fatherly hug, deeply sorry for the brutal way his mother had died. While they were talking, Dr. Marco Rossetti moved slowly toward them, guiding his mother, Lisa Marie, obviously still nervous at being outside of her home.

Mrs. Rossetti offered her hand to Johnny, saying, "I worked with your mother for more years than I'd like to admit. She was a good baker, always cheerful and pleasant to the customers—a hard worker. I liked her. And I'm so sorry about all this ugly business. I'll pray to St. Anthony to help the chief find her killer." Everyone in the room grew quiet as she spoke. They knew the pain that Mrs. Rossetti had borne over her missing children, so for them, she was now endowed with a patina of gravitas.

Johnny bent forward to thank the diminutive woman, and when she put her mother's arms around him, he gave in to his grief. Jablonsky, Joan, and Kate all searched in their pockets for Kleenex. Marco, on the other hand, stood apart, in a posture of watchfulness. His mother let go of Johnny, then slowly walked around the room greeting old friends; Marco approached Jablonsky.

"I understand you have my father's diaries. I hope they can be helpful to your investigation—I went through them years ago but didn't see anything of significance; I was a young man then. I didn't know what might be important."

Jablonsky lowered his voice and responded. "Do you have any papers or diaries of your sister's?"

"I do have a box with some of her things. I don't think there is a diary, but there are papers from her law school years."

"I'm going to want to look at everything you have. Detective DeVille can stop by and pick it up. Where is the box? Is it at your mother's, or at your own condo?" Jablonsky knew that Marco knew that he wanted to look around his condominium. Evidence is not always visible to the civilian eye.

"I'll drop the box by the precinct." Game, set, and match to the doctor. Jablonsky grinned, thanked Marco, and moved over to Kate, who handed him a container with the lunch specialties, dishes that represented Fiona's generation— cheese pierogis with sautéed onions, kielbasa links, a hefty scoop of shepherd's pie, meatballs and sauce, tender greens and beans, and a few slices of homemade nut roll.

As he left for the precinct, he saw Kate and Fitzroy arguing outside the church hall. Stefan slowed his car just in case the argument became more heated, but Johnny appeared at the side door and scolded them. *I wonder what that is about?*, mused the chief. The strain on Kate's face stuck in his mind.

DeVille had returned from talking with a senior salesperson at the lumber yard. He gave his report while Jablonsky ate. "This lumber yard supplied both the hotel project and the Delilah Street townhomes. I asked for any paperwork they might have, and sure enough, the guy went into the back room, opened some boxes, and gave me this."

"I'm surprised they had saved these invoices." As he looked over the invoices, Jablonsky placed some of the sautéed onions on the last pierogi, eating it with relish. "Did he say these were the beams and joists that were actually delivered?"

"I asked him that question. He prevaricated. What he said was that he didn't remember this exact job but did agree that twenty years ago some of the men who worked for Edmonds were sketchy. It is possible, he said, that a few of that crew paid his men on the side to deliver cheaper, flimsier beams." Jablonsky knew that Antoine hadn't yet had lunch, so he slid the meatballs, plus the greens and beans dish, across the desk to him.

"Here. I can't finish these. You have them. So, there is no way of knowing whether the items listed on this invoice were the actual items that were delivered and used." Jablonsky eyed the pieces of nut roll.

"The answers that the guy gave me were vague—obviously motivated to give his company wiggle room in any kind of lawsuit. I think it would be hard to prove, specifically, which inferior products were delivered to either the townhomes or the hotel. Man, these greens and beans are really good." Antoine made short work of the meatballs as well, cleaning the last of the tomato sauce with several slices of Rosalie's Bakery's fresh Italian bread.

"We have to dig deeper and track down any crew members who are still in the vicinity. I want to lean on Luca Lorenzo— get him to name some people. But Thomas Edmonds doesn't know what we have, or don't have, so let's keep fishing

—◦—

Edmonds sat in his home office, his face in his hands. He had had another call from the police for a second interview.

He wasn't worried or scared; he just wanted the whole Rossetti thing to go away. His private cellphone rang It was a number he didn't recognize, so he answered.

"What?" barked Thomas. A familiar woman's voice responded. Edmonds couldn't have been more annoyed. "Is this another burner cell with a new number? What are you calling about now? Let me guess, is it money?"

"Listen, Tom-cat, did you get the invoice for Eleanor's spring tuition?" Jane Louise's tone wasn't nearly as nasty and insulting as it had been in the past, but the call had just begun; there was still time for the mother bear to get rough protecting her cub. "Why must we go through this every time? You only have one daughter. Pay the darn bill."

The phone call was just the red meat Thomas had been craving. If he couldn't chew up the chief of detectives, by God, Jane Louise would be just as tasty. "If I don't pay it, there is absolutely nothing you can do. Nothing. Eleanor is a smart girl; she'll get scholarship money for this last year. The medical school won't let a promising young physician like her drop out because of a few dollars. Besides, she has the money my father left her." Thomas leaned back in his office chair, enjoying having Jane Louise beg.

"There are several things I can do. The first one will be to fly to New York to visit Eugenia, your sweet old mother. While I'm there, I'll show her some pictures. You know the ones, Tomcat. The pictures of a certain room?" Jane Louise had been a very successful litigator; she had trained her voice to be smooth as silk, or as creepy as Hannibal Lecter's.

Her threat found its target. An ominous tingling sensation moved along Thomas's spine. He was silent for several minutes, then responded, "Okay, Jane Louise. You've made your point. I'll pay the darn bill. But, if you ever bring up the room again, I'm going to find a way to hurt you. Are we clear?"

"If I felt like quoting movie dialogue, I'd say, "Crystal." Don't threaten me, Thomas. If something happens to me, an envelope will be delivered to the appropriate people. I'm an attorney, remember? I'm not like those other bimbos you married—the Barbies and Bambis. I have an actual brain. Besides, if I am hurt in any way, you will be hurting our daughter. Think of someone besides yourself for once—think of the one person in the world who loves you unconditionally." Jane Louise knew that appealing to some fatherly feelings in Thomas was fruitless, but for her daughter's sake, she always tried anyway.

"My mother loves me unconditionally." The moment the words came out of his mouth, he knew it was a show of weakness. *"Damn!", he thought. "That witch got me once again."*

Jane Louise burst out laughing and hung up before Thomas got a chance. Her laughter didn't last long—she didn't dismiss his threat to hurt her. Thomas never knew the emotional toll these calls took on his ex-wife. If he had, he probably would enjoy it.

CHAPTER 22

IT WAS THAT WEEK IN WINTER when the temperature modulates, and everyone does two things—they open their windows to let a fresh breeze move through the house and they wash their cars. It was Saturday, and with Eddie's help, the two washed Kate's Mercedes hatchback, plus his heavy-duty Range Rover. Bourbon Ball romped around the cars, chasing a ball, and trying to bite the playful water squirts from the hose.

After the exertion of the morning's car washing activities, BB was stretched out in Kate's sitting room, deep in restorative sleep. Eddie was also asleep, tunneled under the blankets on the bed. Kate, however, was awake, lured into reflection by the soft breeze blowing in through the open window and the reassuring sound of Saturday traffic on Fifth Avenue.

Satisfying sex and meaningful conversation had always come easily between her and Fitzroy; it was the day-to-day living that hadn't. These last months were the longest stretch of time they had spent together in the same city. Today, there had been no arguing about who was going to live where. It had been easy and fun between them, reminiscent of the many times he would return to her from his digs. Would how they had lived in the past be enough for her in the future?

She sighed, having to admit to herself that recently something had been missing in their relationship—so much so that she thought about breaking up with him. That thought always made her shiver with anxiety; Eddie was the link to her loving grandfather; if she finally let go of him, would she experience the loss of her granddad all over again?

Kate wiggled out from under the covers, urging a half-awake Eddie to stay in bed, and went into the kitchen to make coffee. She sometimes worried that she was becoming like many of her colleagues, who were so smart in their work life and so stupid in picking men.

She grabbed her phone to call Johnny. "What time do you want to meet at your mother's house?" she asked, sipping the hot coffee.

"About an hour would work for me." The muffled sound alerted her to the fact that he had tried to cover the phone with his hand, but Kate still recognized a voice filled with tears. She had personal experience with how grief can catch one off guard.

"I'm at your command for whatever you need to be accomplished at the house. I'll order takeout. You bring your favorite coffee." Kate was one of those friends who could be relied upon to help with moving, cleaning out, painting, or even the dreaded task of picking someone up at the airport—all the day-to-day activities that humans take care of. She never forgot that before she moved her grandfather to Pittsburgh, his neighbors and colleagues would go to the grocery store, bring dinners to him, or sometimes just stay to play cards and gossip. Kate saw the difference it made in his life and wanted to pay those human kindnesses forward. Right now, she carried a coffee back to Eddie, who had called Bourbon Ball up onto the bed to wrestle with him.

"Thanks for the coffee, my darling girl. Are you still going over to the house?" Eddie was rarely waited on by a half-dressed, beautiful woman—he showed no signs of getting up. "By the way, you are right, Bourbon Ball's paws really do smell like popcorn. Anyhow, I'll take him out for his walk. I need to work on an article, so if you don't mind, I'll stay here."

After being delayed by a few more amorous kisses, Kate finally escaped into the shower, then dressed, and ordered some Greek takeout to be delivered to Mrs. McCarthy's house. It was a short ten-minute drive to Greenfield. Johnny's car was already parked in the driveway. Since Bill Reeves's forensics team had released the house back to him, there were boxes filled with memorabilia from Johnny's childhood that he wanted to go through, and general packing to do.

Before they could finish digging through his mother's neatly organized household, the food arrived. Instead of coffee, Johnny had brought some cold beer to enjoy with their gyro sandwiches. They talked about the Slope house, the house that Julius and Johnny had renovated on the steep hills above the South Side neighborhood. Now that Johnny had Fiona's money, he could buy Julius's portion and own the house free and clear. In the telephone calls with Julius, arguments had flared over the valuation of the property and some of the things that Julius wanted to have shipped to Paris. Johnny looked haggard.

The only comment that Kate made about Julius was, "As a black man, he suffers with certain unfair practices by the police that you and I did not. Coming back from visiting his parents in DC, you know that he has often been stopped by the police for what he calls "driving while black." It is only fair to acknowledge that insults like that were a significant factor in his wanting to live in Paris."

Johnny looked directly at Kate, responding with, "It is not going to be much better there. Racism is everywhere." Ironically, he didn't realize that his mother had kept the three million dollars for him as protection from prejudice against gay men, but Kate wasn't going to drive that point home when he was so obviously debilitated. And the last thing she was going to share with him today was that Fitzroy wanted her to go the south of France with him. She was exquisitely sensitive to the human state of having suffered "too many losses."

Kate was no stranger to inherited money; her grandfather's estate, and also the insurance money from her parent's deaths, were left to her. The money acted as a cushion against the whims of fate; she wanted her friend to also enjoy that safety net. With some of her inheritance, Kate had bought her beautiful condo and her expensive car; her grandfather would have been so happy that he could do that for her. She tried to explain that Fiona felt the same about her gift of the bank account; it pleased her to know the safety it brought her only son. Johnny listened but did not respond.

Kate spread out Fiona's cookbooks on the kitchen table, focusing on the ones that had the most personal notes. "These are so detailed. She has her own additions and subtractions written in the margins, especially for the pastry recipes. Have you ever seen these before?" Kate's grandfather hadn't been much of a cook, so they always ate at one of Boston's many fine restaurants for the holidays and for special occasions. She did have her maternal grandmother's and her mother's cookbooks; they meant a great deal to her.

"I wonder what this symbol means?" Kate pointed to an x with a circle around it, "I'm not a baker, but an x plus circle usually means something to be left out, or to be wary of. Remember the Mr. Yuck stickers? They were created right here in Pittsburgh at our children's hospital."

For the first time, Johnny really looked at his mother's cookbooks. Kate knew that he was trying to overcome his ambivalence about his mom's double life; the emotional flexibility it took to positively remember all the good times they had together, and not her affair with Andrew Thomas, was a gymnastic feat hard to achieve.

He finally responded. "I would guess that the x inside the circle means caution. There might be some preparations in which one doesn't mix two different herbs or spices together. You know that I don't bake. Any baking knowledge I have has been the result of you and me watching *The Great British Baking Show*. I love to eat, but I'm not the chef Julius is, or you."

Having looked through several of Fiona's cookbooks, Kate had the intuition that certain of the pastry recipes were significant. Rosalie's Bakery, and the people there, were at the heart of Fiona's and the Rossetti's murders. While Johnny went upstairs, Kate thought about calling the chief, but called Joan instead. She was still miffed that he had blocked her from walking the site with Eddie. The information Kate was gathering on the lion symbol and the circle with an x around it might produce clues important to both cases. If she turned up something significant, she would talk to Jablonsky or, to be contrary, she might send it to Dr. Patel.

Joan answered the telephone immediately. "Hey Joan! I'm going to email you some pictures of recipes that I found in Mrs. McCarthy's cookbooks that were used at Rosalie's Bakery. She has a symbol written beside certain ingredients that, combined with others, might make someone sick. Will you have a look, and tell me what you think? Thanks."

Kate sent the recipes, then waited. In a few minutes, Joan called her back. "Well, just off the top of my head, a circle with an x in it is a symbol used in mathematics, for something to do with vectors. I'm more familiar with its use as a symbol for the exclusion principle in data modeling. Also, I remember from my medical history classes that it was used at Ellis Island, either on the forms or on the emigrating person's clothing, to denote insanity. A far-out use is in the comic, Marble Hornets, to signify a character called The Operator, or The Slender Man. I doubt Fiona engaged in reading that online fantasy. When I look at the recipes, I'd say she was indicating that if some ingredients were mixed, they would be poisonous. I'm going to email these recipes to Dr. Patel; she would know the chemical combinations. Does that help?"

"You bet it does. Thanks!" Kate put the recipe books in her briefcase, intending that they would find their way to Jablonsky if there was a quid pro quo of some sort.

———

Jablonsky and DeVille divided the contents of the box of Rosalie's papers that Marco Rossetti had left at the station and began to read through them. They mostly consisted of the A-plus essays she had written for different law courses and an article for the law review. DeVille commented on Rosalie having had a paper published in the review. "It is prestigious to be part of the law review. I guess it is true that she had beauty and brains."

The chief rolled his eyes at his number one's continued infatuation with Rosalie. "Now here is something odd. There are several sheets that have a series of numbers and letters on them, and nothing else. The two men took one sheet each and started to work on the numeric puzzle. Jablonsky finally called out to Annie Lemon, known to be good at coded or encrypted types of evidence.

"What do you make of these, Annie?" She took a page, chewed on the end of her pen, then slowly started to circle groups of numbers. "I think these numbers are dates," she responded.

"You are right! It looks like they start in the year nineteen ninety-nine and run up to the mid-teens."

"And to my eye, this grouping could be invoice numbers— they are in sequence, the way invoices would be. If they are invoice numbers, it would make sense that the initials beside each set are the company." Annie smiled at the chief, always happy to look good in his eyes.

"Coupe, you and Annie go through these sheets and match the initials to the companies we know that did business with Thomas Edmonds. Maybe she really was gathering information on his bribery and fraud activities and not just having a fling. Thanks, Annie."

"It would be sweet if she was," said Antoine. "I didn't even know her and yet it bothers me that she was anywhere near Thomas Edmonds. Boss, these few papers appear to be Marco Rossetti's schoolwork. Here is his name, and here are the problems to be worked. These are symbols from the periodic table—maybe they are from a chemistry class? I know he had skipped some grades—judging from the date on the worksheets, he would have been just twelve or so, taking an advanced class."

"Chemistry papers? Interesting. I want him to identify these sheets as his. I doubt that he even knows these were in his sister's box. Why would anyone save worksheets from a chemistry class?" Poison was never far from Jablonsky's mind.

Stefan slowly unwrapped a piece of cinnamon gum, then offered a stick to Antoine. Annie took the stick offered her and put it in her back pocket, politely saying, "I'll have this later, Boss."

Jablonsky decided to talk with both Bill Reeves and Dr. Patel about the possibility that there are bakery ingredients which are poisonous. Little did he know that because of Joan and Kate, Patel was already looking into whether there are combinations of ingredients that would make a person sick, if not kill them.

CHAPTER 23

THOMAS EDMONDS SAT in the interview room waiting for Jablonsky. Petulance and annoyance were dancing the rumba on his face. Beautifully outfitted in a light alpaca wool sweater and black pants, he pulled a nonexistent thread off his sweater.

Jablonsky set an armful of manila folders, depositions, and his own small notebook on the table. Thomas had shown up for this second interview without an attorney—Jablonsky interpreted that as sheer ego. The chief didn't attempt to soothe Edmonds's annoyance, but he did have DeVille follow him with cups of coffee as a diversion.

"This is detective Antoine DeVille. Here is some coffee. Let's get started."

"Get started with what? Why am I here? I told you last time that I don't know anything about Michael's and Rosalie's disappearance." Edmonds's tone was cold, and his voice dry— he took a sip of the coffee.

"Well, you see, Thomas, I just don't believe you. And this stack of information ties the Edmonds company to nefarious dealings on the hotel site, where we found Michael's and Rosalie's bodies, and the Delilah Street townhomes, where roofs just collapsed. Some of this information was being compiled by your own father; Fiona McCarthy had that evidence in her possession."

"Detective, um, what is it, Ja-blow-ski? Whatever you think you have on me personally, or on the company, will never see the light of a courtroom. I have a stable of highly trained attack attorneys who will have everything thrown out. But if you want to, go ahead and make your case. I'll listen to it." Edmonds leaned back in his chair; a tiny sneer lifted one corner of his mouth.

Jablonsky was very familiar with this ploy. Show me your information so that I can organize my defense to thwart your strategy. The chief wanted Thomas Edmonds to think he was in control; he knew from experience that arrogance distorts a person's perception of reality. Connecting Thomas to building code malfeasance was already in the bag. To connect him to the Rossetti murders and to paying for a hit on Mrs. McCarthy he needed Edmonds to be blinded by arrogance.

DeVille handed Jablonsky a typewritten statement. "Mr. Edmonds, this is an official statement by Luca Lorenzo saying that you asked him to identify local men you could hire who were willing to look the other way concerning building code violations and inferior building supplies. Luca noted that he did in fact identify a few corruptible men for your crew. He also states that you, personally, lied to city inspectors, saying that you were correcting code violations. Mr. Lorenzo was a friend of Michael Rossetti, and of the Alliance. He states that you, personally, asked him to be a mole in that organization, that you wanted him to give a heads-up on their strategies."

Antoine handed two other sheets of paper to the chief, who placed them on the table in front of Thomas Edmonds. Jablonsky continued. "Here are affidavits from Jonathan Price and Jubas Jones, both citing times and places that you were seen in intimate contact with Rosalie Rossetti. You maintain that your relationship was a casual one, based on sex, but we believe that you were in love with her, too blind to see that she was using you to gather information on your company's practices."

Stefan let that last demeaning statement grab this arrogant man in the nether regions—Rosalie was using him, not the other way around. Her betrayal would sting.

"Here is a list of various suppliers of building materials, along with invoice numbers, dates, and names that Rosalie Rossetti compiled while pretending to like you."

Antoine handed the chief two more folders. "Here is the report from the fire department stating that the collapse of two roofs at the Delilah Street townhomes was due to beams and joists which were inadequate to carry a normal load, let alone one with wet snow. The lumber yard owners admit that your men sometimes noted that certain orders met code on the invoice, but in fact, were inferior product."

Jablonsky watched Thomas Edmonds as he presented the case but didn't see any signs that the man was threatened by either the documentation or the accusations, except for that periodic twitch in Edmonds's right eyelid, which he had noticed in their previous interview. Jablonsky continued.

"I've shown you the invoices that your father had gathered on your building practices. He entrusted them to Fiona McCarthy, a woman with whom he had a love relationship for twenty years. Your father left Fiona a great deal of money which, by the way, she never touched. Isn't it a coincidence that right after Michael's and Rosalie's bodies are found at one of your building sites, Fiona is murdered?"

"Detective Jablonsky. I had no reason to murder an old woman who once knew my father. If he left her a few pennies, so be it. It is my experience that one often has to pay women for certain, well, politely put, favors. Land development is a tricky business. It is not for the morally high-minded. But there is a big difference between a few invoices and possible payoffs and committing a murder. Have you finished your story yet?" Thomas Edmonds made no physical move to leave the room, but within his closed expression, Jablonsky detected a hint of anxiety. *Good,* he thought, *anxiety compromises judgment.*

Out of the corner of his eye, the chief could see DeVille unconsciously close his fingers into a fist. To speak about Fiona McCarthy in the manner Edmonds had, indicated nothing about the woman, but did lay bare Thomas's thoroughly corrupt nature. For the first time, Jablonsky wondered if Johnny might be in danger. He and Antoine stood and gathered their papers.

"Mr. Thomas Edmonds, you are the prime suspect in the murders of Michael and Rosalie Rossetti, and in the murder of Fiona McCarthy. Motivated by greed and jealousy, you either perpetrated these murders yourself, or you paid someone to do it for you. You had the opportunity, the motive, and the means to execute all three murders. Today the DA has given your history over to the state and city commissioners, who will examine your business practices under the Ethics and Public Corruption Laws. There is no question you will be charged for widespread malfeasance in your building practices."

Edmonds finally stood and locked eyes with Jablonsky, who warned, "You, Thomas Edmonds, better get those attack attorneys lined up because we are coming for you with first degree murder charges. Remain in the city."

CHAPTER 24

KATE AND JOAN DECIDED TO MEET for dinner at the University Club. Suzie, their usual waitress, had already placed a dry vodka martini, one olive, in front of Kate when Joan arrived. Both women were dressed in finely tailored black suits accented with hand-made artsy jewelry. Little did anyone around them realize that these two professional women were there to discuss murder.

Suzie returned with a sparkling Pelligrino water for Joan, who had surgeries in the morning. Both women decided on a cold weather dinner of ribeye steak, parsley new potatoes, and spinach salad, dressing on the side. They were almost finished eating when someone called Joan's name. "Dr. Weisner. I haven't seen you in quite a while."

Kate looked up to see a tall dark-haired man, dressed in heather gray wool pants, a gray cashmere sweater, and tasseled shoes, offer his hand to Joan. "Kate, this is Dr. Marco Rossetti. Won't you join us? You've already eaten? Have a coffee, then."

It was easy to read Rossetti's hesitant body language, but as Joan pulled out a chair, he gave in to her pressure. While he settled himself, Suzie appeared with a small slice of chocolate cake and a fresh cup of coffee.

Kate could hardly contain her excitement over such a fortuitous meeting; the brother of Michael and Rosalie right in front of her. She knew he had been at Fiona's wake with his mother but she hadn't talked to him. Kate was anxious to ask certain questions but wasn't sure how to approach him, so she waited for the right moment.

"Are you often on this side of the river?" asked Joan.

"I am the principal investigator on a research grant that includes some of the surgeons here at the university, so we often meet at this club for our collaborations and dinner. Plus, my mother still lives in South Oakland." Marco smiled as he cut into the cake. "Suzie always remembers that I have a sweet tooth. You might know that my mother owns a bakery."

"How is your mother doing? What an emotional situation it must have been for her, and for you. Kate attended the funeral at the Cathedral." Kate could have squeezed Joan's hand at her smooth introduction of the Rossetti murders.

Marco tilted his head and looked quizzically at Kate. "You attended the funeral? Did you know my brother and sister?"

"No. But when I was a graduate student here at the university, I was aware of their work with the Alliance. It was always covered in the student newspaper. Your siblings' disappearance shook everyone in the Oakland neighborhoods, including university people like me. I wanted to pay my respects." Kate felt she had offered a coherent story to him; what she couldn't say was that she was also at the funeral because she is an amateur sleuth, connected to detective Jablonsky and his inquiries.

"I see. To answer the question, my mother is doing much better. She has suffered for a long time from what is called traumatic agoraphobia. Since the funeral, she has been going out a little bit. I recently took her to the funeral of an old bakery employee."

Like a miner panning for gold, Kate continued her quest to shake loose any unguarded nuggets of information. "You are talking about Fiona McCarthy. Joan and I saw you and your mother at Mrs. McCarthy's funeral luncheon. Professor Johnny McCarthy is one of my best friends."

Marco looked like he had been caught at something. "Now I remember— you sitting with Joan. I knew Mrs. McCarthy from when she worked at the bakery. Johnny would come around on and off—I can't say I really knew him."

Kate, being the bloodhound that she was, posed the next natural question. "What did you make of her being shot?"

Marco crossed his long legs, pulling the crease of his pants upward so not to wrinkle them. Clearly a man comfortable with a silent pause, he sat quietly and sipped his coffee. Kate thought that he had the chiseled face of an Italian man sipping an espresso at a cafe in Florence.

"Well, like everyone else, I was shocked by it. Her circumstances sparked a conversation with my mother about her continuing to live alone. Like Johnny did for his mother, I look out for mine. She is my only family." Kate was surprised at how unexpectedly soulful his answer was; she didn't know that Jablonsky had had the same impression of him. Apparently, this famously reserved surgeon had another side to him.

Your mother's bakery, her lady employees, and her customers seem to be at the center of the investigation into your siblings' deaths." Like Marco, Kate was also comfortable with putting an idea forth and waiting for an answer, even in the face of another's discomfort.

"I'm not sure how you know that." Kate felt Marco search her face for some indication of the intent of her questions; she guessed that he might be thinking that she was just a gossip. "You must be referring to the fact that the owners of the Edmonds Company and their crews were regulars at the bakery. Members of my family had limited involvement with them—mostly they met over negotiations with the Alliance. Except, well...."

"Except?" Both Joan and Kate spoke at the same time, and then all three laughed nervously. Marco didn't back away from the questions; he stayed in the game.

"Except for Rosalie. There were rumors that the son, Thomas, was interested in her. I saw him flirt with her at the bakery many times. I was just a kid, so I don't know if she responded to his advances. I couldn't imagine why she would want to see him. He was a dick."

"That seems to be the general consensus about him. Considering everything your family was doing to preserve the neighborhood, it must have made you mad that he would presume his attentions would be welcome." Rossetti furrowed his brow, then briefly wiped his face with his napkin; Kate felt he was hiding his emotional pain behind the small piece of heavy damask.

"I was jealous of the men who flocked around my sister. Sometimes I would try to impress them by showing off my brain power—adding up the cost of their purchases in my head, or correcting proportions of an ingredient in a recipe. I loved Rosalie, and often needed her counsel over adolescent stuff; I worried that someone was going to hurt her."

"Or take her away." Kate's four words were a compassionate and empathetic reminder that everyone fears losing the ones they love, a situation with which she was all too familiar. Suzie hung back from approaching the table, sensing something important was happening. She earned her following at the University Club, and her tips.

Once again, Marco tilted his head in a nonverbal gesture of agreement with what Kate had said. "That's right. I both loved her and needed her—she gave me, what's the expression, unconditional love. In the end, no matter how smart I was, I wasn't able to protect her." Marco paused, casting his eyes down in what might be shyness; Kate felt his apprehension created an atmosphere of intimacy which she experienced as both attractive and disturbing. *What is happening here?* she asked herself in annoyance.

Marco stood and pushed his chair under the table. "Well, this was an unexpected conversation. Joan, I was just stopping to say hello, and I end up talking about my love for my sister. Good to see you, fellow surgeon, and to officially meet you, Kate, a woman who knows how to make a man talk. Good evening, ladies."

As Marco walked by the table, he looked directly into Kate's eyes, and smiled. "I hope we run into each other again. This has been wonderfully surprising."

Suzie hustled right over to her two favorite patrons. Kate immediately ordered another martini for herself and a sparkling water for Joan, who remarked, "My contact with Marco Rossetti has been sporadic over the last few years. I see him at surgical conferences, where he is usually the presenter. His public image is of a brilliant but aloof guy, very different from the self-revealing man we saw tonight. What did you make of his talking about his sister and Thomas Edmonds?" Joan, excited by the exchange that had just happened, was vigorously squeezing both lime and lemon into her sparkling water.

"Two things struck me. One, that he was so open about his brotherly dependence on Rosalie, and two, that he showed off his gifted intellectual abilities to the men who flitted around her. He is admitting that even as a young teen he revealed his brilliance, almost like a magician does— as a distraction, "look over here, and not at my sister." It is a sophisticated defense mechanism." Kate paused, sipped her wonderfully cold martini, then added, "I wonder if he poisoned her?"

"You think he might have poisoned his beloved sister?" Joan's voice was free of skepticism. She was used to Kate's suspicious nature and, as a scientist, she loved her for it.

"I don't know him, but in my mind, everyone in the family, and at the bakery, is a suspect. Needing someone is a potent human motive. Any of the men could have heard him spouting off about ingredients and what not to mix together and tucked away that information, perhaps to use at a later time. Joan, I'm going to change the subject. Did you have any more thoughts about the lion symbol etched on the blue topaz stone?"

"Of course. So, as I mentioned before, it is an historic symbol that is variously used to denote the qualities of courage, strength, dignity, et cetera. But in thinking about this case, it can also symbolize justice and wisdom. Many universities use the image of a big cat as part of their corporate identity. Our university uses the panther. The one on Fifth Avenue uses the cougar. The image of the lion is also used by the courts, law schools, law offices, and so forth." Joan sat back, waiting to see if Kate made the same connection she had.

You mean, it could be related to Rosalie being a law student? She had actually graduated and was studying for her law boards." Kate immediately opened her laptop and searched for university rings. "Look at this. On the side of the ring, you can put any design, like this one that has the date of graduation and the scales of justice. So, had the lion etched on the blue topaz been a special-order graduation ring for Rosalie?" Kate could have tap-danced with excitement.

Joan asked, "Was she wearing it in any of the photographs you saw?"

"I don't remember it, but I wasn't really looking. The thickness and carat of the setting would suggest a school ring, though. But if it was hers, it's not much of a clue. We already know it was her skeleton; this would just be more confirmation. Maybe it belonged to someone else."

"But why would she have someone else's class ring? The size of it indicates that it belonged to either a very small man or a woman. You could call Marco and ask him; he showed plenty of interest in you." Kate grimaced at the suggestion. She knew that Joan was right about Marco's interest in her. This man is part of the circle of suspects. How could she possibly be attracted to him? Then, there was Eddie.

Kate was sure that the setting, the blue topaz stone, blue reflecting one of the universities' colors, and the imprint of the lion were provocative clues. How should she approach Jablonsky with the information?

CHAPTER 25

JABLONSKY HAD A QUESTION, and the best people to answer it were the Nonas, Renata and Andrea. He drove into South Oakland and walked the narrow path back to the Grotto. His sturdy shoes crunched the frozen twigs and leaves underfoot—the noise announced his approach. Stefan's intuition was right; Renata and Andrea were seated on the benches, both fingering their rosary beads.

Renata looked up. "Chief Detective! This is a pleasant surprise. Come join us." She motioned to the other cement bench, padding the seat for him with her wool scarf.

"I don't want to interrupt your prayers. But I did come here with a question for both of you, if you don't mind." The implication that he needed their input into the Rossetti murders was like catnip to kitty cats.

"No problem. The Blessed Mother has heard my troubles many times before, so she's probably happy to wait until later to hear them again. What is your question?" Andrea and Renata edged closer, mittened hands clasped together, curiosity softening the creases in their faces.

"You had mentioned to me that Michael and Rosalie came here, to the Grotto, to pray or to talk or just to get away. When was the last time you saw them here?" Jablonsky knew that these women would know the stages of life's timeline, and they would have observed and remembered the details of the younger generation's place on that line.

Andrea spoke first. "I remember seeing them late in the afternoon. You remember, Renata, we came to clean the flower beds and saw them sitting close together on this very bench, talking."

"That's right! They were talking, and I think they had brought coffee. I remember Styrofoam cups with lids, and those wooden stirrers for cream and sugar. They were cheerful, laughing together. I always thought they were like the two parts of a zipper; together they made an unbreakable bond."

"Do you remember how close to their disappearance this was?" Jablonsky took note of the fact that the siblings had had coffee with them.

Renata and Andrea hesitated, casting their minds back to that time, tying to visualize the mark on their calendars that indicated when the terrible search began. Finally, "I think it was just a day before. At least that is how I remember it. What about you, Renata?"

"I believe you are right. I had it circled on my calendar." Both women tightened their coat collars and sighed.

"You said they were drinking coffee. Do you remember if they had brought something to eat? Perhaps a sandwich, or a pastry from the bakery?"

"Maybe. There was a take-out box on the ground in front of them. I don't know if it was theirs, or not. Why? Does it matter?" Simultaneously, it dawned on both of them, and they collectively voiced a drawn-out, 'Ahhh,' and whispered the word "poison." Neither seemed shocked.

"It is just a line of inquiry that I'm pursuing. At that time, who helped clean this area?" The two ladies cast their minds back. "You know, after his kids went missing, Gene Rossetti used to come here to pray. If there was any trash, he would have picked it up." Renata lowered her voice, "He had the compulsions, you know what I mean."

Jablonsky grinned. These two Nonas were the neighborhood shrinks. Having seen Mr. Rossetti's clean basement and beautifully organized diaries, he could well believe that Rossetti had "the compulsions." Unfortunately, the take-out packages would long have rotted in some landfill.

"As always, ladies, you both have been very helpful. I just have one more question. Did any of Michael's and Rosalie's best friends come here to the Grotto?"

Without hesitation, Andrea replied, "Luca Lorenzo used to come. Not that it did him any good. He was, and still is, a criminal." Renata added her affirmative nod.

Jablonsky smiled to himself as he walked along the path to his vehicle. He always felt good after seeing the Nonas. Back at the station, he stood in front of the Rossetti side of the murder board and wrote, "Marco Rossetti's chemistry class."

He turned to Antoine. "No one thought to look for evidence at the Grotto, which we now know was the last place Michael and Rosalie had been seen together before they disappeared. The two grandmothers mentioned that they saw them there, having coffee and something to eat. They said there were cups and take-out containers. It is so frustrating! That evidence might have had traces of a poison on them."

—⁓—

Kate was in Fiona's kitchen systematically boxing dishes, flatware, and pots and pans. Sunlight streamed in through the window over the sink, cascading onto the floor, creating a spring-like atmosphere in the middle of unpredictable March. Bourbon Ball was snoozing by her side, the sunlight bringing out the auburn in his chocolate coat; periodically he snored in total dog relaxation.

She took time out from packing to water the well-nurtured Christmas cactus Fiona had sitting on the counter. Even at this time of year, it was still covered with magenta-colored blossoms. The cheery kitchen sparked memories of packing her grandfather's house. She considered the clearing out of a beloved person's things after death to be a universal bereavement task—necessary but emotionally complex because it could kindle so many memories. For Kate, the person who shared those memories was Eddie Fitzroy.

Johnny had also paused his packing and came to stand in the doorway. "I miss her," he said, his eyes filling with tears. Bourbon Ball raised his large, bear-like head, looked at Johnny, and sniffed. BB moved over to Johnny and was rewarded with an ear massage, an action that relaxed both human and canine.

Kate finished taping the box she had just filled and sat back on her heels. "In the hospital, your mother told me that she always worried someone was going to hurt you. Gay bashing, not just with words, but physically. She also worried that you might lose your job because you are gay. The money in that bank account became her way of protecting you."

"Really? She said that? I never knew. She certainly never interceded when my father harassed me. Apparently, there were a lot of things I never knew about her." Johnny looked down at the floor, sighed, then moved on to another topic. "By the way, one of the neighbor's daughters wants to buy this house. It would be nice to keep it in the street family, so to speak. I think my mother would like that." Kate offered him her biggest smile, but no advice. He had to make his own decision.

She went back to her packing while Johnny began to make coffee. Like the one in his office, the coffee maker was an elaborate appliance that he had bought his mother some time ago, ignoring the fact that she mostly drank tea. Kate watched him grind beans to just the right consistency, then pack them into the metal cup. Shortly, the aroma of the rich espresso filled the air as water steamed through the coffee grounds. Bourbon Ball had moved to the kitchen door, his ears and tail up in an alert stance.

Johnny handed Kate a demitasse and they sipped in silence, each enjoying the meditative atmosphere of the kitchen. BB started a low, menacing growl that turned into barking.

Several loud pop, pop, pop noises, accompanied by shattering glass, exploded into the quiet kitchen. Johnny yelled at Kate to "get down," and then threw himself over her. Neither moved for what seemed like an eternity. Finally, Johnny rolled over, eased his cellphone out of his pocket, and called the police. Bourbon Ball was now jumping at the kitchen door, continuously barking.

Kate remembered Fiona's words. "He'll need you beside him for what is to come." Was this what she meant?

CHAPTER 26

"HOW ARE YOU TWO?" Jablonsky had arrived at the crime scene, realizing that in the short time he has known them these two friends were in mortal peril, again. "Let's move into the living room so forensics can do their job." He motioned to Antoine to stay with the forensics team.

Johnny, looking as if a vampire had feasted on all his blood, sat next to Kate. He was dabbing some peroxide onto a few tiny cuts on her hands. "These are from the flying glass," he commented to the chief. Johnny's clenched jaw let Jablonsky know that he was ready to blow. "Tell me what happened. Kate, you start."

"I was in the kitchen packing. I was kneeling on the floor in front of the kitchen sink. Johnny had finished in the dining room and came to stand in the doorway. We were talking about Fiona. Johnny made us a cup of espresso and we were drinking it when suddenly Bourbon Ball stood at the kitchen door and started to growl and bark. Then there were several popping noises and glass shattering and flying. Johnny told me to get down, and then he lay over me. When it was quiet, we got up and he called you." Kate spoke in a clipped manner. Jablonsky knew her well enough to know that she was trying to hold back her emotions for Johnny's sake.

Is that how you remember it?" Stefan turned slightly in his chair to observe John.

"It was exactly as Kate described. When we were sipping our coffee, Bourbon Ball started to growl and sniff around the kitchen door, then was barking like crazy. He either heard or smelled the shooter."

"Antoine. Have the forensics people let the dog sniff around the outside of the house."

Kate added, "BB isn't a trained sniffer, but he is a retriever. If the person's scent is there, he will remember it. Retrievers can carry hundreds of scents in memory." One of the forensics techs put BB on lead and walked him around the entire perimeter of Fiona's property.

"Detective Jablonsky, what is going on? First my mother is shot and killed, and now someone is after me. I don't understand! You have to give me something to go on, some plausible motive for all this violence." As the adrenaline of outrage coursed through his body, Johnny began to shake.

"John, I think your mother's death was motivated by two things—betrayal and a cover-up."

Kate jumped in. "You mean Andrew Edmonds's betrayal of his wife. And that Fiona had documentation of Thomas's business malfeasance. Correct?"

"That's correct. We believe that we have provided the DA with enough evidence to prosecute Thomas Edmonds under the state Ethics and Public Corruption Laws, using the invoices that your mother had along with details gathered by Rosalie Rossetti. We found her documentation in a box of papers that Marco had." Jablonsky mentioned the evidence in the business case against Thomas but did not share details with these two civilians about the investigation into Fiona's death.

Kate spoke up. "I didn't have a chance to tell you that Joan and I ran into Marco at the University Club. In our conversation, he spoke very emotionally about his love for his sister and his fears that someone would take her away. He also mentioned that he used to show off in front of the older suitors at the bakery like Thomas Edmonds and Jonathan Price."

"How did he show off?" For the second time today, Jablonsky was being given the possibility of new leads.

"He said he would add up someone's large bakery bill in his head, or that he would reveal how much he knew about science by correcting a baker's ingredients. I thought that was really interesting, particularly after the poison markings we noticed in Fiona's cookbooks."

"I agree." He didn't mention Marco's chemistry homework papers found in Rosalie's box. Jablonsky admired Kate's resiliency—she was shot at only an hour ago— now she was focused on the case, weaving together disparate facts. It briefly crossed his mind that with this latest threat Eddie Fitzroy might begin to lobby for her to leave the city, effectively stopping her sleuthing. He found himself hoping she wouldn't go. As difficult it was to keep her in the civilian lane, he enjoyed working with her and Johnny.

Johnny brought the conversation back to his mother. "I can't believe that someone like Thomas Edmonds would shoot my little old mother because he didn't want his business to be sued. It doesn't make sense to me. And further, why try to kill me? I didn't even know about the affair, the invoices, or the bank account." He began to pace around the room in frustration.

"John, we are talking about many, many infractions of building codes—lots of attorneys will be racking big fees. And with the recent roof collapse at the Delilah Street townhomes, we have a clear violation of public safety. The Edmonds Land Company could take a big hit, both financially and in reputation."

In order to further understand why someone would shoot at Johnny, or perhaps even Kate, Jablonsky needed to ask a delicate question. "It was a bold move to shoot through the window in broad daylight. Typically, only a professional hit man has that kind of nerve and skill. Judging from the position of the footprints forensics found outside the kitchen, this person could have killed you both—but didn't."

"So, this was some kind of warning? Warning about what? I don't know anything about anything. I'm an Art History professor!" Johnny cried in frustration.

Kate chimed in. "Would this have to do with the bank account? The three million?"

"John, if you die, who gets the money?" Jablonsky knew that Johnny was an only child—would his estate be divided among cousins, aunts, and uncles, or go to Julius? Or would he gift the university?

"Kate. My estate will go to Kate. Who else would I leave it to?" Johnny shrugged as if Jablonsky had asked a stupid question. The chief noticed that Kate looked stunned at Johnny's statement.

"Understood. Now, I want to talk about your father. I'm just going to ask this straight out—was he your biological dad? No relatives have ever murmured something about your paternity?" Jablonsky knew it was a tough question to hear.

"What? Wait—are you asking me if it is possible that Andrew Edmonds was my father? No. No way. The timeline isn't correct, and my dad and I look exactly alike. Don't you think, Kate?"

Jablonsky could see that Kate was deep in thought. In a distracted manner, she responded with, "I was turning over the possibility that Thomas Edmonds might think that Johnny is his half-brother. That would open a can of worms in terms of inheritance and just plain snobbery. The son of Fiona could never be on the same level as him. And, yes. You look exactly like your father, and nothing like Andrew Edmonds. You could take a DNA test just to rule it out. If Thomas Edmonds is paranoid that he and Johnny are half-brothers, would that be the motive for the intimidation?" She and Johnny both turned toward Jablonsky, needing his insight.

"I'm guessing it is likely related to money, or sheer meanness." The chief was remembering Jane Louise's statement that Thomas liked to toy with her, to hurt her emotionally. "I want you to let forensics take a DNA swab. Let's settle that issue."

"Anything to help understand this insanity. I can't have Kate in danger just because she is my friend." Johnny threw up his hands in frustration.

"One more question. I know that Julius has taken an apartment in Paris, and that things are contentious between you two. I have to ask, is there any chance he would want to scare you, or even hurt you?"

"Wow. I didn't see that coming!" Johnny started to pace the room again. DeVille was standing unobtrusively in the doorway, taking mental notes on how Jablonsky was handling these difficult questions with Johnny.

"It would be a complete departure from his personality. He's never been a violent man. It is true that we have broken up and so are arguing a lot, but to have someone fire a gun at me? No. I'm not sure he even knows anyone who owns a gun, much less knows how to use it. Our friends are mostly gay— we aren't a gun-toting group. Besides, he's in Paris. He didn't even come over for Mom's funeral."

Kate added her two cents. "In terms of the research on abuse and violence, past behavior is the best predictor of future behavior. It's extremely unlikely that Julius would hire someone to hurt Johnny—there is no history there. He might purloin some high-end couture items from Johnny's wardrobe, but that's about the extent of it." Johnny managed a weak smile at the truth of Kate's statement.

One of the forensics crew interrupted the conversation to take Johnny's DNA and secure the swab in the usual tube. Another of the crew came back with BB, who wiggled over to Kate's side and stayed. "There were footprints around the back door, and this pup took a big interest in them. We couldn't find any cigarette butts or fabric, and no shell casings." Kate reiterated that Bourbon Ball would be able to identify the actual boots from having spent so much time sniffing the boot print. "We'll see," said Jablonsky.

Yellow tape had, once again, been wrapped around the house. Jablonsky decided to assign Annie Lemon to guard Johnny since she had come to know the two friends from previous cases. Detective Lemon was summoned.

As was their habit, Kate and Johnny agreed to sweat off their nervous energy by going to Upper Frick Park and working through its extensive obstacle course. Annie Lemon followed them from a distance, discreetly armed. Kate would tell Eddie later what had happened. She dreaded the conversation, knowing that he would amp up his campaign to leave the city; her fears would turn out to be true.

—⁓—

Jablonsky and DeVille did their workout by rearranging items on the murder board.

"We weren't able to say for sure that Luca Lorenzo's flat-black Camaro never left the paint shop, correct?"

"That's correct, boss. The car was parked in their locked garage. It was tucked back in a corner that is outside the range of the security cameras, so someone could have taken it out, shot Mrs. McCarthy, and then driven it back. Unless Lorenzo cops to it, we can't tie him to driving the car." Antoine was writing the details about the new shooting under Fiona's picture.

"Someone would have had to offer Luca a lot of money to chance being arrested for murder. Or maybe someone just wanted to use of his car."

Antoine shook his head in disagreement. "I think it would be too risky to involve someone else as a driver. It makes more sense to me that it was Luca driving his car. Besides, he loves that car so much that I doubt he would let anyone else drive it."

"You are right about how much Luca loves his car. Boys and their toys. Someone could have driven it without his knowledge." Jablonsky began to tap his pen on Thomas Edmonds's picture. "The state Ethics committee has already started to build a case against Edmonds and his company. They issued a warrant for his office files and computers. I still like this guy for murder. I want access to his home—get a warrant. And, while you are at it, get a warrant for Luca Lorenzo's place as well. I want to see if his standard of living has recently improved. Let's give both places a good toss; who knows what might fall out." Jablonsky paused, shifted his weight, then opened a piece of cinnamon gum. Antoine happily accepted the offer of a stick.

"Then there is the problem of our good doctor, Marco Rossetti. Under his picture, Jablonsky wrote, "The chemistry of poisons."

CHAPTER 27

ANTOINE WAS AT THOMAS EDMONDS'S Mount Washington home with the forensics team when they found it. He immediately called Jablonsky. "Chief. You'd better get over here."

The roads to the top of Mount Washington were steep and uphill, no matter which route one took. Luckily, that neighborhood, an eagle's perch above the Ohio River, was only a short drive from the precinct. Jablonsky walked into an architecturally stunning living space—soaring thirty-foot ceilings and several walls of dramatic windows gave the first and second floors a sweeping view of the downtown city. *I guess if you own a construction company, you can design and build anything you want,* thought Jablonsky. *He lives like this and doesn't want to pay for his daughter's education? What a weasel.*

Antoine showed the Chief to the third-floor master bedroom. He went over to the fireplace, stacked stone surrounded by cherrywood paneling, and lightly pushed on one segment of the decorative wood. The panel opened to reveal a security room, filled with hand-crafted built-in drawers that housed expensive watches, a few men's rings, and a stand-alone fireproof data safe. One entire wall of the room was covered with a collage of pictures of Rosalie Rossetti. A hand knitted wool sweater, a hat, mittens, and a shawl hung on a coat tree. Several bottles of perfume sat on one of the built-in shelves, along with a brush with long dark strands of hair still caught in its bristles. Antoine held up a Ziplock plastic bag that contained lacy panties and a brassiere; "And then we found this bag." Both men smirked over the lingerie.

"Additionally, there are these." Antoine held out several envelopes. Jablonsky opened them, finding short notes written by Thomas to Rosalie in which he declared his love for her.

"I guess she wasn't just a local girl he was having some fun with, eh? This is a shrine. No one found any guns? Panties, but no guns. Keep looking, I suspect there is a gun safe somewhere, with a few handguns in it." Jablonsky took a closer look around the room and then returned to the first floor. "Where is he?"

"He's sitting in one of the black-and-whites calling his attorney." Antoine sported a sweet New Orleans, butter wouldn't melt, smile.

"Have forensics email me the photos of the safe room and bring the panties along. Let's let him stew. We can head over to Luca Lorenzo's place." The drive off the steep Mount Washington bluff to the South Side streets took less than thirty minutes.

Jablonsky and DeVille climbed the steep set of wooden steps that led to Luca Lorenzo's apartment. It was situated in the back of a tall, skinny row house, and surprisingly, the door wasn't locked. Both detectives had pulled out their guns as Antoine slowly opened the door, calling out, "Police! Luca Lorenzo, this is the police! We have a warrant to search these premises, and are coming in. Show yourself!"

There were only four rooms—eat-in kitchen, living room, one bedroom, and a bath. DeVille, Jablonsky, and three other detectives squeezed into the small apartment. Two forensics people waited at the bottom of the steps until the apartment was cleared. There couldn't have been a starker contrast between this place and that belonging to Thomas Edmonds. Jablonsky remarked, "If this isn't Main Street versus Wall Street, I don't know what is." He directed the detectives. "You take the kitchen, you take the living room, DeVille and I will take the bedroom and bath."

"This place is so orderly. Look at this closet; all the shirts are washed and ironed, even his jeans have a crease. Every sock is rolled and placed tightly against the others, and his tighty-whities are actually white. My mother would say that "This boy was raised up right." Antoine opened and closed bureau drawers and then the bathroom linen closet, muttering and shaking his head at the orderliness. "Was Luca Lorenzo ever in the service?" he asked the Chief, who answered in the negative.

Jablonsky was looking for family pictures and didn't find any at all. One of his detectives called to him, "Chief, come look at this." In the living room, a small bookcase housed mostly car magazines. But there were a few framed photographs, obviously taken before everyone's phones had cameras. Jablonsky carried all of them to the kitchen table.

"That's Michael Rossetti and Luca, standing in front of Rosalie's Bakery. How young they were."

"Luca wasn't bad looking as a young man. I guess a life of crime ages you. And, after looking in the refrigerator, I'd say the only thing he can bench press is sixteen ounces," smirked Antoine.

"Where was this taken? Do any of you recognize this place?" Jablonsky pointed to a picture of Luca and Michael together on a path in the woods next to a stream. One of his detectives picked up the photo. "I think that might be one of the trails in Schenley Park. That curved arch on the bridge in the background is a dead giveaway. Those are the running trails that start around the Schenley Oval and wind through the park. It's a beautiful place to jog."

Jablonsky stared at the photos. "These young men look relaxed and happy, even intimate. Two friends with privileges?" Jablonsky looked more closely at the photo, then harrumphed to himself. "Neither in Michael's and Rosalie's things, nor in those of Mrs. Rossetti, did I see any pictures like these. I want all the photos bagged, and anything else that they can find, hopefully guns or burner cells."

Antoine was still rifling through Luca's bureau when he discovered a sealed bag with a Styrofoam cup in it. "Hey, Chief! Come look at this."

"Well, I'll be," exclaimed Jablonsky, who could have kissed his number two in joy. "I'll bet this is one of the coffee cups that the Nonas said they saw at the Grotto. Coupe, you know what this means?"

"You bet I do. This places Luca Lorenzo at the Grotto when Michael and Rosalie went missing."

"Not only that. But since he has kept it in pristine condition, we might get DNA, and possibly which poison killed them. This is big." Excited murmurs filled the tiny apartment as the detectives finished their work and forensics began theirs.

CHAPTER 28

IT WAS SUNDAY AFTERNOON, and Kate had finished reading the Sunday New York Times. Her cellphone rang; it was Joan. "Hey Mademoiselle surgeon, what's going on?"

"Well. You won't believe this, but Marco Rossetti called my office this week and asked for your private telephone number."

"Really? Oh, no." She could hear in Joan's voice how much she was enjoying the situation. Kate had felt the electricity between Marco and herself at the university club, and she knew that Joan had felt it as well.

"I think he wants to ask you out."

"Didn't you tell him that I'm practically engaged?" Kate was more than annoyed that Joan didn't mention the existence of Eddie.

"Honestly, I didn't think about Eddie. Sorry. But you have to admit, it is pretty interesting. You could at least have a coffee with him—you might get some new leads in the case." They chatted for a while, made arrangements to meet for dinner the following week, and said their goodbyes.

Eddie had called on Friday saying that he had to stay at the dig in Ligonier, then talked again about the shooting at Mrs. McCarthy's house and Kate's safety. She didn't deny that having been shot at was scary, but she didn't take it to mean she should leave Pittsburgh or stop her sleuthing. After the call, she felt antsy. One of her go-to places to clear her mind was Phipps Conservatory.

It was a beautiful March day, so Kate decided to jog the several miles to the Conservatory. As she ran, she focused her mind on the butterscotch color of the afternoon sunlight and the crisp invigorating air. The more she felt the burn of exertion in her legs and lungs, the more she discharged the lingering worries over Johnny's safety and hers. It was relieving to know that Annie Lemon was guarding him.

Kate wandered through the various rooms of foliage, enjoying the temperate atmosphere and the highly oxygenated air. There was something so soothing to the psyche to be in the desert room or the orchid room while it was only fifty degrees outside. She sat down on a bench to enjoy all of the Chihuly glass sculptures mixed in with the greenery.

"Kate?" Marco Rossetti appeared out of nowhere, with his mother at his side. *He couldn't possibly have known that I would be here,* thought Kate. *And with the mother as well.*

"Dr. Kate Chambers, this is my mother, Lisa Marie Rossetti. Mom has been trying to get out more, so I thought this would be a good place to come. Two of her friends are also here." Marco fumbled around, trying to find something to say. He suspected that Joan might have told Kate that he had asked for her number—it was awkward.

"I come here frequently. I love it." She smiled as his mother was swept away by her two friends, who promised to take Mrs. Rossetti home. They twittered and giggled like three good fairies. Marco remained standing, fingering a schefflera leaf, mumbling something about how his mother's two friends didn't like him. Kate was silent for a few minutes, then decided to throw him a life preserver.

She patted the space next to her on the bench, and started to prattle about Dale Chihuly, the renowned glass artist. Marco visibly relaxed. "I love the giant sunburst that hangs in the entry. I actually own several small pieces of his glass."

The bench was small, so his long leg and broad shoulder touched hers. She felt herself flush, and then flushed more because she was so surprised at her reaction to him. She also noticed that he smelled really good. *What was it? Not aftershave, more like a spicy soap fragrance,* she thought. From Joan, she knew that most surgeons were very clean people. Joan had an entire shelf in her bathroom dedicated to soaps. *I wonder if he has a similar stash,* Kate mused.

After the conversation about Chihuly ran its course, they sat in comfortable silence, people watching. Finally, Marco suggested that they get something to eat at the in-house cafeteria, home of good sandwiches and soups made from organic local produce, breads, and meats. Remembering Joan's remark about leads, Kate couldn't resist the possibility of finding out something new about the Rossetti case, so she agreed.

They ordered, then seated themselves at one of the back tables away from the steady flow of children, parents, and grandparents all out for a Sunday trip. They both had decided on a bowl of mushroom barley soup, an easy selection to talk around—no loose sandwich fixings falling out of the mouth. Their conversation meandered through her work, his work, and the university. Other than Eddie, it had been a long time since Kate had been out with a man that she found interesting; it was strangely exciting, and mighty guilt provoking. She decided to work at clue gathering.

"I was surprised to hear you talk so candidly about loving your sister. I'm an only child—the closest I have to a sibling is my friend Johnny McCarthy, whom you kind of know. It seems everyone adored Rosalie." Kate hoped that he would find her mentioning the subject of his siblings' murders as just as a reference to their conversation at the University Club, and not being macabre.

"It was true that almost everyone loved Rosalie. It's hard to quantify what it was about her—she just had an attractive charm that drew people to her. It didn't hurt that she was gorgeous." Marco laughed at his brotherly, and male, assessment of her charms. "You know, since their funeral, I feel less withdrawn. I'm able to laugh at things again, and get outside of the hospital, like today."

He kept surprising Kate with his emotional openness, and she surprised herself by reciprocating. "There are so many places in the city that are special to me, places where I go to recharge. This conservatory is one place. I like running around the Highland Park Reservoir, I frequently kayak on the Allegheny River, and sometimes I sit in the Heinz Chapel just to absorb the beauty of those stained-glass windows. And perhaps bizarrely, I love to roam around the Homewood Cemetery, which may seem ghoulish to you, considering what you've been through." Kate rarely made a social gaffe, so she felt extremely sensitive that she might have made one now.

"Don't be ridiculous. I'm not that touchy, Kate. Homewood Cemetery is very soothing to walk around—all the interesting and different mausoleums belonging to the industrial rich of our city. I sometimes go there myself." Kate liked the way he said, "Our city."

"Of course, we buried Michael and Rosalie in a Catholic Cemetery. My mom insisted. I didn't care." Kate put the focus back on Marco and the bakery; she didn't trust herself—what would be next, telling this surgeon her Zodiac sign? *Get back to work,* she scolded herself.

"What happened to the people at the bakery after Rosalie and Michael went missing? Did her friends stop going there?" Kate believed that new insights in the case might be gleaned by looking at how the relationships reconfigured during the search for his siblings.

"Now that's a question I hadn't thought about. You definitely spark my imagination, and my memory—you must be a good advisor. Let me see, the crew from Edmonds still came in before the start of their shifts. Rosalie's friends from law school were the ones whom I rarely saw at the bakery during the police search. That fellow, Jonathan Price, stopped coming in altogether. I think I mentioned that he was one of the people I used to show off in front of. Him, and Thomas Edmonds, a man I hated with all my adolescent rage." Marco grinned the kind of grin that gave witness to unexpected self-deprecation.

"You said that the showing off was sometimes about what ingredients to mix, or not to combine. I'm not much of a baker, so it caught me by surprise that there would be things that are dangerous to use. You were a young man to know such things." All of a sudden Marco looked stressed. He started to rearrange the salt and pepper shakers and the container of sugars. With his eyes still lowered, he said, "I've never told anyone this before."

He paused, and then began his confession. "One day, I was helping stack boxes of fresh fruit and I said that I could poison someone with the pits from the fruit." Kate shot him an expression of disbelief.

"Let me explain. In stone fruit, like peaches or plums, for example, there is a chemical called amygdalin. If you grind up the stones and feed the substance to someone, it converts into hydrogen cyanide. A lethal dose would depend on a person's body weight, but with enough, you could kill someone. In other countries, it is sometimes seen as a natural cure for certain kinds of cancer—completely untrue, of course. Surprisingly, you can buy amygdalin in pill form."

"I see. Did you believe that someone heard you and then used the information to poison Michael and Rosalie?" Kate was stunned that this man had carried around that horrible fear and guilt all these years. But was he right to be concerned?

"I believe that it is a possibility. It could have been Jonathan Price, or that neighborhood kid, Luca Lorenzo. Sleazy Thomas Edmonds was standing in the doorway to the stockroom, waiting for Rosalie and her girlfriend to show up after class. He probably heard me. There is no way to prove my suspicions unless someone confesses. Dr. Patel mentioned to me that any form of cyanide would have been degraded beyond recognition by the time they found the bodies." Marco drew in a deep breath, then slowly let it out. "What do you think, Kate?" he asked, his worried eyes searching her face.

"I'm very sorry you have carried this pain and carried it alone. What do I think of your suspicions? I'd have to say they could be right. I'm just not sure what the motives would have been for killing two innocent young people." Kate and Marco fell into another companionable silence, each considering possible motives.

"Marco, do you know if your parents had bought Rosalie a ring when she graduated from law school? A university ring to mark the occasion? Something that would have a blue gemstone in it, maybe with a special engraving on the stone."

"No. Not that I can remember. It would have been unusual for my parents to do something like that. My mom and dad would have given her a string of pearls, or one of my grandmother's rings. I never saw her wear a college ring. What makes you ask?"

"Well, my friend, Eddie Fitzroy, the archeologist, found a ring with a blue topaz gemstone in it at the excavation site. I just wondered if it belonged to Rosalie. The forensics lab has it now." At the mention of Fitzroy's name, Kate suddenly felt awkward. She tried to recover by asking more questions.

"Speaking of law school, were some of Rosalie's friends there women?" Kate was nothing if not persistent in her pursuit of Marco's firsthand knowledge of all the possible suspects.

"She had close girlfriends from undergraduate school, but they didn't pursue advanced education. Nice girls, but girls with no interest in anything besides having children. Rosalie was ambitious—she wanted a career in law, maybe a judgeship. There was one girl from her study group... um, I can't remember her name. Surprisingly, she married Thomas Edmonds while the search was ongoing."

"No kidding! My first reaction is that it is somehow weird that she married Thomas Edmonds; I mean, that a close girlfriend would marry someone Rosalie was dating, well, kind of dating." Kate wondered if Marco would begin to get suspicious over the extent of her knowledge about the case, so she kept to generalizations about relationships.

"Well, the ladies at the bakery all felt that the girl had, how did they put it, gotten herself in trouble. For some unknown reason, they didn't want to use the word pregnant." Marco paused, then added, "You know, it's such a relief to talk like this. As you can imagine, I don't have that many close friends, and at work, I'm the boss of my surgical teams. I don't fraternize there." Marco's dark eyes were warm with genuine friendliness, even libidinous invitation.

"I don't know what I'd do without Johnny and Joan to confide in," was all Kate could muster in reply. As fate would have it, Marco received a text concerning a patient, so he had to leave for the hospital. "This was so pleasurable. I'd really enjoy seeing some of your other favorite places." Marco stood, looked again at his phone, put on his jacket, and left. His tone had become pro forma, communicating that he had switched into his formal surgeon self; it provided her an easy way out of having to say no to future plans, which she was not sure she wanted to do.

Kate didn't immediately leave to jog back to her house. Instead, she ordered another coffee and sat making notes of everything Marco had told her. On a personal level, she wondered if this brilliant man was performing his magic act on her like he had done years ago with Rosalie's suitors. "Look over here, see how soulful and interesting I am." Was he diverting her attention away from really considering him as a viable person of interest in his sibling's death? Could she be attracted to someone who was a suspect?

Kate immediately dialed Jablonsky's number.

"Detective Jablonsky? This is Kate. I have some interesting information for you. I was wondering if Johnny and I could stop at the precinct tomorrow. Today? It is Sunday, remember? Well, okay. If it's really all right with you. See you there in an hour or so."

CHAPTER 29

JOHNNY, KATE, AND JABLONSKY SAT TOGETHER in his spacious office. Although it was the weekend, the precinct was buzzing with detectives scrolling through computer screens and making telephone calls. Before Kate could share her information, Annie Lemon came to the door, motioning to Jablonsky that she had something for him. They stepped out of his office into the bullpen.

Annie Lemon honored the boundary between private citizen and detective, so she lowered her voice to give Jablonsky her report. "Chief, there has been someone lurking around Johnny's Slope house, but not spotted at his mother's house. I've seen that same person at the Fine Arts building, where Johnny has his office. White male, fiftyish, medium build—he sports a baseball cap with no insignias. We've tried to follow him, but he blends in, particularly with all the student traffic. Right now, we are looking at the security video from the Arts building. I'll get back to you."

Johnny had brought his own thermos of coffee; it was enough for the three of them. Jablonsky gratefully accepted a cup of the robust roast but found Johnny and Antoine's fetish about coffee to be amusing.

"Go ahead, Kate, what do you have?"

"I was at Phipps today and ran into Marco Rossetti and his mother. We ended up in the conservatory, talking."

"Was Mrs. Rossetti with you as well?" Johnny sounded hopeful. Being irrationally afraid for her safety, Johnny had already urged Kate to be cautious around Marco. He didn't believe him to be dangerous, but he didn't really know him.

"No. She was there with Marco and some friends, who ultimately took her home."

"Were these friends named Renata and Andrea?" Jablonsky smiled broadly, thinking about the three Nonas roaming around the conservatory with the unmarried doctor, unconsciously looking for marital candidates. Running into an attractive, educated, and eligible woman like Kate would make their day. In their world, hope springs eternal for getting Marco married.

"Why, yes. How did you know? Anyway, as we ate our lunch, I asked Marco about Rosalie and her friends, particularly what happened to them after his siblings went missing. He again referenced how he would show off his high IQ in front of her male suitors. I asked him about the specifics, and he said two interesting things. First, he said he would talk about uncommon poison ingredients that could be used in baking, and mentioned amygdalin, which comes from stone fruits. If you grind the stones, the amygdalin can convert into hydrogen cyanide when ingested. Second, after all these years, he has believed that someone overhead him talking about the chemical and used the information to poison Michael and Rosalie. He never told anyone about his guilt or suspicions."

Jablonsky quickly asked. "Does he remember who was there when he talked about the amygdalin?" In a breach of chewing gum etiquette, the chief unwrapped a piece of cinnamon gun, put it in his mouth, and didn't even bother to offer a stick to Kate or Johnny. He was preoccupied.

"Yes! He remembers Jonathan Price, Thomas Edmonds, and Luca Lorenzo. The bakery ladies would know about the precaution with stone fruit—it would be the reason there was a poison symbol beside certain ingredients listed in Fiona's cookbooks." Kate nodded at Johnny, who looked like he was trying to remember if he knew the chemistry facts about amygdalin.

"What else?" prompted Jablonsky.

"Rosalie had a girlfriend from law school who would sometimes go to the bakery. Shortly after the siblings went missing, she married Thomas Edmonds."

"Her name was Jane Louise Smith. Yes, we know about her. She was wife number one, the first out of four, and the only missus to have a child." Kate was always impressed with Jablonsky's detecting. He continued. "What else did Marco say about this woman?"

"He said that the bakery ladies thought they married because she was pregnant. Marco didn't personally know if she was or wasn't."

"This is excellent information, Kate. Some of it adds to an existing line of inquiry, some of it is new. We will follow up with Marco." Jablonsky spoke in his "You can leave now, because we are busy doing police work" voice.

Kate wasn't going to be dismissed that easily. She set her laptop on Jablonsky's desk, saying, "Then there is the setting itself and the blue topaz stone." She reiterated her and Joan's research into the symbolism of the lion etched on the blue topaz gemstone and showed him some online images of university rings from Rosalie's law school that would match the one Fitzroy had found.

"Marco doesn't think his parents would have bought something like this for his sister. In fact, he doesn't remember Rosalie wearing any ring like this. If it were someone else's ring, it probably would be a fellow student from her law school; given the size of the setting, it most likely belonged to a woman, or a man with small fingers. Why would she have someone else's graduation ring?" Kate presented her question in her best low-key tone but was confident she had provided new information to the case. *Put that in your detective's pipe and smoke it,* she gloated to her everyday citizen self.

"Coupe! Get in here and look at these images. Follow up with this. Is there a friend and fellow student of Rosalie Rossetti's who might have bought this ring?" Jablonsky shot DeVille a withering look and dressed him down in front of Kate and Johnny. "Why didn't you look into the symbolism of the setting and the gemstone? You are the smart, rising star here." Everyone felt the sting of the chief's sarcasm.

"Okay. John, turning to you. Detective Lemon reports that there has been a man spotted at your home and around the Arts building. I want you to be extremely aware of your surroundings. Make sure detective Lemon is always with you when you go out. You remind him, Kate."

Johnny nervously tapped one of his shoes against the desk. "I just can't understand what the motive would be for threatening me."

"We did get the results of your DNA. There is no match between you and Thomas Edmonds. We think that he thinks you are a half-brother. He is a cold man, so I don't put anything past him. He may just be toying with you, or he might have serious harm in mind." The two friends spoke at once. "Will you inform him about the results?"

"Of course," assured Jablonsky. Kate and Johnny left, and Annie Lemon followed them.

Jablonsky moved into the bullpen to note the new information on the murder board. "How did you miss the information on the setting and gemstone, Coupe? I'm disappointed in you. Don't let anything slip again." DeVille lowered his head, then wrote the questions concerning the school ring on the board.

"I've been in touch again with the former Mrs. Edmonds, Jane Louise Smith. She agreed to answer more questions in another Zoom meeting. Okay with you?" Antoine kept the anger at being reprimanded in front of civilians out of his voice.

"That's fine. When?"

"We are ready to go now, if you are." With some fits and starts in connectivity, Jane Louise Smith appeared on the screen. Jablonsky observed her more closely in this interview. Having seen photos of her in her mid-twenties, he thought the south Florida sun hadn't done her any favors in aging gracefully. Jane Louise was a small woman, still slender, once again dressed in bright tropical colors; no more dark attorney suits for her. Today, she had a drink sitting beside her housed in a margarita cup with flamingos on it. Jablonsky began the interview.

"Thank you very much for agreeing to talk with us again. I want to ask about your law school years and the friends you knew then. You and Rosalie Rossetti were in the same year?"

"Yes. We were in the same study group, which in law school parlance means you spend a good deal of time with each other. We were friends." Jablonsky detected reserve in her affect, and her word choice.

"You met Thomas Edmonds through Rosalie, is that correct?"

"Yes." Most women do not parse their words concerning how they met a husband, particularly one that they went on to divorce. *I wonder why she is so reserved, especially since she continues to have trouble with Thomas over tuition payments?* thought Jablonsky.

"It is my understanding that Rosalie and Thomas Edmonds had been dating before she disappeared. Is that true?" The chief watched Jane Louise's lips tighten.

"Yes." She continued her monosyllabic responses but took a deep drink from her margarita glass.

"I'm asking about this because we found a safe room in your ex-husband's home. A room in which he had built a kind of shrine to Rosalie—pictures, letters, some garments. Did you discover that shrine when you were with him? I'm sorry if I am bringing up bad memories." Jablonsky oozed empathy.

Jane Louise Smith Edmonds sighed and began to twist the ends of her bleached blonde hair. "I appreciate that, detective. Shortly after we were married, I found what you just described. I was devastated, and furious. We were about to have a baby, and there he was, mooning over Rosalie." If she could have spat the name, this ex-wife would have.

"It is quite a betrayal for him to have married you in bad faith—that is, while he was still in love with Rosalie. You must have hated him, and her." Jablonsky's voice held a bit more intensity in it; he was hoping to incite her to spill additional information.

"I hated him for what he did to my dreams of a happy life with him and the baby. I resented Rosalie, that's for sure, but... we all thought she was dead." Something in the way she said the word "dead" caught Jablonsky's ear.

"Do you believe that your ex-husband, Thomas Edmonds, was capable of murdering Rosalie? Or of hiring someone to kill her? He had asked her to marry him several times, and she consistently turned him down. If he was that obsessed with her, he might have felt, if I can't have her, no one will." The chief didn't hesitate to plainly lay out the motive.

"Rosalie Rossetti ruined his life, and she ruined my marriage. She may have disappeared for everyone else, but

I still had to live with her every... single... day." Jane Louise paused, appearing to wipe tears—were they tears over thwarted love, or of suppressed rage? Jablonsky wasn't sure which. "I can't answer the question as to whether he was capable of murder. Thomas Edmonds is a man who is used to getting what he wants, like his father before him. I've come to despise him."

"You've come to despise him. Understandable. Did you also come to despise Rosalie?"

"I guess I did. But, if you are asking me if I murdered her, I did not." Jane Louise didn't offer protestations over the question; she had been an attorney and she knew the process. She added, "There were lots of men in law school who wanted to date her, but she was standoffish. A fellow study group member named Jonathan, something, um, Money, no, Price, was also after her. Then there was the cast of characters at her mother's bakery—most of whom I didn't know. I'm afraid I can't help you, detective."

"Did you go to the bakery often?"

"Not really. Sometimes I'd walk over from the law school with Rosalie. I mean, a shop full of pastries—no woman really likes going to a place where she can't have anything they serve, if you take my meaning." Jablonsky chuckled along with her, just to keep the interview congenial.

"Did you have a close relationship with Andrew Edmonds, Thomas's father?"

"He was kind to me when I had the baby. He eased my way financially when Thomas and I divorced. I liked him, but I wouldn't say we were close. I can tell you that Thomas always wanted his father to see him in a good light, but I'm not sure he ever did. That was just my impression. I wasn't around Mr. Edmonds much after the divorce." Jane Louise's face softened when she spoke of her ex-father-in-law.

"When did you leave Pittsburgh?"

"I left when my daughter was two. Actually, I moved to New York State so that Thomas's mother could see her granddaughter. I joined a law practice, and only recently retired to Key West. I live a quiet life, detective."

"Are you still in touch with Mrs. Edmonds?"

"Yes, around the holidays and such. My daughter calls her and sees her regularly. Eugenia is physically frail, but mentally sharp. Thomas got all his drive, and ruthlessness, from her." For the first time in the interview, Jane Louise gave out with a spontaneous laugh. "I like her, and she is good to my daughter. That goes a long way with any mother." Jablonsky could hear where the family alliances were.

"Did you and Eugenia Edmonds talk about Fiona McCarthy?" The picture frame of the computer screen amplified Jane Louise's shocked expression. "Oh. That woman. Everyone knew about her, including Thomas. Eugenia dealt with it like a soldier—women of that generation tolerated men's infidelities in a way my generation doesn't. I will say that she and Thomas hated Fiona McCarthy. Hated, with a capital H."

"Did you, Thomas, or Mrs. Edmonds, believe that Johnny McCarthy was Andrew's son?" Jane Louise reached for her glass and took another long drink.

"There was talk. I remember one Christmas Eve when Thomas was drunk, he asked his father directly. Mr. Edmonds denied it. I mean vehemently denied it—he slammed his hands on the dinner table, and then left the house. I can't remember where I saw a picture of John McCarthy, but I will say that they didn't look at all alike. You would have to ask Eugenia what she believes. Other than my daughter, and Thomas's sister, there were no provisions made for any other child in Mr. Edmonds's will—he left my daughter Eleanor a trust fund. Of course, he could have given money to Fiona in many other ways." Jablonsky could hear the legal training working in her thinking.

"One more question, Jane Louise. Did many law school graduates buy university rings?"

"You mean, graduation rings? It wasn't particularly hip to do that, but I'm sure some did. Why are you asking, Chief Detective?" Jablonsky noted that Jane Louise's face lost its humor.

"Did Rosalie Rossetti own one?"

"I don't remember her having one."

"Did you have one?"

"No. I never bought one. They weren't really my style." Her answer was casual, but not convincing. Jablonsky moved on.

"Thank you so much for your candor and observations. If we need to clarify anything, we will call for a follow-up interview." The Zoom meeting was finished.

"Coupe. What were your impressions?" Jablonsky swiveled his chair around to look at his number one, who was handsomely dressed on this Sunday in a blue and red geometric-patterned sweater, nice jeans, and beautiful leather boots.

"As my grandmother would say, "Honey, that girl is woofin'." Jane Louise was in competition with Rosalie, even after she was missing. Could she have hired someone to kill her? Poison is a woman's weapon, and after Rosalie was out of the way, she did get the rich guy, a wedding ring, and a baby. I'd call that a trifecta of motives."

"I agree that she came across as still holding on to jealousy and resentment of Rosalie. And I detected insecurity over whether Thomas ever even cared for her. Add to it that he is such a jerk over giving his only child tuition support, it makes sense that she hates him. I still like Thomas, though, for the Rossetti murders, and for hiring someone to kill Fiona McCarthy. Has he also hired someone to stalk and terrorize her son? We really have to keep Lemon on John. Digging up the bodies of Rosalie and Michael certainly seems to have made Thomas nervous—if he's killed before, he will do it again, and who better than Johnny McCarthy."

CHAPTER 30

KATE AND JOHNNY HAD FINISHED their early morning run around the blue-green waters of the Highland Park reservoir. It was spring break at the university, so neither had to be in their office. The morning held the promise of warmer weather; on their way back to Kate's condo, both exclaimed over rows of brilliant yellow daffodils in neighborhood yards. Their sunny beauty felt like a reprieve from all the death and loss. They decided to breakfast on her small side terrace, a decision that provided Bourbon Ball the chance to chase his squeaky ball with exuberance. Johnny's playlist that morning was all Sam Smith with his throbbing voice and break up lyrics. "Too Good at Goodbyes" played as they set the bistro table. "I guess he is thinking of Julius," thought Kate.

Johnny poured himself a second cup of coffee. "You know who called me? It was Jean-Luc Bernard. I guess he knew about Julius's plans long before I did and just wanted to say sorry and to check on me. He's been to Julius's apartment in Paris, so he described it to me. And you know, it really helped to visualize him in his new place—I could see that he left for a different kind of life. I don't begrudge him that."

"I hope we don't lose contact with our intrepid French Consul; he is such a dear man and helpful on previous cases. Kate lazily buttered some toast, giving half of it to BB, breaking her "don't feed the dog at the table" rule.

"Detective Lemon, what's going on?" Annie Lemon, who had been walking the perimeter of Kate's property, appeared at the terrace gate with a serious look on her face.

"Johnny, your office was broken into. Antoine DeVille is with the university police now. I'd like you to come over to campus and take a look around. I'm so sorry. At least no one was hurt." Lemon sounded frustrated.

Johnny broke into tears. "This is just too much! My mom's death, Julius leaving, someone shooting at you and me, and now a person has broken into my sanctuary. I can't take much more of this." Kate put her arms around her friend, waiting until his sobs subsided; she totally agreed—it was all too much. *Who is behind this latest attack against Johnny?* she wondered.

"I'll drive." They motored the short distance into Oakland, where she parked in Johnny's university space and they quick-stepped it to the Arts building.

"Oh, my God!" Kate saw nothing but malicious carnage in his office. Thousands of dollars' worth of fine art books were strewn everywhere, some cut up or with pages ripped apart. The perpetrator had taken shears to his beautiful oriental rug, and then made gouges in the wood desk. Luckily, Johnny never left his laptop at the office, so all his files were safe and backed-up.

The chief showed his badge to university security officers. Right behind him came Bill Reeves's forensic team—everyone cleared the room so they could work. "There are chairs in the hall that we can use," said Johnny.

"I'm sorry, John. This is brutal. Someone clearly wants to unnerve you. It is, however, an atypical style of intimidation. The person starts with shooting a gun at you, and instead of accelerating into more physical violence, he steps back, and does this—not that this isn't bad enough." Jablonsky shook his head in empathy.

Not to be left out of the conversation, Kate chimed in. "I agree. It seems someone is messing with you—just to make your life miserable." She then preempted the chief's next question. "Johnny, can you think of anyone who might want to disrupt your life like this—a disgruntled student, a gay-hating fellow professor, a wacky family member?" Jablonsky nodded at her as he opened his small paper notebook.

"Right now, I'm only teaching graduate courses and directing a few dissertations. I have a great group of students this year—all their projects are going well, there isn't a mean-spirited person among them. Chief, I think you and Kate are right—this harassment started when Mom died and I inherited the money. It's got to be tied to Edmonds."

"Who has access to this office?"

"No one. Since the September 11th terrorist attacks, new university safety rules prohibit students from freely moving in and out of a professor's office, as well as having unfettered access to this historic building. I choose to do my own housekeeping. Whoever did this must have posed as either a building maintenance person or maybe as a parent looking for me." The forensics team announced that they had found many good fingerprints and would run them through the system for a match.

Jablonsky lingered, speaking to one of the technicians while Kate was insisting that Johnny stay at her place. "Detective Lemon can keep better track of you if your movements are limited to traveling back and forth from my condo to the university." Lemon whole-heartedly agreed.

Several hours later, Bill Reeves called Jablonsky at the precinct. "We got a hit on the fingerprints from Johnny's office. Local crook, has a history of being a bag man, stealing cars, breaking and entering, stuff like that. He goes by the name of BoBo Ramone."

"Thanks, Bill! Great work, as always." Jablonsky stood in the doorway to the bullpen and yelled, "Coupe, with me."

"Does the name BoBo Ramone ring any bells for you? I know I've seen it somewhere in our investigation." Jablonsky twirled his coffee cup, and when that didn't help spark a connection, he brought out some cinnamon gum and began to chew.

"I remember, it was in one of Mr. Rossetti's diaries. I think I know where he mentioned Mr. Ramone. While I reread the entry, you go find this guy and bring him in. He might be Johnny's stalker."

———∿∿∿———

DeVille was still in the bullpen at the precinct when he got the tip that a neighborhood cop saw BoBo Ramone at his favorite watering hole. Coupe and another detective zoomed out of the city and over the Hot Metal Bridge into the South Side. He and his partner pulled up to the bar and parked the car out of sight of any patron looking out the window. They casually entered the establishment and sure enough, there sat BoBo downing boilermakers. The bartender knew a cop when he saw one and alerted Ramone to their presence by a nod of the head. BoBo ran out the back door and a classic car chase ensued.

BoBo drove an old beat-up 1970 Dodge Charger R/T. The car didn't look pretty, but it had a 440 Magnum V8 under the hood—this car could fly. With one hand loosely draped over the large steering wheel and sitting low in the long front seat, Ramone sped down the center of the narrow cobblestone side streets, ran two red lights, almost hit a pedestrian in the crosswalk, and then gunned it over the bridge toward the six-lane parkway.

BoBo was buzzed, but he didn't need clear thinking to handle his car—no police vehicle could catch him at high speed. DeVille had called for backup, so when the Charger blew up the ramp leading to the parkway, two black-and-whites had blocked the entrance. Even in his altered state, BoBo was able to coax a perfect one-eighty out of his car, only to find that he was facing the detectives who gave chase.

"Get out of the car, BoBo. Jablonsky wants you downtown." Antoine holstered his gun. While the police handcuffed Ramone, he spewed such a colorful set of expletives that DeVille and his partner laughed out loud, later regaling their fellow officers with some of them.

———

Jablonsky and Antoine watched Ramone on the closed-circuit television screen. The chief had read the reference to him in Rossetti's diaries; Mr. Rossetti had listed him as one of the men who drove the mob-owned delivery trucks. Jablonsky wasn't sure why he thought it important enough to mention Ramone by name. In the margin of that entry, Rossetti had written, "All might be guilty." Jablonsky had no idea what he meant by that phrase.

The chief also read through the sleeve on BoBo, and now was getting some sense of the man. He was fifty-eight, sported a buzz cut, and had a beer belly that hung over the waistband of his worn blue jeans. Unlike younger criminals, BoBo had no tattoos, but did have a row of silver hooped earrings that curled up both of his earlobes, and several chains with the Italian horn, the evil eye, and the hand of Fatima charms hanging on them. When they brought him into the precinct, he spent a long time relieving himself in the bathroom, then requested several bottles of water to "help him focus." *Good,* thought Stefan, *the bottle is a DNA opportunity,* and he tucked an evidence bag into his pocket.

Jablonsky entered the interview room, placing BoBo's record on the table, then carefully opened it, pretending he had never seen it before. He sat, and slowly read, knowing this would jangle BoBo's nerves.

"Ah... hey, chief. Why am I here?" Ramone took a deep drink of the water, wiping his mouth with the back of his hand. He was a naturally disgusting man.

"Mr. Ramone, I think you know why you are here. One name, Professor Johnny McCarthy. You've been busy running around town terrorizing him. It will go easier on you if you just give me the name of the man who hired you. That's really who we want. What do you say?" Jablonsky continued to run his right pointer finger down the text in BoBo's record, remarking "Ah-ha," under his breath; it was a little theatre to push BoBo along.

"I can't say that I know any professors. I'm just a working stiff, I don't travel with any hoity-toity types. What am I supposed to have done to this so-called professor?" BoBo tried to focus his blurry eyes on the paper Jablonsky was reading.

"Well, first you fired some shots at him while he and a friend were clearing out his dead mother's house. That was in Greenfield. Then, you went to his office at the university and destroyed valuable books, cut an expensive rug, and gouged his desk with some kind of shears. We have your fingerprints from the office, and we have the bullets you fired into the house. They match the Saturday Night Special you have been known to carry, without any registration, I might add. Oh, by the way, we will need those boots you are wearing. One of our sniffer dogs will have a go at them. We have you, BoBo.

Give us the name of the man who hired you and it will go easier on you at sentencing."

BoBo Ramone wasn't a strong man, nor a loyal one. He was strictly a fee-for-service toady, making just enough to subsist and keep his muscle car running. Jablonsky watched him grunt as he leaned over to untie his boots, clearly using the time to reason out how he could get away with no jail time, which, according to his sheet, was his modus operandi. He'd finger anyone for no jail time. An officer came in and retrieved the boots; an unpleasant dirty sock odor filled the room. *"Could this man be any more* gross?" thought Jablonsky, wishing there was a window he could open.

BoBo pursed his lips, took another drink of water, and then leaned toward the chief, speaking earnestly, the way inebriated people do. "I ain't no killer. I never killed the professor's mother or hurt her son. You have my word. If I give you a name, what's in it for me?"

"I didn't mention Mrs. McCarthy's murder. But since you mentioned it, did you kill her?" Jablonsky cocked his head to one side.

"Come on, chief. It was all over the news. Like I told you, I ain't no murderer. So, what about this deal you are offering?" BoBo burped loudly.

"You will be charged for all your criminal activities, but your cooperation will be taken into consideration. Who hired you to terrorize the professor?" Jablonsky was getting irritated with this old punk's indecision.

"I want no jail time, just probation."

"Mr. Ramone, you shot at two people—that's way beyond a B & E and destroying property."

"Come on, Chief. I didn't kill the professor, now did I? It was just a little scare. You can get me no jail time." Jablonsky closed the folder and started to stand up. "Take your chances with the judge, BoBo."

"All right, all right. Just give me a minute." Ramone stretched his arms over his head, issued another burp, then blew his nose on a snot-encrusted handkerchief. He finally answered. "I was approached by Luca Lorenzo, a kind of colleague of mine, who said that someone wanted the professor hassled but not hurt. Just make him nervous. Luca said that the money came from a guy named Thomas Edmonds, some big muck who owns a construction company. He was the guy who ordered the job."

"Did Luca say why Edmonds wanted the professor to be harassed?"

"I asked the same question. Luca gave this answer, 'Just because.' Yeah. That was the answer, 'Just because.' How do you like that?" BoBo began to laugh so hard that he started to compulsively cough. Jablonsky watched him, disgusted.

"Did you know a Mr. Rossetti who used to own a beer distributorship over in the North Side?" Clearly the question took BoBo by surprise.

"Well, yeah. I sometimes drove for the trucking company that hauled the beer. I'd drive the goods in, give the invoice to Rossetti, and leave. He paid the company directly. I did that work years ago. I thought he died. What's the story?"

"Did you know Michael and Rosalie Rossetti?"

"You mean his kids? The ones that went missing, and whose bodies were just found? Like everyone else in the city, I knew about them, but I never saw them at the shop. I only knew what I read in the paper." Jablonsky was inclined to believe BoBo Ramone on that score.

"After you sign your formal statement, this officer will take you to booking. You know the routine, Mr. Ramone, you've done it often enough. You'll get a legal aid attorney."

"Wait a minute! What about my boots?"

"You'll get them back." The chief didn't wait for BoBo's statement. He left the room, feeling like he needed a shower. Antoine met him in the hallway, shaking his head, repeating, "Just because?"

"Is the dog here? Good. Let's get some film of the dog around the boots."

Kate and Johnny were waiting in another interview room with a placid, almost snoozing, Bourbon Ball. Antoine, who was filming the dog's reaction to the boots, Stefan, and the detective with the bag of boots were all in the room. The minute the bag was opened, BB went over to it and sniffed his way around it. Then the boots came out, and BB started to bark and wiggle his butt. "I'd call that a hit. Did you get that video, Coupe?"

Jablonsky dismissed Kate and Johnny with thanks, but no offer to fill them in on BoBo Ramone's interview. He knew that an untrained sniffer dog was a stretch in court, but it added to the case against Ramone. And it was dramatic.

Antoine commented, "It was lucky that one of Johnny's neighbors found those shell casings. They weren't in Fiona's yard when forensics looked. And we were able to dig out the bullets from the kitchen wall."

"Okay. Get Thomas Edmonds back in here, Mirandize him, and then charge him with paying Ramone to terrorize Johnny. Then we need to talk with Lorenzo again."

Jablonsky walked back to his office thinking, *We've got Edmonds on terrorizing Johnny, but we still don't know who shot Mrs. McCarthy or murdered Michael and Rosalie.* He went back to the murder board and began to rearrange certain of the pictures. Antoine appeared and stood beside him as Jablonsky pinned a picture of Jane Louise Edmonds under Thomas's photo. He drew a line from her photo to that of

Jonathan Price, and wrote, "Both in law school with Rosalie." He then drew lines from Luca Lorenzo to Michael Rossetti and Thomas Edmonds. He wrote, "Lorenzo procured for Edmonds—people for hire."

Jablonsky paused, opened a piece of cinnamon gum, and then drew a line from Thomas Edmonds's picture on the Rossetti side of the board all the way across to Fiona McCarthy. He wrote, "No DNA match with Johnny McCarthy. Did Lorenzo procure Mrs. McCarthy's killer for Thomas Edmonds?"

Antoine picked up a marker, and beside Thomas Edmonds's picture wrote, "Because he could."

CHAPTER 31

KATE LIKED PUTTERING AROUND her condo doing household chores. She always made sure her home was clean and welcoming for her friends, but today was extra special. Eddie was traveling back from Ligonier in an unexpected midweek visit. Although they had been having heated conversations about the dangers of her sleuthing and his leaving again for yet another dig, a deep love underpinned their push and pull. It was because of that love, and their many years of shared history, that Kate was having trouble telling Eddie that she wanted to end their relationship. Maybe if she could create the right atmosphere, she would be able to tolerate the pain in his eyes that she knew would follow her words.

She placed a few vases of white spider mums in the dining room and then filled the house with the smell of good cooking. She was making one of Eddie's favorite meals, Moroccan chicken Tagine with couscous.

Kate had already seasoned and braised the chicken in her favorite Dutch oven and cooked the onions. She added the lemon zest, garlic, cloves, and a bit of fast-dissolving flour, then chicken broth and honey. The carrots, green olives, and preserved lemons were added last. The more the dish sat, the better the marriage of the flavors. She would make the couscous once Eddie arrived.

The temperature had been in the high forties, so all the snow had melted, leaving the city streets wet. In the Laurel Highlands, however, winter had returned, with the temperature dropping below freezing. Kate always worried about the s-curves on the turnpike coupled with the level of eighteen-wheeler traffic. Today was no different. She decided to cope with her anxiety by giving Bourbon Ball a long walk.

Johnny texted her that he had sent a special romantic playlist to her for the evening. When she took a look, she found old and new slow dance standards: the Flamingos, 'I Only Have Eyes for You'; Queen Latifah, 'At Last'; Norah Jones, 'Come Away with Me'; Madeleine Peyroux, 'Dance Me to the End of Love.' Kate started to laugh as she scrolled down his list—Johnny was much more romantic than she. He wanted this relationship to work out for her, but he also knew she was struggling with Fitzroy's long absences.

The table was set, and the house was perfumed by the lemons and paprika in the chicken Tagine. Kate put on a comfortable black tunic and leggings and swept her dark hair into a French twist. She had the uncharitable thought that she might as well look good just so that he would recall that picture of her when he was alone at his new work site.

Her cellphone rang. It was Joan. "Kate. I'm at the hospital in the emergency room. Eddie was in a very bad accident with a trailer truck. He was airlifted here to our trauma center. He's going to need extensive surgery. You are listed as his next of kin. I want your permission to call Marco Rossetti—he's the best surgeon in town to address some of Eddie's injuries." Joan waited while Kate tried to absorb what she had just said.

"I can't believe this! Another car accident. Okay, um... yes, call Dr. Rossetti if you think he is the best surgeon for Eddie. I'm on my way." Kate felt the room begin to spin, so she grabbed onto the kitchen counter to steady herself. Bourbon

Ball, sensing something was wrong, came close and leaned his weight against her.

"Kate. Listen to me. I called Johnny first. He is on his way to pick you up. I don't want you to drive. Either wait for him or walk to the hospital. We will talk when you get here." Joan ended the call precipitously.

I can't focus, thought Kate. *I can't focus my eyes. I can't breathe.* Just when she thought she was going to faint, Johnny charged through the kitchen door and grabbed her.

"You are okay. Listen to me. Get your coat and gloves. We need to go right away and you need to be strong when we get there."

"Why does everyone I love get hurt?" Kate's eyes grew wide with fear.

"I love you, and no one's killed me yet. Let's go right now. We can philosophize later." They left Bourbon Ball lying in the kitchen with his head between his paws. Just as she had done for him when Mrs. McCarthy was shot, Johnny dropped her off at the emergency room while he drove around looking for a parking spot. When she said who she was, a nurse took her right to a surgical pod.

Both Marco Rossetti and Joan came out to speak to her before scrubbing for the surgery. Joan took the lead.

"I'm afraid Eddie's injuries are many and severe. In a nutshell, the roads froze suddenly, and one of the eighteen-wheelers hit some black ice, flipped on its side, then skidded into Eddie's Range Rover, spinning it around and slamming it into the guard rail. He was unconscious at the scene, and still is." Joan held both of Kate's hands as she delivered the bad news.

Kate looked from Joan to Marco. "He will survive, right?" She started to hyperventilate, so Joan called for one of her nurses. "Sit her down, head between her knees. Give her five milligrams of Diazepam, right now, and a prescription to take with her."

When Eddie was brought into the trauma center, Joan had quickly filled Marco in on his relationship with Kate. When Marco spoke to Kate for the first time, his voice was very calm, and his dark eyes were kind. "Kate, the surgery will be lengthy. And there may be more than one. You have to settle in with Johnny. As soon as Eddie is out of surgery, we will let you know. Joan and I will use all of our skills, and every available technology, to save his life." Marco's visage changed from empathic to serious as he turned to enter the surgical suite.

The nurse assured Kate that she would receive a text when the surgery was over, but that it could be many hours. She encouraged her and Johnny to either go to the cafeteria or, since she lived so close to the hospital, to go home.

"Come on, Katie. Let's go back to your place. We've spent enough time in this hospital lately. We can be back here in fifteen minutes." Kate did not know that when Joan called Johnny, she had told him that Eddie's injuries were catastrophic.

The house was still as inviting and warm as when she left it. Johnny immediately made some strong coffee and added a bit of Irish, then carried it into Kate's private sitting room. They sat on her mustard-colored love seat together, silently drinking the fortified coffee and petting BB, who had his head protectively on Kate's feet. The doorbell shattered the quiet. "I'll get it," said Johnny, who was followed into the hallway by a barking Bourbon Ball. He opened the door to find Antoine DeVille.

"The boss wanted me to come and tell you exactly what happened tonight on the turnpike. Sometimes knowing the facts helps." Johnny called to Kate, and all three settled in the living room with more cups of coffee.

As Antoine went through the report from the Pennsylvania State Police and Kate had a chance to ask questions, she slowly began to organize herself emotionally. From his description of the accident, it was clear to her that Eddie's injuries were serious, perhaps even lethal. She knew that she needed to marshal all of her inner resources to stand up to the next weeks, or months, of what would be extensive rehabilitation. Antoine reassured her that, so far in the investigation, the accident was just that—an accident. It was not related to any of the cases in which she or Johnny were involved. Kate felt an undercurrent of guilt drain from her; she had been worried about just that issue.

"That section of the turnpike is known to be very dangerous. Big trucks traveling at high speed on those curves, and rapid changes in weather, make it very dangerous year-round." Kate nodded in recognition of that reality, but in the back of her mind she thought, *If Eddie hadn't come to Pittsburgh to see about me, he never would have been hurt. I might want to break up with him, but I don't want him to die.*

The hours passed, and Antoine left. Johnny took Bourbon Ball out for a short walk around the grounds and then fell asleep on the couch. Kate looked at the beautiful meal she had prepared for Eddie, then slowly began to scoop it into containers; with each scoop, she felt like she was packing away her heart.

It was four in the morning when she received the call from Joan. "Eddie is out of surgery. He will stay in our suite and then be moved to the intensive care unit. He won't be conscious for many hours. I'm coming to see you now." Kate woke up the sleeping Johnny and told him the news.

She busied herself with making some breakfast for her friends—cheesy scrambled eggs, ham slices, rye toast and jam, and more hot coffee. Over the years, she had found cooking to be efficacious in quieting emotional pain. Joan let herself in the kitchen door—the two friends hugged for a long time. They all moved to the dining room table, where Johnny and Joan attacked the food, but Kate could barely choke down a bit of toast; her mind kept drifting sideways.

"Marco knew I was stopping here to talk to you, so he went home to get some sleep. Eddie was taken care of by one of the best surgeons, well frankly, in the world. I hadn't seen him operate recently—pretty darn amazing." As usual, she was blunt, but not uncaring. Kate was glad it was Joan who gave her the details of Eddie's state of being. Men could shilly-shally around with platitudes and metaphors, but in Kate's experience, it was women who spoke plainly about tragic realities.

"Will he recover?" Kate looked directly into Joan's eyes, giving her permission to tell the truth.

"I don't know. We have to wait and see."

Johnny, who had so recently been in Kate's position of having to "wait and see," commented. "Antoine DeVille was here earlier with the State Police report of the accident. Both of us forgot to ask if the truck driver survived. Do you know?"

"I was told he was airlifted to another hospital. He didn't make it out of surgery."

The whoosh of early rush hour traffic permeated the quiet of Kate's condo. Joan went home and Johnny took a shower, then crawled into the guest bed. Kate loaded the dishwasher. She was agitated; her skin felt too tightly stretched over her bones, and there was a slight tingling in her arms. She took one of the diazepam pills, then left Johnny a note that she had taken Bourbon Ball out.

As she and BB jogged through the neighborhood, the breaking dawn lit the sidewalks with a slight tint of misty pink. The beautiful light, the drug, and the run helped Kate calm down. Like the stylus in the groove of a vinyl record, Kate had a recurring thought. *If Eddie dies, the person who was witness to the first third of my life will disappear. He was the only one left who had memories of me as a young girl. I guess Marco Rossetti felt something like that when his siblings went missing.*

CHAPTER 32

"WE ARE GETTING CLOSE. I'm about to find out who shot Mrs. McCarthy." Jablonsky poured more milk on his hot oatmeal, stirred it vigorously, then layered in several packets of sugar. He and Aashi Patel were having their usual breakfast at Sophie's Cafe.

Dr. Patel's velvet-brown eyes grew bright with keen interest. "Oh, yes?" She cut into her poached egg and waited for him to continue.

"I'm re-interviewing Thomas Edmonds today. This will be the third, and I hope last, time. We took the measure of him in the first interview. In the second interview we presented enough evidence to him, the DA, and the State Ethics committee to secure convictions on building code malfeasance and endangering the public's safety. Today, between BoBo Ramone's statement and that of Luca Lorenzo, we have him for terrorizing Johnny McCarthy."

Jablonsky paused, then, as if it were a statement of fact, said, "I'm going to get him to confess that he was responsible for Fiona McCarthy's death. Here's a quote from Ramone's interview, talking about Edmonds's motive, 'He wanted him terrorized—just because.'"

Aashi sipped her hot tea, and then tackled the fresh fruit plate. "If anyone can get a perp to confess, it is you, Stefan. So, we were speaking about amygdalin in fruit stones or seeds, which breaks down into hydrogen cyanide when you eat it."

"Do you think it is possible to poison someone that way?"

"Yes. But one would have to know the proportions of weight relative to amount of ground stones or seeds. Unfortunately, the victim's bones won't confirm it was cyanide." Dr. Patel finished her fruit plate, no stone fruits involved, and sat back in the booth.

"We will wait to see what the Styrofoam cup gives us. There might still be a trace," remarked Patel. Jablonsky was aware that the poison probably was in the pastries, not the coffee, but it was worth the cost to have it processed anyway.

"I'm going to change the subject. You heard about Eddie Fitzroy's tragic car accident?" Jablonsky nodded in the affirmative. "I handled the postmortem on the truck driver. There was Adderall XR in his system—you know, the common amphetamine used for attention deficit disorder. No alcohol. I'm not sure the Adderall would have contributed to the accident. It looks like he hit a patch of black ice and spun out. What is happening with Dr. Fitzroy?"

"I asked DeVille to stop and see Kate last night, just to give her the official State Police interpretation of the crash. As you can imagine, when an eighteen-wheeler and an SUV collide, it's never good for anyone. Fitzroy is in very bad shape. DeVille mentioned that Marco Rossetti performed the surgery. Interesting, isn't it? Fitzroy helps identify the remains of Rossetti's siblings, then a few weeks later, Marco might save his life."

"Rossetti is known all over the world for having developed certain lifesaving surgical techniques, especially for use in war zones. I'm glad he was available for the surgery." Jablonsky and Patel finished their breakfast, then left to address their always pressing business. The chief winked at Jeanne and added a few more dollars to the tip Dr. Patel had left for her. It is small kindnesses that make a day worthwhile.

Jablonsky wanted Thomas Edmonds. There was plenty of evidence to tie him to Johnny, but none so far to tie him to Fiona or the Rossetti siblings. He was going to have to confess. Stefan felt he could get him there—he had a theory.

As usual, Thomas Edmonds was expensively dressed, but Jablonsky's outfit of gray flannel pants and a sky-blue shirt matched with a blue/gray patterned tie, was just as natty. His effort, however, was for Dr. Patel. The chief had splashed on a little of his bay rum aftershave and was satisfied that Aashi had noticed its fresh scent. Right now, Stefan was physically and mentally ready for the ensuing chess game.

"Mr. Edmonds. And hello to you, Attorney Rosen. Your client has been Mirandized? Good. We are here to discuss the statement given by BoBo Ramone." He placed the typewritten document in front of Thomas.

"I don't know anyone named BoBo Ramone." Edmonds pushed the statement over to his attorney, Elise Rosen, who took her time reading it.

"You are lying, Mr. Edmonds. Ramone claims that your toady, Luca Lorenzo, was asked to approach him to do a job for you. He also stated that the payment came directly from you." Rosen remained quiet, waiting for the next move.

"I'm not responsible for what Luca Lorenzo says about me. You cannot trace any cash money back to me. Lorenzo is a liar and a crook."

"That's the pot calling the kettle black, isn't it?" Showing his amusement, the chief smirked as he placed Lorenzo's statement in front of Rosen.

"Please don't denigrate my client, Chief Detective. If you have concrete evidence, aside from these statements from two known hoodlums, please present it." Attorney Rosen kept a blank expression; she and the chief had known each other from many other cases.

"Where are we going with all this?" Elise asked.

"Mr. Edmonds, I have here a list of the telephone calls you made to your mother the weeks before the attack on Mrs. Fiona McCarthy and then later, around the time you hired BoBo Ramone to terrorize her son, Professor McCarthy. There are a great many of them."

"So, he frequently calls his mother? Mrs. Edmonds is a frail, elderly person. Come on Jablonsky, what is the point here?" There was an uncharacteristic note of concern that tinged Rosen's voice. It told Jablonsky that he was getting somewhere.

For the first time in all the interviews, Thomas Edmonds broke with his studied air of dismissal, moved forward toward the chief, and threatened him. "You leave my mother out of this, or else," he growled.

"Or what? What are you going to do, Edmonds? Send one of your goons to terrorize me? Sit back. I'm not finished, not by a long shot." Jablonsky's eyes were stone cold; Rosen whispered Thomas's name as a reminder to stay in control.

"I believe your mother asked you to find someone to kill Fiona McCarthy. I believe that she didn't want to go to her own death knowing her husband's mistress would continue to enjoy life. I believe you decided to flip the ask—you'd shoot Mrs. McCarthy yourself and hire out the terrorizing of her son to one of your local crooks. You hated Mrs. McCarthy as much as your mother did. You weren't going to give anyone else the pleasure of killing her."

"This is absurd, Chief Detective. Where is the evidence?" This is simply an unsubstantiated conspiracy theory." Rosen kept her hand on Edmonds's arm as she demanded more evidence.

Jablonsky pointed to the telephone log where he had highlighted the name of the detailing shop that painted Luca Lorenzo's flat-black Camaro. "The day before Mrs. McCarthy was shot, your mother spoke with the owner of Diamond Detailing. Why would an elderly woman, who lives out of state, call that particular paint company? Why would she do that, Edmonds?"

The color drained from Edmonds's face. "I'd like a bottle of water, please," his dry mouth croaking out the request. Jablonsky lifted his right hand into the air and snapped his fingers. DeVille opened the door, placed a bottle of water on the table, then left.

"Now that you are finished deflecting, what was your mother doing speaking with the owner of Diamond Detailing the day before Fiona McCarthy was shot? That day, a young medical resident was out jogging around dawn and identified a flat-black Chevy Camaro on the street and part of the license plate number; the rest of the plate number was given by a neighbor who was taking out his trash. Answer the question, Mr. Edmonds." The demanding harsh tone in Jablonsky's voice heightened the tension of their chess match. He was remembering how Thomas had spoken about Mrs. McCarthy and was just plain mad.

"I have no idea how my mother would know this auto business, or why she would call there. You'd have to ask her." Edmonds had finished half of the bottle of water, but his voice still cracked.

"Well, we asked the owner. Here is his statement. It says that your mother called to say she was thinking of bringing an expensive car in for a new paint job and wanted to know about security—what kind the business had and where the cameras were placed. She specifically asked if her car would ever be out of sight of the cameras. He said she sounded like a sweet grandma. But that's not what she is, is she, Edmonds? Your mother is a co-conspirator in murder, and we are going to charge her as such." Jablonsky moved his queen into position.

Thomas Edmonds jumped out of his chair as if a fire were burning his butt. "You bastard!" he shouted and punched his fists across the table at Jablonsky. DeVille and two uniformed officers raced into the room and grabbed Edmonds. Jablonsky slowly slid his chair back from the table, remained seated, and nonchalantly crossed his legs.

"I can charge her, and I will charge her. I can have officers at her house today with a warrant. They will take your elderly mother from her comfortable home to the police station, where they will book her and let her sit in a stinking cold cell."

Edmonds was breathing so hard he couldn't speak. Rosen intervened. "What do you want, Jablonsky?"

"I want the truth! Did you pay someone to heist Lorenzo's car, drive to Mrs. McCarthy's home, shoot her, and then return the car to Diamond Detailing?" Jablonsky's body was relaxed, but his voice had a tone that reached into Edmonds's throat to rip out a confession.

"Still silent? All right, then." The chief raised his arm and snapped his fingers, again summoning DeVille. "Call the New York police and have them arrest Eugenia Edmonds."

"Wait! You are a bastard, Jablonsky! This is hitting below the belt!" screamed Edmonds as the officers restrained him. Finally, he got ahold of himself and sat down. Attorney Rosen attempted to intervene, but Edmonds waved her off.

"Okay, Jablonsky. You are right. I hated Fiona McCarthy and her tawdry affair with my father. When I found out that he had left her three million dollars, I wanted to do something about it. I didn't know that she had some of my father's papers, but that just added fuel to the fire." Edmonds paused, and Rosen urged him to stop talking. Treating her like a servant, Thomas told her to shut up.

"Did you and your mother believe that Johnny McCarthy is your half-brother?" Edmonds waited before answering. "It was a possibility."

"By the way," remarked Jablonsky, "he isn't." Rosen looked from her client to Jablonsky but didn't comment on the paternity issue. Jablonsky continued, "Does your mother know Luca Lorenzo?"

"Yes. She knew him from the early days here in Pittsburgh. She had asked him to do small favors for her before."

"Come on, Edmonds. What favors?" Jablonsky was uncharacteristically impatient.

"One time when I was home for the holidays, I mentioned his name. She remembered it and contacted Lorenzo to routinely give her information on Mrs. McCarthy and my father. My mother is old. She wanted the score settled. She told me she was planning on having Luca find a shooter." He paused again. Suddenly, Edmonds became extremely animated—his eyes shone bright with pupils dilated and his face filled with delight like child looking at a Christmas tree.

"I decided to kill her myself. I knew that old bitch's habits; I had cased her place. I paid one of the employees at the shop to get me Lorenzo's car and I drove to her home, and I... shot... her. It was the best day of my life! Forget the money—I took away her life. My mother and I laughed and laughed."

It was as if a dam broke, and Edmonds's confession just poured out. "Then I found BoBo Ramone and had a good old time with that fag Johnny. Mother really enjoyed hearing how the professor's office was destroyed. But what she really loved was having someone shooting at Johnny while he was clearing out Fiona's house. Man, that was sweet."

Thomas Edmonds smiled at Jablonsky; a sick, arrogant smile, the kind that gives normal people the creeps. Elise Rosen quietly closed her laptop.

Jablonsky stood. "Thomas Edmonds, I am arresting you for the murder of Fiona McCarthy. These officers will take you to booking. Oh, maybe you can wear Rosalie's underwear in prison. Your cellmate might like that."

Back in his office, he and DeVille reviewed the chess game. Thomas Edmonds was being investigated for his building practices, he was charged with terrorizing Johnny, and now he was charged with murdering Fiona McCarthy.

"Getting the confession from Thomas Edmonds brings closure, and justice, to Johnny," remarked DeVille. A bottle of Jameson Black and two rocks glasses appeared from Jablonsky's bottom desk drawer.

"Any news on Eddie Fitzroy's condition?" Jablonsky poured two generous fingers of the whisky for each. "No," answered DeVille. "I checked with Johnny this morning and he said that Fitzroy still isn't conscious. Johnny worries that Dr. Fitzroy will die before he regains consciousness. It's pretty terrible for Kate."

The two detectives sipped their Jameson, its warmth making Edmonds's confession even bigger and better. "We got Thomas Edmonds. But," said Jablonsky, as he polished off his glass of whiskey, "who murdered Michael and Rosalie Rossetti?"

CHAPTER 33

RETRIEVING HER MEMORIES of Eddie Fitzroy was like opening the small windows on an Advent calendar. Open this window, and they were playing volleyball on the beach in Nantucket; open that window, and they were sitting at her grandfather's kitchen table playing Hearts; open another window, and they were laughing together in bed.

Sitting at his bedside, Kate vigilantly scanned his face for any signs of consciousness. But there was nothing, just the continuous beeping of all the machines. She stood and stretched. There were several other patients in the intensive care unit, so she walked into the waiting room and then out into the long hallway. A tall, dark-haired man, wearing a physician's white coat, was walking toward her. It was Marco Rossetti. "Kate, I'm glad you are here. We didn't get a chance to talk the other night. Let's sit."

Slowly and quietly, Rossetti spoke about Eddie's surgery, what was done, and what his team wasn't able to do. It was similar to Joan's description, only in much more detail. Kate listened, but as he talked, she felt a deep fatigue begin to engulf her. *He's telling me that the chances are high that Eddie won't survive,* she thought.

When Marco finished his report, Kate noticed that he seemed to be waiting for something. He reached into the pocket of his white coat and pulled out a ring box. "This was among his things. I wanted to make sure it didn't go missing."

Kate took the box and slowly opened the lid. Inside was a large emerald set in platinum. Its' pure dark green color, with just a tinge of blue, was like a stand of trees in the forest lit by sunlight. This surely was a family heirloom, and just as surely, Eddie's offering as an engagement ring. She looked at the engraving, "For Kate, my darling girl."

"Your man has exquisite taste. That's a stunning heirloom."

"I guess he had a special weekend planned." Kate thought it was ironic that while her weekend plans were to talk about ending their relationship, his were to officially propose. She kept staring at the beautiful ring. In a low, soothing voice, Marco began to reminisce.

"When Rosalie went missing, I would remember the strangest details. There was a rhyme she would recite, and then always leave the last two words for me to say. I would remember that she would make coffee in my mother's kitchen and ask me if I wanted a 'Caffeine rocket for my back pocket.' They are silly memories, but very precious to me."

"Eddie always calls me 'my darling girl.'" Kate closed the ring box, keeping it cupped in her hands. "Marco, is he going to wake up?"

"I was able to repair the worst of his orthopedic injuries, but his head took quite a beating in the accident. His internal injuries are massive. Time will give us the answer to your question. Is there anything we can do for you? I really mean me—anything I can do for you." Kate thought that Marco's manner was kind without being maudlin, and she suddenly found herself confiding in him.

"You have an idea of where I am, emotionally, I mean. I'm trying to come to terms with the possibility I might lose him.

You know, if he dies, it will be like losing my grandfather all over again. It may sound strange to you, but Eddie and my grandfather are linked together for me, almost like they were different halves of the same person, one older, one younger. It's odd. But then, I had an odd upbringing—no parents or siblings, just my grandfather. He loved Eddie so much, and in part, I loved Eddie because of that. I'm not sure I can survive this... so many losses." There was no self-pity in her statement, just profound exhaustion.

"I felt the same way when it became clear that Rosalie and Michael weren't coming back." Marco shifted in his seat to face Kate directly. "But I did survive it. I haven't known you very long, but I believe you are mentally strong enough to handle it if he doesn't make it. Kate, his death will not be the same as the loss of your grandfather."

Kate grew silent, thoughtful. Finally, she spoke. "I believe that everyone needs an elder. My grandfather was mine, and after he died, he remained my imaginary elder. I think that the elderly provide us with unconditional love, sweetness, and an irreverence that comes from the long view of life. I miss him so."

"I've never heard it conceptualized like that before, but I know what you mean about the importance of having an elder in one's life. Mine still is my mother, and maybe her two friends, who don't really like me." Marco shot her a sheepish grin.

They both heard footsteps, turned, and saw Jablonsky walking toward them, so the intimate conversation ended. Marco's office had texted him that the chief wanted a meeting—there was no escape now.

"Chief Detective. I understand you wanted to see me. There is a private consultation room down the hall, we can go there." Marco pointed out the way, and then left Jablonsky alone to speak with Kate.

"Now that he is out of surgery, is it a waiting game?" Jablonsky felt terrible for his young amateur sleuth and tried to communicate his concern to her. They spoke for a few minutes, he gave her a fatherly hug, and then he left to talk with Dr. Rossetti.

The consulting room was comfortably furnished with a small table and several chairs, soft lighting, and a few magazines. It was a space where surgeons like Marco and Joan delivered either good news or bad. Jablonsky wondered which it would be for Eddie Fitzroy.

"I'll get right to the point. We have a working theory that Michael and Rosalie were poisoned. In the box of Rosalie's things that you gave us were sheets of chemistry homework, your chemistry homework. Here they are. Do you recognize them as yours?"

Marco scanned the yellowed homework papers. "Yes. These are mine."

"Did you ever talk about amygdalin at the bakery—more specifically, did you ever say that it transforms into cyanide when ingested? Kate mentioned that you might have spoken about hydrogen cyanide." Jablonsky's tone wasn't accusatory, rather it was clear that he was soliciting facts.

"Yes, I'm afraid I did. I was a teenager showing off my erudition. For years I have suspected that my narcissism might have been the cause of my siblings' deaths. I just don't know what the motive for killing them would have been." Marco spoke of his youthful folly without shyness or excuses. Jablonsky's prejudices about surgeons continued to be challenged by this man.

"Who would have overheard you?" The chief wanted to be doubly sure of who overheard Marco before he went into his next round of interviews.

"Jonathan Price, a girlfriend of Rosalie's from law school, Thomas Edmonds, and maybe, Luca Lorenzo, but I'm not sure about him."

"Did the women who worked at the bakery know about this particular chemical reaction?" Jablonsky didn't really believe that one of the ladies would have deliberately murdered the owner's two children, but he had to cover all bases.

"Yes, they knew the fact of it, but not how the chemicals functioned. It is listed in the Food Safety Hazard Guidebook that my mother kept at the store. An updated copy is still there. I was taught that hydrogen cyanide is not heat stable. Because of that, there is little risk that a baked pastry could poison."

Jablonsky pressed him. "If you were use amygdalin as a poison, with pastries as the vehicle, how would you do it?"

"Either I would grind the fruit stone into powder myself, or I would buy it already ground. Then, I would find out how much my victim weighed and calculate how much I would need to kill him, not just to make him sick. You would have to mix it into a cold ingredient within a pastry—say for instance, the cream in cannoli. It would take smarts and attention to detail to do the job correctly." It was obvious to Jablonsky that Marco had thought about the many different kinds of poisons that could have killed his siblings.

"You are mirroring what Dr. Patel said. Unfortunately, as you know, there is no forensic evidence left. A confession must be obtained."

"Are you close to a confession?" Marco's urgency was palpable.

"Maybe. I really can't comment, but I do have to ask this question. Dr. Rossetti, you had the knowledge, means, and opportunity—did you poison your brother and sister?"

"No. I did not." Jablonsky noted that Marco didn't resent the question. *He probably knew it was coming,* thought Stefan. *He seems almost relieved to be directly asked at the question— and to reply to it.*

The chief pulled out four pictures and placed them in front of Marco. "Do you recognize any of these women?" Rossetti touched each picture with one of his beautiful, strong fingers. "This girl looks familiar. I think this was Rosalie's girlfriend from law school. She had two names— Jeanne something, or Julie something—?" He turned over the photo to see if there was writing on the back. "That's right, it is Jane Louise. Jane Louise Smith. She married Thomas Edmonds. Who are these other women?"

The chief snickered. "These are Edmonds's other three wives."

"Would you mind if I showed a few pictures of Rosalie and her law school friends to your mother? I don't want to upset her unnecessarily, but it would really help with one of our lines of inquiry."

"I'll let her know that you will be calling, and why. My mother is pretty tough. She will say yes, especially if it will help in your investigation."

Both men rose at the same time and shook hands. "What about Eddie Fitzroy?" asked Jablonsky.

"We don't know yet. He sustained very serious injuries. While he's not an old man, he's not a young one either. I have no other answer for you, or Kate. It is in the hands of fate."

Jablonsky speculated that, like a detective, a surgeon would know about fate. On his way back to the office, the Chief called DeVille, who had been re- interviewing all of

Thomas Edmonds's ex-wives. "I just saw Dr. Rossetti at the hospital. He identified the chemistry homework as his and did confirm that someone might have overheard him talking about amygdalin. There are a few things I want to go over with Kate and Johnny. Tomorrow will be soon enough."

CHAPTER 34

KATE HAD TAKEN VACATION TIME from work so that she could be at the hospital pretty much all the time. Today it was early evening when she walked back to her condo. The streetlights were on, casting shadows on the roads and the passing pedestrians. The chiaroscuro suited her mood.

Once home, she was standing in the kitchen, leaning on the open refrigerator door and staring at its contents, when Johnny let himself in the door. "How are you doing?" He looked at her with concern. Kate knew she looked terrible—it seemed impossible, but over the last several days she had lost eight pounds, and every bit of that loss showed in her drawn face.

Johnny let Bourbon Ball out into the fenced yard for an evening pee and a sniff around his kingdom. Kate slowly became aware that John clearly had something on his mind.

"What's up?" she asked.

"Well, I know it is a lot to ask, but Jablonsky called me and wants me to come to the precinct. They have arrested the man who murdered my mom—he wants to discuss the situation. I wondered if you feel up to going with me. You don't have to, Kate. Really."

"Of course, I will go. This is wonderful news! Is it that slime ball, Thomas?" Kate grabbed her friend, and in the French habit, she kissed him on both cheeks.

"It is. It is Thomas Edmonds. He didn't hire someone, he killed her himself." Kate watched as the impact of that last statement fully hit him; he covered his face and gasped for air. BB appeared at the door, whining to come in and comfort his friend. The pup leaned his seventy pounds against Johnny; then Kate put her arms around him, sandwiching BB in between. The three of them remained close until Johnny recovered his equilibrium. Kate was once again reminded of Fiona's statement that Johnny would need her beside him— Fiona didn't realize that no one had to ask Kate to stand with him because along with generosity, loyalty was one of her strongest qualities.

"Johnny, you can see Jablonsky tomorrow, after you have had time to process everything. There is no shame in delaying—you are not a machine; you are a human being who just learned the identity of the person who murdered your mother. You are allowed to have a reaction."

"No. I want to go. I want to hear him tell the story. It will help me."

"Okay, then. I'll freshen-up while you feed Bourbon Ball. Deal? Good." A quick shower and change of clothes helped wash off the otherworldly vibes of the intensive care unit. While the hot water of her shower cascaded over her, Kate felt a tremendous emotional relief—justice had been served for Fiona.

Kate and Johnny arrived at the always busy precinct. Antoine escorted them to the chief's office. Jablonsky's handshake was so vigorous and enthusiastic that Johnny had to pull his hand away. Antoine brought in four excellent cups of coffee made from his elaborate brew machine.

Jablonsky detailed the two-pronged case against Thomas Edmonds, starting with the investigation into his building practices and ending with the final interview, where he confessed. "In the end, John, he was driven by hatred of his father's betrayal of his mother, and his own misplaced loyalty to his mother, Eugenia." Johnny had many questions, so while the chief gave him the time to ask them all, Kate opened her laptop and googled the engagement and wedding pictures of Thomas Edmonds's first marriage.

She looked again at the society pages in the local paper, and then she viewed the pictures printed in the paper from the small town in New York where Mr. and Mrs. Edmonds kept their main house. The coverage was surprisingly extensive.

Several pictures caught her attention—there was Jonathan Price, whom she recognized from Fiona's album, standing with some of the wedding party, and there was a smallish, thin man, visible only in profile, lurking in the background. Kate thought he looked familiar.

When there was a lull in the conversation, she pointed to the man in profile and asked, "Do you recognize this man?" They all scrutinized the computer screen, then the chief remarked, "I think that is Luca Lorenzo." Johnny, who knew Luca from the bakery, squinted, and moved the screen closer to him. "Yeah. That's Lorenzo, all right. What would he be doing at Edmonds's wedding?"

"Was he security?" Kate offered.

"He very well might have been. We didn't notice this when we scrolled through the wedding pictures." Jablonsky gave Antoine an annoyed look.

Kate quickly clarified, "These are pictures from the local New York paper—the Pittsburgh paper didn't run them."

"You should have known to look at the New York coverage, Antoine. Another missed detail." Before Jablonsky could warm to dressing down his number one, Kate tried to intercede by posing another question.

"But why have a known thug at a society wedding? Johnny, you kind of knew him, right? What do you think?" Kate found that focusing on the Rossetti case was like a tonic for her brain; for the time being, it blocked her fears about Eddie.

Jablonsky hadn't revealed all that they had uncovered about the convoluted relationship between Lorenzo and the Edmonds company. The investigation into the Rossetti murders was still ongoing.

"I mostly knew about Lorenzo from my mother. She referred to him as a neighborhood criminal, who worked for the Edmonds company in some 'procurement capacity,' her words. She said he spent most of his time with Michael Rossetti and the Alliance. Mom said that wherever Michael went, Luca went. It very well could be that Edmonds hired him as security for the wedding—maybe they thought there would be threats. They were hated in the South Oakland community." Johnny shook his head, clearly not knowing where to go from there.

"In this third shot of the wedding, Lorenzo seems to be having a pretty intense conversation with someone. She's half in the shadows, right here." Kate pointed to an elegantly dressed older woman, who had her hand on Luca's arm. "Let me try to zoom in on this section." Kate enlarged the two figures in the photo.

"I'll be," said Jablonsky. "That's Eugenia Edmonds, Thomas's mother. This confirms that Lorenzo and the Missus knew each other as early as the wedding. Antoine, you and Annie missed this information." DeVille looked as guilty as a dog who had just chewed the master's shoe.

"John, this shores up certain aspects of the case against Thomas Edmonds." All four sat back, enjoying the moment. Another nail in the Edmonds's coffin—it just felt good.

"There is one more thing," added Kate. "When I read the list of pictured attendees, they listed Jonathan Price as an attorney for the Edmonds company. Johnny, when we went through your mother's work album, she talked as if there were two warring camps—the development company and the Alliance people. In these photos, we see Lorenzo, Mrs. Edmonds, and Jonathan Price—all mixing in together, nicey-nice. I find that curious."

"So do I," remarked Jablonsky. Later he pulled Antoine aside and gave him instructions in a tone of voice that indicated his number one was definitely in the doghouse. "Find Luca Lorenzo and get him into the station. Then, bring me Jonathan Price. And I want the web photos of the wedding made into actual pictures."

CHAPTER 35

LORENZO'S FLAT-BLACK CAMARO was spotted cruising down the narrow side street to his digs. DeVille and the uniforms were already at his apartment when he was seen. Luca pulled over, locked his car, and started on a serpentine escape route through the back streets of the South Side. He was like spilled mercury; every time the police thought they had him, he shape-shifted out of their grasp.

The chase went on for some time. Luca knew every rooftop that could be reached from the fire escape ladders, and he used them. He was like a jewel thief, disappearing into the shadows of chimneys and dormers, and then reappearing in the next block. He worked his way down to the railroad tracks that ran along the Monongahela River, then sprinted across one of the bridges and disappeared into a questionable bar on Bates Street. The owner knew him and knew that he was always in trouble. "Get in the back," he growled.

"Hello officers, how may I help you?" The bar owner, and his few patrons, looked innocently at the police when they entered the establishment.

"Have you seen this man? No worries, we just want to talk to him." Antoine held up a picture of Luca on his phone. "We just want a conversation."

The owner's expression made clear his disbelief, but he agreed anyway. "Yeah, okay, in the back." He jabbed his right thumb over his shoulder, so Antoine dispersed several officers to cover the rear exits before he walked down the hallway to the storage room. His Glock was at his side.

"Come on out, Luca. We just want to talk. No one has to get hurt here. Just step into the hall and we can head to the precinct and see Jablonsky." Everyone, including DeVille, was sweating from the adrenaline pump.

Finally, the storeroom door opened, and Luca called out, "I'm unarmed. I'm coming out. Don't shoot!" A collective exhale was breathed as Luca was handcuffed and marched out of the bar. "Screw you, man," were his parting words to the barkeep.

—⋘⋙—

"Luca, I hear you were quite the escape artist today, climbing up ladders and tiptoeing over roofs." Jablonsky placed a cup of coffee in front of Lorenzo and, remembering the last interview, laid down a dozen or so sugar packets. He watched as Luca stirred most of them into his small cup.

"Chief, why am I here again?"

"So many reasons, Luca, it's hard to know where to begin counting. We've arrested Thomas Edmonds, who confessed to the murder of Fiona McCarthy, and for hiring your pal, BoBo Ramone, for terrorizing her son, Professor McCarthy. Both BoBo and Edmonds had very interesting things to say about you, Mr. Lorenzo. But let's start with these pictures. See anyone you know?" Jablonsky took his time placing the pictures of the Edmonds's wedding on the table in front of Luca.

"Yeah, so I was there. Thomas Edmonds hired me as additional security for the, what do they say, the nup-ti-als. Nothing illegal in that." Luca's leathered skin almost cracked as he gave the chief his best screw-you grin.

"And this woman?" Jablonsky pointed to Eugenia Edmonds. "You agreed to do some work for her. Tell me about that."

"You're the man with all the answers. You tell me."

"Luca, I'm in no mood to play this game. We have statements from three different people that you were very involved with the Edmonds company and family. You spied on Andrew Edmonds and Fiona McCarthy for Eugenia Edmonds. You supplied Thomas with crew members who would look the other way on building codes. Recently, Eugenia Edmonds was in touch with you again, looking for a shooter to kill Mrs. McCarthy. Of course, there is BoBo Ramone. You are like the Fredo of "I know a guy." We have plenty on you, Luca, and I'm afraid you will not be free to go today."

"Wait just a minute, Chief. What are you saying?" Luca's voice held a tinge of hysteria.

Jablonsky pushed his chair back from the table, stretched his long legs, then continued. "Aside from those charges, you are here today because I think you know who killed Michael and Rosalie Rossetti and you've kept it quiet all these years. You've been paid handsomely for your silence, haven't you? How else could you afford your car and your apartment? You certainly don't file a W-2. Who is it, Luca? It is time to come clean about who murdered your good friend, Michael, and his sister. Let's go. Give me the truth."

Skinny Luca was fast on his feet. He jumped out of his chair and banged his hands on the table like a frustrated baby banging on his highchair tray. "I don't have any freaking idea who murdered Michael!" he screamed. "You're a jackass, Jablonsky! You wouldn't know the truth if it bit you on the ass." Before a uniformed cop could get into the room, Lorenzo broke into a combination of hiccups and sobs. When DeVille entered, Jablonsky signaled to him to sit down and remain in the room.

Both detectives watched as Luca remained bent over the table, tears streaming down his face while he continued to gasp for breath. Jablonsky stood and, like a clock pendulum, slowly walked back and forth. It was rare that a criminal like Luca would cry during an interview. Lorenzo had loved Michael; he had admitted it in their very first interview. Just as surely as the sun rises in the east, Jablonsky knew that this reaction was grief over lost love.

The chief placed a few of the pictures they had found at Luca's apartment on the table. "You told me that Michael was your best friend and, like a best friend, you loved him. These photographs tell the story of how close the two of you were. In this picture I saw that you both were wearing leather bracelets. You have yours on today. We found a matching bracelet by Michael's body. The bracelets meant something to you both, didn't they?"

Luca looked as if someone had ripped open his guts. He whispered, "Yes. They meant something to both of us," and covered his face with his hands.

And then there was this." Jablonsky laid down a picture of the evidence bag containing the Styrofoam cup. "Tell me about this cup. Set the record straight on what happened to the best friend you've ever had. What happened to Michael and Rosalie?"

Jablonsky remained standing; then, in a threatening posture, leaned over the table toward Luca and growled, "Give me the truth!"

Luca kept his face in his hands, continuing to choke for breath. Finally, he got ahold of himself and looked at the photos. Almost entreating the chief, he said, "I want these back. Agreed?" Jablonsky nodded his agreement. "I'm still waiting."

"What's in it for me?"

"Relief. Relief is what's in it for you. Beyond that, I can't offer anything." Jablonsky gave his response calmly, not breaking his eye contact with Luca. Minutes passed.

"Lorenzo. Let me be clear. Given your past and present associations, I can make a case against you. I can arrest you for both murders. Today, right now, I can charge you with double homicide. Don't think I won't." It was as if the proverbial iceberg hit the Titanic, gouging a hole, out of which streamed Luca's story.

"I didn't kill them! I loved Michael, and he loved me. We weren't fags, you understand, there was just something between us. We fell in love with each other. Then, well... one thing led to another." Lorenzo's chest heaved a huge sigh. His jaw relaxed, then drooped, and suddenly he looked a decade older.

"I tried to tell Michael that he was pushing Thomas Edmonds too much, but he wouldn't hear me. Rosalie was even worse. She wanted, and got, dirt on Thomas Edmonds, but I was never sure whether she told Michael how she had gotten her information on his code violations. Michael would have hated that she was playing footsie with Edmonds." Jablonsky pushed a bottle of water over to Luca, who took a long, deep drink.

"So, what happened?"

"I found them. That's right. Yeah. I found their bodies." Luca stared straight at the chief and Antoine, as if he was trying to communicate what that felt like.

"Where?"

"At the Grotto. I found them at the Grotto. Both dead. I knew that Michael and Rosalie were going there to talk; it was their private place. So, I followed them. They must have been sitting on the benches and slid off, because Michael was lying half on Rosalie, half off. It was awful. I didn't know what had happened. They weren't shot, they weren't bleeding... they were just, dead."

"What did you do?" Jablonsky was careful to not interrupt Luca's flow of memory with too many questions.

"I pulled my car as close to the path as possible. I dragged Michael, and then carried Rosalie, and put them in my car. I just drove around with them for a couple of hours. I didn't know what to do. Finally, it was dark, and I was still in South Oakland, drinking. I keep a fifth in my car. I was driving by the hotel excavation site, and it dawned on me that I could put their bodies there, in the hole. So, that's what I did. I laid them side by side, and then covered them with a blanket from the car, then I shoveled some dirt on them. Oh, man, it was the worst day of my life. I can still see their faces—Michael was so beautiful." Luca had another fit of coughing and sobbing.

"Why didn't you just leave them at the Grotto?"

Luca looked down at his hands. He kept his eyes averted and answered. "I thought it was disrespectful. If I left them there, Michael would be cut up in an autopsy. I didn't want that. He was so handsome—he was my beautiful boy."

Inexplicably, Jablonsky found himself feeling sorry for Lorenzo. He pushed another bottle of water over to him. "Take your time."

"I don't know who killed them. For years I tried to wheedle it out of Thomas Edmonds, who I figured did the deed, or else had hired someone to do it. No dice. I'm telling you the truth, Chief, I don't know who killed them. I moved the bodies, but they were already dead when I got to the Grotto."

"When you found them, Luca, there were cups and take-out cartons lying around. This was one of the cups. Why did you keep it?"

"It was the last thing that his lips touched." Jablonsky and DeVille were surprised at the intimate expression of Luca's love for Michael. Suddenly, the reason for Jablonsky's interest in the cup and take-out cartons, dawned on Lorenzo.

"You think they were poisoned! Ho-lee shit! But the boxes were from the bakery; what kind of poison would be in baked goods?" Lorenzo looked shocked. He couldn't reason it out.

"It's a line of inquiry we are pursuing. Did you see anyone else there?"

"No. I was really careful. I looked around because I had to take the bodies along the path. Sometimes when Michael was at the Grotto, there were two old ladies he knew from the neighborhood who would talk to him. I didn't see them when I was there."

Jablonsky tapped his fingers on the table for a few minutes. "I want you to write this down, Lorenzo. We are going to hold you for a day or two, really for your own safety. One of the public defenders will talk with you about the other charges."

"What do you mean, for my own safety? I had nothing to do with their deaths."

"You know Luca, I think I believe you. But maybe some others won't." Jablonsky left a sputtering Lorenzo to write his statement.

Back at the murder board, Jablonsky offered Antoine a piece of cinnamon gum. "That's one piece of the puzzle in place. I can use this information in our next interview, Jonathan Price."

CHAPTER 36

KATE QUIETLY READ through the details of Thomas Edmonds's life on her laptop. It gave her something to do while she sat at Eddie's bedside. There had been no change; he was still unconscious. They had moved him out of intensive care into a private room, but all the monitors remained the same. She frequently watched them, considering the beeping and movement of the different colored lines to be "proof of life."

There is something we are missing, she thought, as she went through the wedding pictures again. She looked closely at the guests on the periphery of the wedding party. There was Jonathan Price, Luca Lorenzo as security, and various other guests identified as cousins, or aunts and uncles. Kate kept returning to the question she had asked Marco. "Who were Rosalie's good friends from law school? Jane Louise Smith was one, but who were the others?"

Thomas Edmonds's wedding was a big society shindig. The pictures revealed a wedding party made up of Thomas Edmonds, the groom; Jane Louise, the bride; Thomas Edmonds's sister, as maid of honor; and finally, a friend of Thomas's, as the best man. Kate knew that a wedding like this would typically have had at least three bridesmaids and a matching number of groomsmen. Why were there no other law school classmates?

Kate's thinking about friends went to character. If neither Thomas nor Jane Louise had friends outside of family or church members, what did that say about them? Kate believed it indicated something neurotic, something in a person's character that wasn't fully developed or fulfilled.

She couldn't move off the subject of love and friendship. In postgraduate programs, everyone is of the age where strong young adult friendships are forged out of similar professional interests, dating and mating issues, and overall support during the years of specialty education. Graduate student groups are close and dishy. Kate felt that there was no question that Rosalie would have shared most aspects of her life with several of her core study group. Who else was in the group?

Rosalie's Law Review article was an examination of Pennsylvania's committees for the legal enforcement of building permits, inspections, and the general and specific processes of commercial construction, especially related to public safety. While she was researching the article, all of Rosalie's study group would have known that that was her area of interest. Her closest friends must have known that it was specific to the Alliance, and the Edmonds company.

Kate walked to the ladies' room, washed her hands, and splashed water on her face, hoping to spur more thinking. When she came out of the bathroom, she found Marco Rossetti looking at Eddie's chart.

"Marco. Anything I need to know?" Kate looked as exhausted as she felt, but she didn't want to be absent if Eddie woke up.

"I'm afraid not. You look like you could use a bite to eat and a coffee. Let's go get something in the cafeteria. The food isn't too bad." Marco was unaware of how much time Kate had recently spent with Fiona McCarthy in the hospital; she could walk to the cafeteria blindfolded.

Over a half-eaten bagel and a smear of cream cheese, Kate revisited the topic of Rosalie and her law school friends. "You mentioned Jane Louise, who went on to marry Thomas Edmonds, now in jail, as you know. Was it your impression that she confided in her closest friends about her law review article? Was there an aura of intimacy or special confidences in any of the relationships?"

"Well, when you put it like that, I'd say yes. Certainly Jane Louise, probably Jonathan Price, and there were a few others. I can get those names for you." Marco was intrigued, in part because he was typically the smartest person in the room, and here was Kate, moving in a direction about his siblings' disappearance that he hadn't considered.

"It is odd to me that Jane Louise didn't have any study group friends at her wedding. Why would that be, and is it related to Rosalie's disappearance?" Kate looked at Marco, hoping he had something to say about Rosalie's friends.

Marco tried to follow her reasoning. "Are you suggesting that one of the people in Rosalie's study group told Thomas that she was researching his company and so he had her killed? I'm not sure that works for me. In all these years, either the old Chief Detective, or Jablonsky's current team, would have gotten some leads on that. They didn't arrest Thomas Edmonds for the murder of my siblings."

"True enough. But there is something here. Something that has to do with love, jealousy, betrayal—those kinds of motives." Kate's sluggish brain couldn't articulate what she was intuiting.

"Okay, agreed. All those strong human emotions are potent motives. But which person in this cast of characters was so driven by those emotions that she, or he, would kill over them?" It was now a pattern that when Kate was making a point with Marco, his phone announced a text. "I have to go. You should talk to Jablonsky about your theory." Kate could see that Marco clearly reduced her emphasis on aspects of love and friendship to Eddie Fitzroy's condition.

Just when Kate was getting her phone out of her purse to call the chief, he walked into the cafeteria. "The nurses told me you and Marco were here. How are things going?"

"No change with Eddie's condition." Kate immediately launched into her theory that one of Rosalie's study group told Thomas Edmonds that Rosalie was only seeing Eddie in order to garner information about his building practices, and her curiosity about why there were no other female friends at his wedding. "Dr. Rossetti was just here. He said that he would get a list of Rosalie's entire study group."

Jablonsky listened. He knew not to dismiss Kate's intuitions. "You know, Mrs. Rossetti and her friends did say that Thomas Edmonds was not only in love with Rosalie but was crazy about her."

Kate perked up when she heard that phrase. "Mrs. Rossetti used that language? Crazy about her? Now see, I find that really interesting. I think it supports my theory that somehow Michael's and Rosalie's disappearance was about betrayal and jealousy."

Jablonsky didn't mention that Thomas Edmonds had kept a shrine to Rosalie, or that Luca and Michael were in a relationship, much less that Luca had found and buried the bodies. When all was over, he would disclose those facts. That information was closed to this amateur sleuth, but her intuition concerning motives was right on the money.

Kate continued with her speculations. "I have these two pictures from Mrs. McCarthy's work album. I've been carrying them around in my purse, meaning to give them to you. I think they might be important. Take a look... see what I mean?" Jablonsky looked at the people Kate pointed at and immediately understood her reasoning. He pocketed the photographs.

"I'll have DeVille contact Marco about the study group list." Kate knew that Jablonsky was closing the evidence circle, keeping her on the outside. *It was my lead,* she thought, too tired to argue with him.

"Go home and get some sleep, Kate. The hospital will let you know when Eddie wakes up." Jablonsky left the cafeteria thinking that he would go home himself, work on completing his model of the USS Missouri, and consider the motives of love, betrayal, and jealousy.

CHAPTER 37

JABLONSKY DID COMPLETE the USS Missouri model that night. It was perfect, even if he said so himself. In the midst of gluing the tiny bits of the warship together, he decided how he was going to shape the interview with Jonathan Price.

At the precinct the next morning, Jablonsky heard DeVille on the telephone with Dr. Rossetti, getting the list of the study group members. *Good,* thought the Chief, *he needs a fire lit in his belly. He's been lax in crossing the t's and dotting the i's in this case. Amateur Kate has been doing his work.*

"He's here, Boss. Interview room number two. I'll bring some coffee and water." DeVille handed several files to Jablonsky, who opened the door, ready for the verbal tug-of-war that eliciting information from this suspect for the Rossetti murders would take. Kate had forwarded Rosalie's Law Review article; Stefan had a few other tricks up his sleeve.

"Thank you for coming in, Mr. Price."

"I didn't know I had a choice. I was Mirandized. Should I have my attorney with me?" Price's posture was defensive, arms crossed over his chest, legs also crossed. His fingers slowly pressed his hair back on either side of his head—Jablonsky remembered that nervous tick.

"You can call your attorney at any time. It is usual for us to read an interviewee his rights. Of course, you are an attorney, so you know more than most." Jablonsky was sure that Price was too stupid to realize he was being handled.

"You are right. I do know more than most, about almost everything." With that bit of narcissism, Price rubbed his hands together, clicking his annoying pinky rings. Jablonsky remembered that nervous habit as well.

"Here are some pictures of Thomas Edmonds's wedding. As you know, he married one of the members of your law school study group, Jane Louise Smith. Here she is, here you are, and here is—who?" Jablonsky pointed to Luca Lorenzo.

"I believe that is a man who used to always be around Michael Rossetti. Um, his name is... Luca. Where did you get these pictures? I haven't seen these people in years. I look so young, and, I must say, handsome."

"Mr. Price, why were you the only one from the study group that was at the wedding? Here are the names of everyone else that you were close to for the three years of law school—of course, Jane Louise, Rosalie is dead—here are the rest." The chief slowly enunciated all five names.

"Well, you would have to ask Jane Louise and Thomas Edmonds. It was their wedding." Price pulled his collar away from his neck. *Already getting warm,* mused Jablonsky to himself.

"Why did Thomas Edmonds offer you a position with his team of attorneys? You knew Jane Louise, but you mentioned that you only had met Thomas a few times at Rosalie's Bakery. How did those few hellos translate into a job?"

"Jane gave me a great review. Why not me? My specialty was real estate law. I only worked for him briefly, then decided to open my own shop. I feel it is best to be the boss, wouldn't you agree? As you know, I've been quite successful."

"So you've said. Here is a copy of Rosalie's Law Review article. I'm assuming she talked with you about her interest in public safety and building practices?"

"Well, while she was writing the article, she did talk about certain points of it with the study group. She didn't go into much detail. Writers are always afraid that someone is going to steal their ideas." Price laughed at his last statement; he found himself to be quite amusing.

"Did you tell Thomas Edmonds about Rosalie's article and her interest in his building practices in particular?" Jablonsky turned up the heat.

"Can't say that I remember that. Law Review is a big deal. He probably heard about the article from someone else and put two and two together." In what he thought was a subtle motion, Price kept smoothing his hair.

"I just don't believe you, Mr. Price. I believe that you told Thomas Edmonds about Rosalie's interest in his company's practices and, to keep that information flowing, he hired you."

"No! That's not the way it went. Jane told him what a brilliant law student I was, and he wanted me in his stable, with the other thoroughbreds. I didn't have to report on anyone. Besides, Rosalie would never have stayed with him; everyone knew that."

"Who was everyone? When was the last time you saw any of the people on this list? And I don't mean just Rosalie." Once again, the chief said the names of the study group out loud, just to make Price antsy.

"I haven't seen any of them for years. They all went into other areas of law; some stayed in the city, but most left. Including Jane Louise. After the divorce, she went to New York state. I don't know where she is now."

"Well now, you see, Jonathan, we know that's a lie. Didn't you recently receive some pastries at your office?" The chief slid an order sheet across the table.

"Several cherry and apricot pastries from Rosalie's Bakery were delivered to your office. Miss Nivens, your assistant, has made a statement to that fact. As you can see, they were ordered, and paid for, by... this is a name you know."

Price sputtered. "How did you...?"

"How did we know? I'm as good at my job as you say you are at yours, that's how. These pastries were sent to you as a warning to keep your mouth shut. So, Jonathan, now is the time for you to tell me the story of what you know about the murders of Michael and Rosalie Rossetti. Now!" Jablonsky slammed the palm of his hand on the table.

The room was warm in temperature, and now warmer in emotional intensity. "I want to call my attorney. I know my rights!"

"Go ahead, Jonathan, call your attorney. Just remember, this will go easier on you if you willingly come forth with information on your own. Once your attorney is involved, I'm going to have to arrest you for the double homicide of Michael and Rosalie. There will be no deals made, none. You'll spend the rest of your life in prison—not jail—but prison. A man like you will be a tasty morsel there, I can assure you." Jablonsky didn't want things to calm down; he painted a picture of what Price's life would be like in prison. It had Jonathan obsessively smoothing his hair.

"As a young chemistry student, Marco Rossetti showed off to Rosalie's suitors, of which you were one, by talking about stone fruit and poisons. You were at the bakery for Marco's mini-lectures." Price's face tuned white.

"I was not! I don't know anything about Marco Rossetti or poisons!" Click, click, click went Price's pinky rings, as he rubbed his hands together.

"You are lying again, Jonathan. You knew that amygdalin turned into hydrogen cyanide."

"Someone else told me about it. I would never have known how to make a poison. I'm telling you the truth, damn it, and you don't even recognize it! Screw you, Jablonsky."

"Why did you decide to murder Rosalie? Was it because you couldn't have her, and that swine Thomas did? Come on, man-to-man, you loved her, but that love eventually turned into hate." Jablonsky played the "we are all guys here" card.

"It wasn't me! I didn't do anything!" Jonathan Price began counting his breaths—five in, five out, five in, five out. Finally, he said, "Someone else made the preparation to make Rosalie a little sick, just so she couldn't see Thomas. That's all it was supposed to be—a little vomiting, headaches, diarrhea, like that! Oh, my God! That's all it was meant to be! You have to believe me! I didn't kill them!"

"You gave Rosalie the box of pastries. You knew they were headed to the Grotto for some private time, so you handed her the pastries that she and her brother ate."

"Yes, but—but I never knew how much would make them sick. I didn't prepare any poison. I'm completely and utterly innocent of any wrongdoing."

"No, Mr. Price. You are guilty of wrongdoing." Jablonsky just shook his head at Jonathan's ability to let himself off the hook.

"Jonathan Price, we are arresting you as a co-conspirator in the murders of Rosalie and Michael Rossetti. Now, you should call your attorney."

Jablonsky and Antoine walked back to the chief's office. "Is she here in the city yet?" Stefan asked. "Yeah. She's here," answered his number one.

She had landed at the Pittsburgh Airport just as Jonathan Price was being interviewed, escorted by out of state police, then handed off to the Pittsburgh city detectives. Overwhelmed by having been summarily taken from her comfortable home, she shivered during the ride to the police department and to the interrogation of her life.

CHAPTER 38

AROUND THE SAME TIME the prime suspect's plane touched down, Eddie Fitzroy opened his eyes. Kate glanced up from her reading, not expecting to see his blue eyes staring at her. "Eddie, you're awake! Welcome back, my darling!" He looked around the hospital room, trying to understand where he was; then his gaze returned to rest on Kate. She buzzed for the nurses, who immediately swarmed into the room and began their ministrations.

One of the nurses oriented him. "Mr. Fitzroy, Edward, you have been in a bad car accident, and were brought here to the hospital. You've had surgery for your injuries. You are in Pittsburgh, Pennsylvania. Today is Wednesday, March 21st. Sip this, please." The nurse handed him a cup of some concoction that would soothe his throat.

Kate texted Joan that Eddie was awake, then stood back and let the professionals do their job. Finally, she sat beside him tightly grasping his hand. He tried to speak, but his voice was dry and cracked. Through the ubiquitous bent straw, she gave him several more sips of the nurse's brew. Eddie fixed his azure blues firmly on her face.

The first words that he croaked out were, "I love you, my darling girl. Will you marry me?"

"Well...as soon as you are able."

Fitzroy's hand shook as he took another drink from the straw. "No. Now. I want to marry you, now. I had a ring. Where is it?" The nurses looked at each other and grinned; in the midst of the day-to-day uncertainties of acute care, this was a scene movies were made of.

"A minister is down the hall, visiting another patient. I'll just step out and get him." The nurse flew out of the room. Joan arrived and, unexpectedly, so did Johnny.

"What's going on?" asked Joan, looking at Kate. She moved to the bed, shined a small light in Eddie's eyes, then asked him to follow her finger as she slowly traced an invisible line back and forth in the air. "Good," was all she said. Eddie touched her hand, and whispered, "Thank you, for taking care of me and my girl."

"We are getting married." Kate looked like she had swallowed a feather and didn't know whether it was tickling her insides or making her choke. She only knew that she had to say yes to the proposal.

She was oblivious to the fact that her marital outfit would be old jeans, a black tee shirt, hair pulled high into a top knot, and no makeup. Johnny grabbed some flowers from a vase and handed them to her. Kate retrieved the emerald ring from her purse, where she had been keeping it, and let Eddie slide it onto her finger.

The atmosphere in the room suddenly and inexplicably was charged with the sweet anticipation that always descends on everyone witnessing a nuptial ceremony. The indirect light around the bed's headboard softened the lines of fatigue on Kate's face and muted the reddish-brown hue of Fitzroy's bruises. To everyone there, they were transformed into a beautiful bride and handsome groom.

Without elaborate ceremony, the minister pronounced the ancient words and heard the "I do" responses.

Unsentimental Joan, and very sentimental Johnny, let the tears flow unhindered. The nurses clapped and the minister gently shook hands with Eddie. Whatever would happen in the future, in this moment, Kate knew she had made the right decision.

—⁓—

The woman who walked into the interview room looked much older than the last time he had seen her—Jablonsky barely recognized Jane Louise Edmonds from their Zoom conferences. Her tan was sallow under the fluorescent lights and her multiple pieces of gold jewelry appeared garish. Antoine and his boss watched on the closed-circuit televisions as the officer settled her in the interview room. "Let's get it," urged an energized chief. "Let's get justice for Michael and Rosalie Rossetti."

"Jane Louise Smith Edmonds, you have been read your rights, both in Florida and here at the precinct. You have declined to have an attorney present? That is your prerogative." Jablonsky laid the same bill of sale on the table that he had presented to Jonathan Price.

"What can you tell me about this order for pastries from Rosalie's Bakery? An order that you recently had delivered to Jonathan Price's office?" Stefan had placed his small paper notebook beside him but had no need to open it.

"I wanted to send an old friend some pastries." Although tired, Jane Louise was in enough control of herself to not give any extraneous information in her answers. Jablonsky thought, *She probably was a very good attorney.*

"Jane Louise, we know that that is a lie. You sent the pastries as a warning to Jonathan Price, a warning to keep quiet about the poisoning of Michael and Rosalie."

"You can't back up that statement with even a scintilla of evidence, Chief Detective. It is pure supposition." Jane Louise unconsciously started to rotate one of the gold bracelets on her wrist.

"Do you recognize this?" Jablonsky laid the ring with the blue topaz stone on the table.

"It looks like a university ring." Jane Louise made no move to touch or examine it.

"You notice the lion etched in the topaz. It stands for justice. At least, that was what I was told by your elderly mother. She also said it is your ring size—a six."

"You contacted my mother? How dare you!" Jane Louise flushed with anger, and there was something else—the hint of a gasp.

"I dare to because I am pursuing a murderer. Your mother and father bought this ring for you as a gift for when you passed the bar exam. They had ordered it from the jewelry center at the university bookstore and had asked Rosalie to pick it up and to hold onto it until they came into town. She had stopped by the bookstore the day she and Michael went to the Grotto. Apparently, she had tried it on to show her brother, because when her bones were found, they also found the ring. As her flesh rotted, the ring fell off—but I didn't mention that part to your mother."

The chief placed her mother's statement in front of Jane Louise, who did not read it. "Your mother mentioned in her statement that she never knew what had happened to the ring. When she asked, you denied ever seeing it, which in fact was the truth." Jane Louise stared at Jablonsky, but he knew she wasn't seeing him—she was looking back into the past.

"We have arrested Jonathan Price as a co-conspirator in the murders of Michael and Rosalie Rossetti. He has fingered you as the one who poisoned them. The motive was one of the oldest in the world—jealousy. You wanted Thomas Edmonds for yourself, so you needed Rosalie out of the picture. Jonathan wanted Rosalie and needed Thomas out of her life. That's a perfect storm. Where did you acquire the grounds from the cherry and apricot stones? Did you buy them online? Did you grind them yourself?"

"I had nothing to do with their deaths. I don't care what deal Mr. Price made with you. I am not, I repeat, not, a murderer! Really Jablonsky, I'm surprised at you, a Chief of Detectives in a big city, flies a suspect in from another state and presents a ring that an elderly woman thinks she remembers she bought twenty years ago?" Jane Louise settled back in her chair and examined her painted fingernails.

"The ring, and your mother's statement, are just the beginning of our evidence. To start with, here is Jonathan Price's sworn affidavit, detailing that you knew about the poisonous qualities of amygdalin, obtained some, put it into chilled cream, and stuffed cannoli with it. You knew that Rosalie and her brother were going to the Grotto, so you gave the box to Price so he could give it to Rosalie. He remembers that Rosalie thanked him, that Rosalie even commented on what a good friend you were to think of the pastries. But you weren't a good friend, were you, Jane Louise?"

"That is a pack of lies. How would I know about, what did you call it... amygdalin? Price is trying to save his own ass."

"Do you recognize this woman?" Jablonsky placed several pictures from Mrs. McCarthy's work album in front of Jane Louise. They were the pictures that Kate had thought were relevant to the investigation.

"No. I don't know these women."

"This is Fiona McCarthy, and her boss, Lisa Marie Rossetti, and this is a younger you. You were at Rosalie's Bakery with them, in the kitchen at the back of the building.

Here is the picture enlarged—these are apricots, here are cherries, plums, and peaches, all in baskets on the counter. Mrs. Rossetti remembers that she and her employee, Mrs. McCarthy, gave you a baking lesson, a lesson that included the perils of stone fruit. Here is her sworn statement." Jablonsky presented the statement to Jane Louise, handling it as if it were made of rubies.

"In her statement, Mrs. Rossetti refers to the fact that she knew you were pregnant, so she and Mrs. McCarthy wanted to make sure that you were healthy and safe, eating only good things during your pregnancy. Hideously ironic, isn't it? These two mothers were looking out for you, while you were learning how to poison Mrs. Rossetti's daughter."

Jablonsky again slammed the palm of his hand on the table; the sound of it cut through Jane Louise's carefully crafted facade, leaving her shaking like a wet cat. She looked closely at the pictures, then turned them over, face down.

Jablonsky slowly turned the photographs face up again. "You can't look away any longer, Jane Louise. This is the mother of the two young people you murdered. This is the mother who grieved so badly that for years she couldn't leave her house. And this is you. A young murderer, standing right next to her, defiling her kitchen and her life. All because you wanted that piece of crap, Thomas Edmonds. Take a good look at yourself!"

Jane Louise's shaking became worse, and she started to hyperventilate. She pushed herself out of the chair and screamed across the table at Jablonsky, "I just wanted to make her sick! I never thought about killing her! Or Michael, whom I hardly knew!"

Jablonsky stood as well. "You are lying! What was it, Jane Louise? What was the trigger? Come on, you know the trigger, come on, say it." Jablonsky's intensity was like a hatchet, slicing and shredding the false story she had been telling herself for decades.

Jane Louise's face contorted with pain. Then for the first time in twenty years, she shouted out the truth. "He called her name! The night we had sex, the night we made our daughter, he called her name! He called out, "Rosalie!" Oh, my God! It was grotesque. In his mind, he was with Rosalie! Beautiful, smart, elusive Rosalie, who didn't even want him! Can you imagine? She didn't—even—want—him!" Jane Louise's words filled the room with pain and rage—she collapsed back into her chair, rocking and sobbing.

Jablonsky remained standing but pocketed his small notebook. Two officers came into the room, lifted Jane Louise out of her chair, and handcuffed her. "Book her, for the murders of Michael and Rosalie Rossetti." The chief didn't even bother to stay in the room while they took her away. He had one more loose end to tie up.

"Coupe. Get Jubas Jones in here."

CHAPTER 39

KATE RECOGNIZED THE BRAND and color of one of the envelopes that came in the mail. A heartfelt condolence note from Pittsburgh's French Consul had been written on the same stationary. This time, it was an invitation to brunch at Jean-Luc Bernard's home. She smiled at the beautiful script on the light blue notecard from G. Lalo Mode de Paris's stationery.

Eddie Fitzroy died twenty-four hours after they were married. Even though she had tried to prepare herself that he might die, it still felt like his death was shockingly unexpected, and madly unfair; Kate was shaken to her core. In the weeks that followed, after consulting what little extended family he had in Britain, she decided to take his ashes to Nantucket Island. It was the place where, under the approving eye of her grandfather, she and Eddie had begun their courtship. Johnny and Joan went with her, all three huddling together on the outside benches, shivering through the hour-long ferry ride from Hyannis Harbor to the island.

So many friends and colleagues of Eddie's wanted to be there with her to celebrate his life that she rented a pleasure yacht and took everyone for a late afternoon cruise, during which she would spread his ashes in the north Atlantic. There was a glowing red sunset that evening, a sunset that slowly transformed into streaks of pink iridescent light, finally resolving into a pearly gray twilight. The sea was calm, and a salty, soft breeze amplified the scent of the ocean. As it is at all funeral wakes, people stood talking, drinking, and eating—to her and Johnny's specifications, the crew had prepared a buffet of grilled meats, fresh fish and seafood, and salads. Archeologists are born storytellers, so many Fitzroy stories were shared by his colleagues and recorded by Johnny.

As if on cue from a movie director, a school of dolphins swam alongside the boat, leaping in play. "Eddie would have loved that," everyone said. Kate smiled and nodded, but inside, she just felt numb. Out of view of the guests, Kate stood at the railing with Johnny and Joan, tilted the urn that contained Eddie's ashes, and slowly poured them into the sea.

In Boston, one of his colleagues helped her sort through his published papers, which he had wanted to donate to his alma mater, the same university to which her grandfather had given his life's work. In Kate's mind, there was a certain symmetry in that that pleased her.

Johnny found a box containing most of her love letters, written to Fitzroy while he was off at various digs; the last ten years of her life were chronicled in them. Those she took with her, to savor once she could read them without feeling unbearably empty.

After the two weeks in Boston, she and Johnny flew back to Pittsburgh. She returned to work and Johnny returned to preparing classes for the summer semester. Kate floundered, unsure as to how to begin rebuilding her emotional life. She felt like Sisyphus and the rock, doomed to keep reliving the heartbreak of losing family, over and over again. Surprisingly, it was a conversation with Marco Rossetti that offered her true empathy and practical advice for the way forward.

"I was much younger than you when Michael and Rosalie disappeared. For what it is worth, here's what I did to cope with the emptiness and grief—I worked like hell. I immersed myself in my studies. I operated as much as I could. Later, I added on treating the homeless, so the only downtime I had was when I slept. I'd advise you to do the same. Your academic advising is important and meaningful work. You have loving friends. You are an athlete. Push yourself in all three areas. Keep and cherish your memories, Kate, but look forward."

What good advice, she thought. Kate was a very practical person, so his suggestions appealed to her. She knew that Marco liked her, but right now, her heart was simply the pump that pushed blood through her veins. It was closed to new love.

"Hey, lady!" Johnny shouted as he came in the kitchen door, interrupting her reveries. "I see you got an invitation to Jean-Luc's brunch. When he is in Paris he always sees Julian, then takes the time to tell me what was said and what's going on. I called him to ask what we could bring, and to find out who was invited. The guest list includes you and me, Joan, Jablonsky, and Dr. Patel. I asked him if it would be all right if we added Antoine DeVille. Of course, he said yes."

"Oh, Antoine DeVille? The tall, handsome, charming detective from New Orleans? That Antoine DeVille?" Kate gave Johnny a little pat on the cheek, saying, "I approve."

"How did he get Jablonsky to agree to come? You know how the chief is about the line between the police and civilians. You and I have watched him take a big piece of chalk and draw that line as thick as possible—well, metaphorically speaking." Kate laughed at her own image.

"He enjoys Jean-Luc and as you know, he has helped Jablonsky on a few cases. More than that, I think the chief has a commitment to community relations. With us as the community members, it's an easy gig for him—he likes all of us. And Antoine said that there are a few more facts to be revealed about the Rossetti murders."

The morning of the Sunday brunch, Kate dressed in a long, periwinkle silk shirt with a matching short skirt. The color reminded her of Eddie's eyes. She chose the diamond tennis bracelet that Fiona McCarthy had given her, coordinating it with her mother's diamond stud earrings. She wore Eddie's emerald engagement/wedding ring. *These pieces of jewelry were gifts from people who loved and cared for me. I need their energy around me now,* she thought.

BB had been invited to the brunch, so Kate made sure that he was clean, brushed, and sprayed with her favorite doggie groom aid. They walked the mile to Bernard's home; Kate hadn't been out socially since the Nantucket trip, so she needed the walk to discharge her nervous energy.

Jean-Luc opened the door and immediately enclosed her in a warm embrace, whispering something sweet in French. BB knew his manners; there was no jumping, just some head butts and the friendly wag of that otter tail.

Kate knew that Jean-Luc enjoyed baking, and in his circle had achieved some regard as a pastry chef. It seemed ironic that pastries and bakeries had been in their lives for months now—she refrained from mentioning the murders.

The Consul's dining room table was tastefully set with French dinnerware by Bernardaud, ecru linen placemats and napkins, and tall crystal champagne glasses. Johnny commented on the beauty of the table setting while they sipped the bubbly.

"Only one glass, please," said Kate, as Johnny went to refill her glass. "You know what I always say. One drink sharpens your wit. Two drinks make you a philosopher. Three drinks or more just makes you stupid." Johnny rolled his eyes over the saying that he had heard many times before; he filled his flute a second time.

"Yum. Look at this fabulous brunch! Onion tarts, lots of ham and bacon, toasted brioche, salmon, and then there are the pastries." Johnny grinned like a schoolboy; he was his mother's son when it came to baked goods. Kate knew he was happy to see her out socially and also happy that Antoine DeVille had accepted the invitation.

It was the men who were crowded into the kitchen, watching Jean-Luc plate his exquisite breakfast breads. There were pain aux raisins, or raison bread; chausson aux pommes, or apple slippers; and abricots à l'anglais, or apricot log. It was the apricot log that brought the conversation around to Michael and Rosalie Rossetti.

When everyone was sated and hot cups of coffee had been passed around, Johnny asked Jablonsky to talk about the conclusion of the case. "How did you ever nail Jane Louise Edmonds when there was only the ring as physical evidence? Even Dr. Patel couldn't get blood from the stone—you know, traces of hydrogen cyanide from old bones." Everyone groaned at Johnny's analogy.

Jablonsky explained. "I had her in my sights from the time we found your mother's work album. All those pictures helped us organize the various configurations of suspects. But it was our sleuth Kate who produced the nail that we used to hammer shut Jane Louise's coffin. She found the incriminating photo." Kate beamed over the praise for her insight.

"It was the picture of Jane Louise getting an impromptu baking lesson from your mother, John, and, more importantly, from Mrs. Rossetti. There were all the stone fruits laid out on the counter, so the two bakers would have had to give warnings about amygdalin. When I took the picture to Mrs. Rossetti, she remembered the day, the girl, and the baking lesson. She was instrumental in putting the murderer of her two children behind bars, and helping the whole neighborhood finally heal." Jablonsky smiled, and lightly tapped the table with one fist, accenting his pleasure at the closure of this twenty-year-old cold case.

Kate stirred some sugar into her coffee, then asked. "Do you think Jane Louise Edmonds really intended to poison Rosalie? Or do you believe her when she said that she only wanted to make her sick?"

"That is the million-dollar question. A good attorney will use that to show she had not formed murderous intent. Her attorney will apply it to her, and Jonathan Price's will say the same thing about him—no intent to murder."

"Whatever the intent, two beautiful young people ended up buried in an excavation site." Dr. Patel had no use for legal hair-splitting, and everyone at the table murmured support for her point of view. "Plus, they died because that woman didn't know her science!" Her statement elicited embarrassed chuckles—compared to Aashi and Joan, everyone at the table felt inadequate in the science department.

"But there is one more aspect to the story that I haven't mentioned. As you know, Luca Lorenzo, who loved, and had an affair with, Michael Rossetti, found the two bodies, and dragged them to his car. What niggled at me was that it is one thing to get the bodies from the Grotto to a car, but another to get the bodies down into the excavation site. Dead weight is heavy. He had to have had help." Jablonsky paused, enjoying everyone's rapt attention.

"And he did. By coincidence, Jubas Jones was at the site, poking around, looking for any visible infractions of the agreements Thomas Edmonds had made with city planning. He saw Luca trying to get the bodies out of the car."

"And he helped him?" asked a stunned Kate. "Instead of calling the police?"

"Yes. Because he had been half in love with Rosalie, he understood when Luca pleaded with him to not let them cut Michael in an autopsy. Jubas didn't want that for the beautiful Rosalie either. So together they carried the bodies and carefully laid them side by side, then covered them with a blanket and soil. He kept his actions a secret all these years."

"Eddie always said that someone had taken care with the bodies," Kate softly whispered.

"Your Eddie was right. Luca and Jubas did just that; they took care in how they handled them." The group grew quiet as they considered the picture of the unlikely duo being gentle and respectful with the bodies of Michael and Rosalie Rossetti.

As they cleared the table, Johnny, Antoine, and Jean-Luc began to talk about Paris and Julius. Joan was in deep conversation with Aashi Patel, again talking about the Pirates' new pitcher, Cheeks Maloukas, and his prowess at training camp in Florida. Jablonsky sat down next to Kate, who was petting Bourbon Ball while she mentally drifted.

"You were right, Kate. The Rossetti case was all about love, betrayal, and jealousy. I'd have to throw in some greed as well, in Thomas Edmonds's case."

"What will happen to Luca Lorenzo? And Jubas Jones? They didn't kill anyone."

"Luca will do some jail time for his role with Thomas Edmonds and BoBo Ramone. And, no matter what their intentions were in moving, transporting, and then burying Michael's and Rosalie's bodies, it was illegal. For his part, Jubas will only get a slap on the wrist—I think that is fair."

Kate saw that Jablonsky had something else he wanted to say, so she leaned back in her comfy chair and waited. The chief began by mentioning that "In one of Mr. Rossetti's diaries, he had a note that said something like, "All might be guilty.""

She perked up. "Why, that's a reference to Shakespeare's Romeo and Juliet. It implies that both the feuding families, the friends, and the town were complicit in their deaths." Kate was intrigued.

Jablonsky continued. "That phrase helped me look at the entire group of people who surrounded Michael and Rosalie—Lorenzo, Price, Thomas Edmonds, Andrew Edmonds, Mrs. McCarthy, Jane Louise, Jubas Jones—the lot of them all kept secrets and told lies. Two innocent young people, Michael and Rosalie went to the Grotto to spend time together, ate some pastries from their mother's bakery, and died.

With palpable sarcasm, Kate remarked, "Dying because you are in the wrong place at the wrong time—I'm familiar with that situation," She saw that she had made Jablonsky feel guilty over his remarks, so she added, "In the end, I've come to admire Fiona McCarthy and Lisa Marie Rossetti. I want to be as strong as they were." Keeping her head down, Kate twirled the emerald ring on her finger.

Just as Jablonsky was about to respond, his cellphone rang. He answered with his usual, "Talk to me." He listened to detective Lemon, then replied, "I'm heading out now." He pocketed the phone and called into the kitchen. "Coupe, with me. There's a body."

Kate raised her head, her eyes sparkled for the first time that afternoon. "A body? How can I help?"

THE END

ABOUT THE AUTHOR

REBECCA A. MILES (STEPEK) was raised, educated, and established her career in the city of Pittsburgh, Pennsylvania. From her work as a psychologist specializing in Behavioral Medicine in Oncology, she became a recognized expert and presenter on grief, the grieving process, and the psychology of dealing with loss.

She believes that all forms of criminality are about loss— the loss of the rule of law and its subsequent effect on the community, the loss of privacy and security in one's home, the loss of control over one's body, the death of dear friends and family due to criminal acts, or the loss of meaningful family possessions.

Through the fictional characters in *Ground Truth: A Pittsburgh Murder Mystery,* she explores the themes of loss and love, two states that she considers to be universal in human experience. Her writing about murder describes loss and our ability to come through it, scarred but stronger.

When not at her dining room table writing, you will find Rebecca untying knotty plot issues by lapping in the swimming pool at her local YMCA or by running the family dogs on the beach.

Rebecca A. Miles holds a doctorate in psychology from Duquesne University.

Connect with and follow Rebecca:

rebeccaamilesmysterywriter.com
twitter.com/RMmysteries
goodreads.com/author/show/5028437.Rebecca_Miles
amazon.com/Rebecca-Miles/e/B06Y4ZJPJ2

CPSIA information can be obtained
at www.ICGtesting.com
Printed in the USA
LVHW110843290422
717027LV00002B/73